Hillbrooke New Beginnings

The work of Beverly Joy Roberts

ISBN: 1530581303
ISBN 13: 9781530581306

Dedicated to my children, Aaron, Trenton, Amber,
and to my grandchildren and all who come after them.
Never forget your Pentecostal heritage.
It's who we are!
In 1927, the message of salvation came
to your great-grand parents in Flint, Michigan.
They believed and received!

Acknowledgements

Dear Reader,

This work of fiction is not based on any person living or dead. The idea to write this book came about through the many long car trips my husband and I took during our travels as missionaries. It has been in the works since 1999. We enjoyed discussing the story line, plot twists and the complicated lives of the characters.

It wasn't until 2015 following a message my husband preached that I felt the prompting of the Lord to finish the book. It has been a roller-coaster ride of ups and downs. Many times I questioned if I had the talent to write anything. I told myself, don't do this—everyone will know you can't write. You'll be found out! I prayed—a lot. Then forged on believing in the message of the book—***redemption through the work of the Holy Spirit***. This message is too important not to share.

When I was in writer mode, I became so connected with the characters that I had to remind myself that (Spoiler Alert!☺) these aren't real people. After a full day of writing, my husband would come home from the office and I'd greet him at the door with this line, "You're never gonna believe what happened in Hillbrooke…today!" Then I would proceed to tell him about the drama in the lives of the characters. Oh, the power of the pen.

The issues the characters experience in the book will cause you to fall in love with most of them, but not all of them. Remember even the

Bible has a villain. My villains are just working on their testimonies. We are all human and fall short. When we fail, the big question is—will we allow God to redeem the mess we've made—then move on?

My purpose in writing the book was for my children and grandchildren to know my passion about these four things; the power of the Word of God (the Bible), the gift of the Holy Spirit to empower the Believer to partner with Him, flawed people can be used by God and the need for the altar—a place of surrender.

It is my prayer that all who read this book will finish it with a better understanding of the Lord's enduring and long-suffering love for us. Once you come into relationship with the Lord, there is a powerful gift called the baptism in the Holy Spirit that is available to you! Ask for it—receive it—be empowered by it.

A word of thanks to Barb Cody, my sister, who has read this book more times than I care to say, helping me with the wording, punctuation and spelling—feel free to blame her if you find a mistake. Also, thanks to the many others who helped. Dolores Anderson *who is with Jesus now*—*miss you*, Diana Wiehe, Sharon Chambers, the ladies of the New Life Book Club—you are awesome and many others who read the rough (and I do mean ROUGH) manuscript. Bless you all. These ladies helped me through the tedious process of proof reading.

A huge thank you to Teresa Crumpton for offering a free writing class at our church to inspire would be writers—like me. You were an enormous encouragement to press on.

Thank you to my wonderful husband, Bob Roberts, the love of my life. You believe I am the most capable woman in the world—sometimes I believe you!

I hope you will enjoy reading this *fiction book* that deals with real spiritual issues.

Beverly Joy Roberts

Character Cheat Sheet!
You're gonna need this! ☺

Major Characters
Rey Douglas-Pastor, married to Callan
Callan Douglas-Pastor's Wife, mother of Zander and Ty
Tom and Jean Brown-Small group leaders and Vice President at *Superior Solar Energy Plant*
James Fields-husband of Marilyn, owns *Fields Insurance*, Chairman of the Board at *Community Outreach Church*
Marilyn Fields- James's wife, mother to **Carl and Emily Fields**
Kota Edwards-friend of Carl Fields (Carl changes his name to Zak Parker.)

Minor Characters
Mike and Tina Morris-friends of Tom and Jean Brown
Daniel and Naomi Walters-Callan's Parents
Melvin and Ruth Douglas-Rey's Parents
Bill Edwards-father of Kota
Mary Edwards-mother of Kota
Snake-inmate at the prison
Heidi Hogan (Alden)-works with Marilyn/church friend of James Fields

Community Outreach Board Members:
John and Heidi (Hogan) *Alden*
Peter and Katherine Carver-buddy of James Fields
Henry and Dorothy Samson-PHDs at local college
Harold and Esther Smith-older couple

Community Outreach Church Staff:
Heidi Alden-Church Office Manager, wife of John Alden and friend of Marilyn when they were younger.
Grace-Secretary
Tiffany-Secretary
Dusty Anderson-Youth Pastor
Matthew Lewis-Children's Pastor
Eldon Chambers-Music/Media Pastor

CHAPTER 1

The Lord Has Marked Him Good & Faithful

*"...I know what I'm doing. I have it all planned out—plans
to take care of you,
not abandon you, plans to give you the future you hope for.
When you call on me, when you come and pray to me,
I'll listen.
When you come looking for me, you'll find me."*

Jeremiah 29:11-14 The Message Bible (MSG)

Pastor Rey Douglas drove along the slick two-lane road in absolute silence. Swirling through his mind, like the bitter wind of a winter storm, stinging questions rushed in. How did things go so wrong? If I had stayed the course and stuck to my plan, my wife would be at my side and my church would not be in turmoil. He slammed both hands onto the steering wheel, "What was I thinking?"

An hour ago the radio had ceased to entertain him. Utterly alone he drove on. The tires repeated their unique rhythm on the snow covered highway. An endless path of pine trees lined the road far into the horizon. The dashboard clock showed it had been 45 minutes since his view had changed. Everything remained the same. Snow piled high on both sides of the road and pine trees—never-ending pine trees.

His grip tightened around the leather steering wheel until he felt a tingling in his fingers. Why didn't I pull my iPod out of my briefcase? He chastised himself. Worship music or an encouraging sermon might be just the distraction I need to give me a few hours of reprieve from all this blasted thinking!

Pastor Rey drove on; he pushed away the thought of unpacking his iPod hidden away somewhere. He breathed in through his nose a deep cleansing breath, forcing it out through his clenched teeth. He pressed onward. A feeling of urgency crept in—anxious like a panic attack.

Only nine months ago Pastor Rey Douglas, his wife, Callan, along with their two young sons, Zander and Ty moved to the community of Hillbrooke, Michigan. This mid-sized town had everything a young family needed to build a thriving church. A flourishing local industry had just moved to town bringing with them young professionals—some looking for a home church. The state university had an extension campus in town as well as the thriving community college. The public school system was one of the best in the state. The recipe for a mega church was lacking just one ingredient, a young, progressive-thinking pastor.

James Fields, the chairman of the church board, believed Rey Douglas would be the perfect fit. Everyone felt a church growth explosion was on the horizon. All the pieces had fallen perfectly into place.

Pastor Rey was in agreement with the goals of the church leadership. This young pastoral family was greeted with expectation upon their arrival in Hillbrooke, but something had changed.

The road was desolate. Nothing could distract Pastor Rey from his own thoughts. A churning sea of confusion overwhelmed him. A sudden gust of wind mixed with falling snow caused a momentary whiteout. Rey pulled himself forward with the steering wheel, leaning in towards the windshield. Here I am driving to 'no man's land' with my tail tucked. Is everything I worked for in vain? Will this time of solitude change anything? A snow plow speeding by sent a load of wet snow over the jeep jolting Rey back to the present.

Pastor Rey knew he had failed. He allowed people to lead him and not God. People were hurt. "Why didn't I seek the Lord's counsel instead of allowing myself to become a puppet? Why didn't I do the right thing? Would a few days alone seeking the Lord really make a difference?"

Rey pondered; can any of this be repaired? Will I be able to salvage what is left of my fragmented congregation—and my marriage? He'd never felt this low in his 29 years of life. He'd always been the golden boy; abundantly talented and destined for success. He'd believed he would do great things in the name of the Lord. He'd believed the power of his words would move people to greatness. He'd believed it would be Callan at his side—beautiful and accomplished.

Rey broke the silence with a frustrated shout, "Will these pine trees ever end?"

CHAPTER 2

Tom and Jean Brown

*The LORD grants success to the one whose behavior he
finds commendable.*

Psalm 37:23 New English Translation (NET)

*N*ine months earlier, nestled at the end of Cabin Creek Trail the comfortable brick home of Tom and Jean Brown looked empty except for their silhouettes viewable through the front window. Tom slid his arm around his wife's waist and drew her close. Together they peered out the dining room window at the SOLD sign in their front yard. It was a stark reminder that this chapter of their lives was ending

Tom said, "Are you ready for another move?"

"The first few weeks at any new place brings adjustments. I'm feeling like a professional packer." Jean sighed deeply. "Each move helps me look at things with a discerning eye and ask the question…"

Tom finished her sentence, "Do we really need that?" He paused. "I'm just saying, there's a lot of *my things* that have come up missing in the past 36 years. It makes me wonder, was it really lost or maybe a 'discerning eye' decided I didn't need my lucky golf shoes."

Jean gave Tom her most innocent look followed by a quick hug. She hurried into the kitchen to finish setting out the paper plates and cups.

Tom entered the kitchen just steps behind her. "Where did the past four years go? I can barely believe we've been together with this group for that long."

Jean continued arranging the plastic silverware. "I never dreamed it was possible to open my heart like this. They are like family. I can't bear to say goodbye."

Tom felt the same pain of separation. He reached out to hold her for a moment. Jean laid her head on his chest and whispered, "The things we have all gone through these past years; personal struggles and battles, but we never had to walk through any of them alone."

"When one member felt spiritually in need…"

Tom added, "Another stepped up to encourage them."

The sound of a car pulling into the driveway brought the couple back to their task. They looked at each other, hugged one more time, and prepared themselves emotionally for their last small group meeting. It would be an evening of goodbyes with their spiritual family.

The Brown family was on their way to a new job, new city, new home, and new church. This time it was Michigan!

Tom's company was taking advantage of some friendly tax breaks this struggling state was offering. He would supervise the opening of the new solar energy plant in Hillbrooke. Tom never questioned a job transfer, but accepted each move as a new opportunity from the Lord to use them.

The four previous moves the Lord had used to stretch them spiritually. In Midland, Texas as a newly married couple they first realized their need for a Savior and accepted Jesus. In sunny Ocala, Florida, their two daughters were born. In Florida, Jean and Tom began attending the Friday prayer group. It was there they received a gift from the Lord. Something they never dreamed possible. In Fenton, Missouri, Tom taught the adult Sunday school class and occasionally filled in for the pastor on Wednesday evenings. The Browns grew spiritually deeper in their relationship with the Lord during these years.

When the Browns landed in Springfield, Illinois, it was without their two married daughters. In this city they became small group leaders for the first time. Their family grew to include three couples and four singles. The prayer time at the close of each meeting was powerful. This small group had a reputation in the community as people who knew God, knew how to pray, and whose prayers were answered.

After their small group prayed for a child in the community with cancer, the child was miraculously healed. They began receiving written prayer requests tucked inside their front doors, left on their windshields, and handed to them in the grocery store. This small, diverse group was committed to making a difference in as many lives as they could touch.

At the last gathering before moving day, all members of the small group were present. Tom welcomed everyone and opened in prayer. He looked around the room at each dear face and sensed a profound sadness. "Jean and I moved frequently throughout our marriage. Each time the Lord was gracious. This has been no exception. We have grown in ways we didn't know possible. There isn't enough time to share how much you have impacted our lives. This has been an amazing time of spiritual growth for both of us." Tom paused, picked up the styrofoam cup that held his warm coffee, took a sip and continued. "Mike and Tina Morris will be taking over this group. I'd like them to come now and share."

Mike and Tina Morris were the fulfilment of the scripture; *the Lord will restore what the locusts have eaten.* Mike a recovering alcoholic and Tina a former unfaithful wife never believed they could rise above the death of their only child. They were redeemed, restored, and in love with the Lord and each other. Here they stood in front of this small group ready to take the baton.

Tina and Mike stood side by side. Mike spoke first, "We know it's only by God's great mercy that we stand here today."

He took his wife's hand. "His love is immeasurable and his compassions are new every morning. Many mornings I couldn't get out of bed, and Tina hadn't come home at all the night before but God..." Mike stopped talking. Something was happening in that living room. He waited. No one spoke. There was a stirring in the air. The members of the group began to close their eyes. Some bowed their heads. Soft muffled cries began to grow into moans.

The words of adoration and praise started out in soft, whispers.

"We adore you."

"Thank you, Jesus."

"I love you, Lord."

The volume of praise grew as the presence of the Holy Spirit filled the room.

It was undeniable. It was powerful. It was all-consuming.

Then as quickly as the praise began, it stopped.

A prophetic word was given. It was clear and precise. *"Through the years your feet have taken you many places and your words have touched the hearts of many people. But this time your purpose will be to touch the life of one. Then the Lord will use him to touch the lives of many. The harvest will be like leaves falling from trees and waves crashing on the shore. Be watchful, be alert, and seek the Lord in all you do. Pray continuously. Your prayers will be his covering; your prayers will be his rear guard. The enemy has marked him for destruction, but the Lord has marked him as a Good and Faithful Servant."*

After the prayer time, all ten members knew that God had a plan for the Browns in Hillbrooke, Michigan that exceeded and surpassed that of secular employment.

CHAPTER 3

Rey meets Callan

*GOD said to Joshua, "This very day I will begin to make you
great in the eyes of all Israel. They'll see for themselves that
I'm with you in the same way that I was with Moses."*

Joshua 3:7   The Message Bible (MSG)

he door of the house slammed behind Rey Douglas as he
walked in long strides towards the waiting van. His parents, Melvin and Ruth Douglas smiled at Rey from the front seat.
Ruth called to Rey from the open car window. The same tender
voice that had guided him through childhood drew him in like a
sweet aroma, "Rey, Dad and I are so proud of you. It's not every day
a high school graduate is asked to speak to the adult congregation. I
can't think of one other college bound freshmen ever given such an
honor."

Rey slid into the back and fastened his seat belt. He tried to
ignore the waves of nausea rumbling in his stomach. "Oh, Mom,
you've always been my biggest fan. Pray for me when I'm speaking
this morning."

"You know I will, Son."

"I'm prepared, but without the blessing of the Lord…it's all in vain." Rey's shoulders were tense causing them to draw upward towards his ears. He forced himself to relax into a more comfortable position.

His dad was the quiet type. Words were only used when necessary and Melvin doled them out sparingly throughout Rey's life. Today was no different; Melvin looked over his shoulder while slowly backing out of the driveway. He reached back, found Rey's knee and gave his son's leg three soft taps. Rey swallowed hard, emotion welled up. This small gesture spoke more to Rey than a thousand accolades. In just a few weeks, Rey would leave for Calvary Seminary.

Rey's childhood had been nothing short of Opie Taylor (Andy Griffith Show) mixed with Kevin Arnold (The Wonder Years). He grew up in the church under the tutelage of Sunday school teachers, youth pastors and senior pastors who for the most part knew how to rightly divide the Word of Truth. Rey had watched and learned well. He was an articulate speaker for one so young, vocalist, and he played the keyboard. He could turn a phrase and tell a story. The old men winked and nodded their approval, the old women dabbed at the corners of their eyes. The young girls hoped that Rey would look their way. Every mom wished her daughter would be the one who turned his head.

Rey was liked and respected by his peer group of young men in the church. He had set goals for himself while he was still young, and he was not afraid to set them high. He knew how to walk a fine line without tumbling off into destruction.

Rey had a few strict rules of conduct he had set for himself. Number 1: Never misuse or mistreat a girl. Number 2: He took the warnings about pornography seriously and had an accountability partner on the computer. Number 3: Foul language or jokes were never funny to him or worth repeating. Number 4: Do your body no harm. He did try smoking with some guys when he was fourteen. The smoking thing didn't make any sense.

Once at an overnight party, when Rey was 16 he tasted beer with his buddies. It was fowl tasting. Some of the other boys became intoxicated leaving Rey to clean up vomit and tuck sick pups into bed. Just like the cigarettes, it didn't make much sense.

The thing that put Rey on the path to ministry and impacted him more than anything else in his young life happened at the close of a Sunday night youth service. The speaker had challenged the youth to partner with God in a new and powerful way. He challenged the teens to be "God Pleasers" and not "Man Pleasers." Rey listened to the words of the speaker. He was a powerful communicator. His words found a home in Rey's heart. He stayed in his seat, head bowed and prayed— following the prayer of the guest speaker. While he prayed something wonderful happened. This was the *game changer* moment for Rey.

A week later, Rey finally got the courage to share with his youth pastor about his experience. It wasn't hard to find the words because the experience was still fresh. "It felt like I was standing in water. The water moved and swirled around my ankles. I felt compelled to go deeper. I walked a few steps, but stopped. I wanted more. I wanted to be fully immersed in whatever this was, but I stopped. I was scared. It was unknown." Rey looked at his youth pastor's face whose mouth was turned up on one side in a half smile. Rey wondered if he was pondering what he was saying or if he was mocking him. He was hard to read.

Rey pressed on. He had to know. "Do you know what that was? Have you ever experienced anything like it? I've never heard anyone speak about something like this. I want to understand it. Can you help me?"

The youth pastor relaxed his mouth. He spoke slowly. "Sounds like God may be calling you into relationship with Him. I'd be careful who you shared the water thing with. Not everyone believes or accepts these kinds of experiences. You wouldn't want to be labeled as a weirdo or religious fanatic. You may want to take a year at seminary to get a better understanding of the Bible." He slapped Rey on the back. "Don't forget about the youth overnighter. It's going to be a blast. You should bring a friend."

"I'll look into that seminary thing." Rey could not deny the desire he felt. There was something more out there and he wanted it. And so it began, like a smoldering coal. It was a passion in his innermost being.

Rey believed it would be at seminary that he would find the key to unlock the source.

Callan Walters grew up in a nominal Christian home where good moral values were loosely enforced. From the outside looking in, this *Christian* family seemed to have it all. They went to church and lived in a beautiful home. The nucleus of this family was intact, but the facade was as thin as an egg shell.

Daniel and Naomi Walters choose Callan's name because they loved the meaning, *powerful in battle*. Callan grew up a fighter. On the outside she appeared strong, confident and powerful. On the inside there was simmering conflict. Her struggle was with being accepted for who she was, not just for her abilities or appearance. The conflict to follow her heart or people please started early for Callan.

When she was eight years old Callan was invited by a school friend to attend a church summer camp. She begged and pleaded with her parents until they relented and let her go. After Callan left for camp, her parents were actually happy she was gone for five days.

The day she returned from camp, Naomi waited in the unfamiliar church parking lot. She glanced around at the other families waiting to retrieve their campers. She didn't know any of them nor did she want to know them. When the bus finally rolled into the parking lot, Naomi's wall rolled up with it.

The bus doors eased open. Kids with messy hair, dirty clothes and smiling faces spilled out onto the pavement ready to greet their families. Callan came into view. Naomi gave a regal wave to get her daughter's attention. Callan spotted her mom, following the lead of the other children she ran to greet her. Naomi stiffened as Callan approached. She stopped her daughter's impending hug with both hands extended in front of her.

Recognizing the firm boundaries set up by her mother, Callan stopped short of impact. Callan's voice did not show the disappointment she felt on the inside. Her words were breathy with excitement. "Mom, camp was so fun. The best thing ever happened." She gulped air as the words poured out. "Last night at the closing service I prayed—at the altar—in front of everybody. I asked Jesus to be my Savior." Callan looked at her mom. Expecting the news was worthy of a cheer or maybe a pat on the back. She wanted to throw herself into her mother's arms, but she didn't. She kept her place an arm's length away.

"Wait." Naomi glanced from left to right and lowered her voice. "You did what?"

"In the service, at the end, everyone who had never asked Jesus into their heart could come to the front. I never prayed that prayer—so I went. Look there's my counselor." Callan pointed in the direction of a teenage girl not more than twenty. "Gina, prayed with me. You want to meet her?"

"No!" Naomi's words were tense and cut off. "Where is your suitcase?"

"In the back of the bus—the counselors will get them out for us." Callan tried to keep that happy feeling from camp in her heart.

"Go wait for your suitcase. I'll be at the car over there." Her mom gestured in the general direction of the crowded parking lot.

"Okay. I'll be right back." Callan walked towards the church bus. She watched the other kids with their families exchanging hugs, kisses, smiles, and happy chatter.

She retrieved her suitcase and tugged it into the parking lot. Scoping the sea of cars, Callan spotted hers. Sitting in the driver's seat, looking straight ahead, her mom rested her hands on the steering wheel.

As Callan approached the car, she heard the click of the doors unlocking. She opened the heavy door and pushed her suitcase into the back seat. Then she scooted in beside it, shut her door and buckled-up.

"Mom."

"Not now Callan. We'll talk about this later." Her mom started the car and pulled away.

Never again was Callan allowed to attend her friend's church or to go to summer camp.

Even though her parents tried to extinguish that little flame that flickered within her—she did not forget how she was compelled to go to the altar or the words that she prayed. Callan hid every moment like this one in her heart.

Daniel and Naomi Walters raised their children in church; however, their main focus was not living a Christ-like life. The Walters chose to focus all their attention on the elite families in the church. They valued nice clothes, high-end automobiles with all the bells and whistles, and people with clout. Her parents held prestigious jobs in the community, and were college educated. Higher education was extremely important in the Walters' household. Everyone would go to college; a minimum of four years was expected.

Callan realized at thirteen that she was blessed with all the best physical features of her Scandinavian mother and German father.

Her blond hair reached her waist and swung back and forth when she walked. Her green eyes twinkled and had a hint of mischief present at all times. She was five foot seven with a slender frame. Callan learned to use all of these traits for her own benefit.

When she was in her teens, her two sisters shared a closet with her. All the clothes inside were meant to be shared. It was Callan's practice to steal away some of the nicer items to make sure they were clean and in good condition when she needed them. She had a way of dismissing the cries of her sisters when their needs conflicted with hers. After all, she sang the special music in front of the church. It was important during her presentations at the school assemblies to "dress for success." In her piano competition, general appearance was 10% of the judging. Looks were important to Callan, but what she treasured most was the praise of others.

Rey and Callan met the beginning of her sophomore year at Cornerstone University. Rey was a senior at Calvary Seminary. Their chance meeting was at the first sporting event of the year. The two colleges located in the same town were rivals.

Their relationship moved quickly and by March a summer marriage was in the works.

Rey's seminary obligations kept him from going home with Callan for her February Winter Break. This would be the time she would break the news to her parents.

The winter snow storm outside seemed like a sunny beach day compared to the chill at the Walter's home when Callan broke the news.

"Dad, Mom, can we talk?"

"Is this about that ridicules phone call from your boyfriend yesterday? Mr. what's his name?" Daniel lowered the newspaper and made eye contact with Callan.

Callan's heart tightened in her chest. "Rey called? Did he ask you?" She knew he was trying to soften the blow for her, but it didn't help. Her parents were never going to make anything in her life easy.

"He asked. But I didn't say, yes. I don't even know this boy."

"Rey and I are in love and we want to get married this summer after he graduates." Callan felt her breathing increase.

Her father's eyes narrowed to a squint. He didn't say another word only scowled at her.

"Callan, why?" Her mother's voice was higher and louder than normal, "You could have done so much with your life. You could marry someone with money. Don't settle for second best or third best."

Naomi shook her head then looked down at the floor. After a few seconds, she jerked her head back up and spoke with a voice full of accusation, "Are you pregnant?"

"No, Mom, I'm not pregnant."

"Daniel, what will we tell our friends?" Naomi snapped. "Who gets married at 20 without being in a hurry?"

"Really! I'm not pregnant."

Callan lowered her voice to a whisper. "We're waiting. We believe in keeping ourselves pure for marriage. It's been hard, but we've been careful not to put ourselves in compromising situations."

"Okay, sure, whatever!" Naomi rolled her eyes like a mocking teenager.

"I really love Rey. He treats me like a princess and he's amazing with people and when he speaks there's a power. It moves me."

No one spoke.

Callan blurted out. "You liked him when he visited at Thanksgiving."

"That was different. We thought he was just a friend—nothing serious."

"Just give him a chance."

Naomi added, "If you really aren't pregnant then why not wait for a few more years. I'm just so disappointed with you." Naomi sat on the opposite end of the couch from her daughter. She turned her back to Callan.

Callan sat speechless.

"Well, why a pastor of all professions?" Daniel asked. His tone was somewhere between disgust and anger. "Aren't there any doctors or lawyers left in Illinois or a financial investor or business owner?" Sarcasm replaced the anger, "No, our daughter brings home a preacher!" He shook his head.

Callan spoke soft but firm. "Rey and I *are* getting married. I hope you both can *get onboard* with this because I want you at my wedding."

"You think you're in love now, but this love thing will only last so long. Then you are going to want all the comforts of life. You have never known a day of sacrifice!" Daniel shook out the newspaper and disappeared behind it. He spit the words out in disgust, "A preacher!"

Naomi turned back towards her daughter and pointed her finger. "You are going to regret this decision and we will not be here to pick up the pieces. You've been warned!"

From this day forward, Daniel and Naomi made sure Callan knew their disappointed with her life choice for a mate. The wedding would be in July following Rey's graduation. Callan knew that the only way Rey would ever gain her parents respect was with success both in his career and financially.

Rey sat on the stage waiting his turn to speak. It was graduation day at Calvary Seminary. The past four years rushed by like a flash of light on a radar screen.

One of his greatest victories while at seminary was being elected student pastor his senior year. This role carried with it honor and prestige. Plus, it looked great on his resume. He would graduate with a year of ministerial experience giving him the edge over his less experienced classmates.

Once a week he spoke in the chapel service to the seminary students. His messages were skillfully honed and Biblically based with a flawless presentation. On a few occasions he counseled younger students and worried he was the only sane person left in the universe. The few sick students he visited at the hospital allowed him to polish his visitation skills. While visiting the sick, Rey experienced a closeness to the Lord that reminded him of that special experience when he was a teen. Times like these confirmed to him his calling. He wanted to help people and be appreciated. His ministry experience so far had brought an abundance of praise with no discord.

The sun's direction changed casting a spotlight on the stage where Rey sat. He lifted his hand to shield his eyes. He refocused his thoughts. This was graduation day!

The president of the seminary, Dr. Hall, stepped up to the podium, "It is my privilege to introduce to you our graduation speaker. He is no stranger to our student body or faculty. He has been a key player on this campus for the past four years."

After a few more flattering comments it was finally Rey's turn. He stood confidently, shoulders back, and walked to the podium. He was a head taller than Dr. Hall. He gave his mentor a bear hug followed by a firm pat on the back. Rey glanced back at the seminary faculty and school benefactors seated on the stage. He gave them a nod. Then he turned to face the 73 graduating seniors, their families, friends, and seminary alumni. Rey looked across the vast collection of people in attendance. He cleared his throat and with authority he spoke from memory.

"Dr. Hall, honored faculty, fellow graduating seniors, family and friends, it was Mark Twain who said, 'no one likes change except a baby in a wet diaper.' And yet we who are graduating today are about to experience one of the biggest changes in our lives. We are going from the studying of life to the living of it.

There are three roads clearly marked before each graduating senior; success, mediocrity or failure.

Let me ask each of you this question. Is it possible to become the person God wants you to be without being willing to change? Amazingly, this change is brought about by a God, who testifies of Himself, that He cannot change.

Change is coming—and on the heels of change is fear. In the course of our lives we will all wrestle with fear in different ways. The fear of failure, the fear of what others think, and the fear of the unknown will insidiously slither up to us endeavoring to choke out God's purpose for our lives." Rey paused for effect. "We cannot move forward until we crush the head of the serpent of fear!" He slammed his heel down on the wooden stage. He watched with pleasure as heads jerked to attention. All eyes were focused on him.

Rey went on for eight more minutes keeping his time exactly to the allotted minute. At the conclusion of his speech the graduates gave him a roaring standing ovation. He returned to his seat intoxicated by his own accomplishment. Rey confidently looked out at his peers unaware that in six short years this same serpent of fear would coil itself around him attempting to destroy his life and ministry.

CHAPTER 4

James and Marilyn Fields

*"... The crops are in, the summer is over, but for us noth-
ing's changed. We're still waiting to be rescued. For my dear
broken people, I'm heartbroken. I weep, seized by grief. Are
there no healing ointments in Gilead? Isn't there a doctor in
the house? So why can't something be done to heal and save
my dear, dear people?"*

Jeremiah 8:18-19 The Message Bible (MSG)

*J*ames Carl Fields opened the door of his brand new Lincoln
Continental. It was black, sleek and shouted, 'I'm a SUCCESS!'
He eased into the luxurious driver's seat and mumbled to himself,
"Well, this trip wasn't a *total* bust." James nodded his head and smiled
as he thought, that Rey Douglas can certainly preach, and it doesn't
hurt that he is distinguished looking and smart.

James had been the natural choice for the past ten years to attend
the commencement exercises at Calvary Seminary. His position as
the chairman of the church board at Community Outreach Church
in Hillbrooke, Michigan, gave him the privilege to assign another to
attend. But, he liked getting away and looking at new talent. Pastor
Wingate was pushing 60 and would want to retire in the next few years.

James was already compiling a short list of candidates. The name Rey Douglas was now—a definite contender.

James started the car. He touched the phone icon on the dashboard screen. A short list of phone numbers appeared. He selected HOME. The irritating tone sounds of the number dialing darkened James's mood. The phone rang a few times then James hit the red phone icon disconnecting the call. He wondered where Marilyn was and why she didn't answer. He glanced in his review mirror at the disappearing Calvary Seminary.

The two-story, 4,000 square foot, brick home of James and Marilyn Fields seemed unusually quiet for a Friday afternoon. This was the last day of school before summer vacation. No visual lights were on in the house, no movement, no cars in the driveway, no teens swimming, or playing basketball.

Marilyn Fields sat at the kitchen table looking at the back door. The grandfather clock in the living room was playing its familiar song marking the 15 minute intervals with chiming bells. It was 4:45 P.M. and Carl wasn't home from school. Carl hadn't been home for two days. He left in a dark cloud of anger with only the clothes on his back following another verbal assault by his father.

Marilyn couldn't remember how things had escalated. She usually had time to deflect James's attention from their son to her or something else, but this time it happened like a sniper attack. There wasn't time to bandage the wounded. Carl was gone.

Marilyn chastised herself. Why had she allowed her husband to treat their son like this? Why didn't she stop him? What son could be expected to stand mute while his own father yet again spewed a cruel liturgy of demeaning and damaging words all over him?

Carl's own words directed at his father still hung in the air, "You don't love me. I hate you. I wish you were dead! You can go to HELL!" Carl used both hands to flip an inappropriate finger gesture at his father, then glanced briefly back at his mother one last time. Then he turned and ran out before his father had a chance to react.

Marilyn learned early in her nineteen year marriage with James that it was best to never verbally disagree with her husband. His presence was both intellectual and physical. He had never abused her with physical force, but there was always a deeply rooted sense she was mere seconds away from that first blow. The threatening way he stood leaning in towards her as he spoke. Her personal space invaded by his hot, angry breath as he worked at verbally breaking her spirit. His jaw would tense up and his hands would form a fist. Then he would relax slowly pondering his next move. She wanted no part of that life again. Marilyn's quiet, gentle spirit longed for a home of love and peace.

When she married James at the young age of nineteen, she thought her life's road would be paved with happiness. She had been rescued, delivered from the home of her abusive father. Her mother had escaped years ago leaving Marilyn and her brother defenseless to fend for themselves.

During those pre-teen years, Marilyn learned the art of being invisible, quiet, and undetectable to her father's radar. She was average in height about five foot six. She kept her dark curly hair cut short because she was once told it flattered her face. Marilyn's well-formed figure was a problem often attracting unwanted attention. When she walked there was a grace and presence about her.

Marilyn was introduced to James Fields at church. The introduction came through a co-worker at her first job as a bank teller. Heidi

Hogan was happy and friendly. She seemed like a safe person. When Heidi invited her to attend a special meeting at her church, Marilyn quickly consented. It would keep her out of the house until late—away from her father's unpredictable anger.

Arriving at church, Marilyn and Heidi looked for a place to sit. This was the first encounter Marilyn had with the tall, handsome young man with jet black, wavy hair and big blue eyes. Marilyn felt uncomfortable with the way he seemed to be taking in every inch of her with his eyes. She wondered what kind of church she had consented to attend.

Heidi noticed that James Fields was looking at Marilyn with great interest. She leaned in close to her friend and whispered, "Lucky you. James Fields is a great guy with a promising future. I think he likes what he sees. I'll introduce you after the service."

Marilyn didn't expect to find the two loves of her life that day, but at the close of the service she desperately wanted to know more about the peace and forgiveness that the minister had talked about.

After the service Heidi introduced James and Marilyn. They talked about going out to eat at a restaurant, but Marilyn made her excuses and asked Heidi to take her home. In the car, Heidi insanely prattled on about James Fields.

Marilyn interrupted her, "Heidi, what do you know about being saved?"

"Oh Marilyn, don't think about that so much. What did you think of James Fields? He is the best catch at church. You know he comes from money, but it's a sad story." Heidi avoided the topic again.

"Are you saved, Heidi?"

Heidi was defensive, "Of course I am."

"I've never felt like I did tonight. Heidi, I was just wondering what you can tell me about being saved or born-again like the preacher was talking about." Marilyn's inquiry was followed by an uncomfortable silence. She thought, maybe this was something a person only spoke with a minister about. Maybe it was too complicated for the church members to discuss without a minister present.

"Listen Marilyn, I have something stuck in my Bible that tells all about being saved. It explains the whole thing in detail; if you want to read it you can have it. Now let's get back to James. What did you think of him?"

"I'm kind of tired and can't really think about James Fields tonight. Maybe tomorrow at work we can talk about him." She glanced in the back seat and saw Heidi's Bible. She hoped the "something" Heidi was talking about really would explain the emptiness she felt.

"Right there is my house." Marilyn pointed at a small home with a broken fence in the front. No lights were on. Not even a porch light. "Is it safe to go in there? It's so dark."

"My dad and brother must be out. I have a key." Marilyn dug in her purse and pulled out a key chain. She looked directly at Heidi and asked. "If you have that information about being saved, I'd like to read that, if you can find it?"

Heidi reached over the seat and grabbed the Bible. She fumbled through it until she came to a small pamphlet. "Go ahead and read this but don't get all holy-holy on me. We're young and should be having fun. I've learned that church is a great place to meet guys, but don't get all caught up in the rules and regulations." She handed the folded paper to Marilyn. "Okay, see you at work tomorrow. Let's eat lunch together. We have lots to talk about."

Holding the pamphlet, Marilyn looked down at the title. Printed in bold letters across the top it said, **ABC's** *of Salvation,* below the title was a red heart with a black cross inside.

In the quietness of her bedroom that night she read the pamphlet from cover to cover—twice. Then she read the printed prayer out loud, **"Dear God, I admit I am a sinner and I need your help. Please forgive me of all my sins. Thank you for the promise** of eternal life with you in Heaven someday. I believe Jesus died and rose again for my sins. I confess Jesus as Lord and Savior of my life. Thank you for saving me. In Jesus' name I pray, Amen."

Before turning out the light Marilyn read the pamphlet for the third time, but she didn't feel any different. The tract had Bible verses to look up to encourage all who prayed the prayer, but Marilyn didn't own a Bible. At least she couldn't recall ever seeing one in her house. She certainly wasn't about to root around looking for one in fear of being questioned by her father.

The next morning Marilyn awoke with an unexplainable peace. This was not the beginning of a typical day. Usually when she readied herself for work there was a gripping fear that followed her until she was safely locked inside her car, but this day was different. She felt safe and protected, not helpless. Marilyn couldn't understand why she felt as she did. She wondered, if the peace she sensed had anything to do with the prayer she prayed last night. Something was different! There was a sweet, calm presence that surrounded her as she drove to work.

The bank tellers arrived at 8:15 A.M. and the doors were unlocked at 8:30 A.M. on the dot. Marilyn looked up from her computer to see her first customer walking towards her with a smile. It was James Fields. As he approached her window, she felt her face grow warm. Before she could speak—he did.

"I noticed you didn't have a Bible last night at church. I have this extra one and was wondering if you'd like it?" His tone was kind and reassuring.

Marilyn's hands were shaking as she reached for the book. Somehow, she knew, this book held all the answers and would help her navigate through life. Just before the blue leather book was safe in her grasp, James jokingly pulled it away. Marilyn felt embarrassed as she looked at her empty hands.

He then teased, "But first you must agree to go out with me Friday night." He smiled and placed the treasured book in her waiting hands. "I'm just kidding! The Bible is yours to keep, but I still would like to take you out for dinner and a movie, if you're willing?"

Marilyn stood, stunned for a moment, with the heavy book resting in the palm of her hands. As she opened her mouth to reply, Heidi joined them and said laughingly, "Oh, James of course she'll go out with you."

Marilyn looked up and smiled. Something had changed in James Fields sometime between that beautiful day she held that Bible in her hands and now, but Marilyn could never quite pinpoint what it was or when it tragically happened.

Six months after their first date, almost to the day, she was saying "I Do" on a quiet beach in Jamaica. They eloped, just the two of them. Looking back at the lack of family and friends, Marilyn should have guessed something wasn't right.

In the kitchen of her expansive home, Marilyn desperately looked at the back door while she sipped her lukewarm coffee. If only she could *will* that door to open, to see her son's face, and hear his voice. Her mother's heart began to rush with terrifying thoughts, is he safe? Is he hungry? Is he in trouble? Does he need me? Please, Dear Lord, let him be okay!

The annoying ring of her IPhone brought Marilyn back to the present. She looked at the screen and saw a picture from last summer of her husband grilling hot dogs his name spelled out in block letters, JAMES, across the picture.

Marilyn thought, he must be in the car on his way home. He never carries his cell phone with him. He always says that the cell phone is for my convenience not anyone else's. He used it mainly in the car for business.

Marilyn answered the phone without expression or emotion, "Hello." Her eyes were fixed on that door, that unmoving, stationary, motionless back door.

"Marilyn, did you hear me! Where are you?"

"I'm home." Marilyn answered.

"Why didn't you pick up the house phone when I called a bit ago?"

"I'm sorry. I didn't hear it."

"I'll be home in about five hours." James's voice was caustic with anger. Marilyn had prayed the Lord would soften her husband's heart. She hoped he would use his time on the road to reflect on their son, Carl.

Marilyn listened again to the tenor of James' voice and could almost see his teeth clenched as he slowly over-pronounced each word, "MARILYN, WHAT IS WRONG WITH YOU? A SIMPLE ACKNOWLEDGEMENT ISN'T TOO MUCH TO ASK FOR—IS IT?"

An awkward silence followed! Marilyn felt the stinging pain of his demeaning tone. She thought, well, you obviously haven't been using the passing hours on the road to inquire of the Lord for godly direction in the matter of our son. The futility of her situation stung like a slap to the face.

Marilyn responded just in time, "I'm here. I-I heard what you said. I'll see you tonight when you get in." She paused. Her voice was softer and hopeful. "I haven't heard from Carl and you told me not to call the police, but I think we should? Don't you?"

There was no pause in the sharp reply, "Are you on drugs? Are you crazy? The boy walked out on us. Leaving was his choice. He's not a child. He's 17 years old and he has major issues. If he wants to come back into *my* house, ***ever again***, he'll be living by *my* rules and you will not be pampering him. He's not a baby. You've been too soft on him, undermining my authority. *NOW* you're worried, *NOW* you're concerned about him, well, you should have thought of that before!"

Click! There was no mistaking the sound of dead air. This disconnect was not a dropped call by the cell phone company or a dead cell phone battery. This was a deliberate end to a one sided conversation.

CHAPTER 5

The Beginning of Compromise

"You may be poor and young. But if you are wise,
you are better off than a foolish old king who won't listen
to advice."

Ecclesiastes 4:13 Contemporary English Version (CEV)

World for Christ Church (WCC) was conveniently located 40 minutes north of downtown Chicago. It was a scenic drive along the shoreline of Lake Michigan to the well-to-do community in the suburbs. Attendance Sunday morning easily exceeded a thousand.

After graduation, three inner-city churches had contacted Rey and Callan about being their youth pastors. They visited two and drove by the other one. The needs in these communities were overwhelming and Rey felt drawn to minister at a church like one of these. When they discussed the idea of doing inner-city ministry Callan was very persuasive with her concerns. She was uncomfortable with the pay package, location of the church and the economic condition of the parishioners. Rey finally gave in to his bride's demands. The youth in the suburbs needed youth pastors too. Callan wanted to be safe, accepted and appreciated.

World for Christ Church had met and exceeded Callan's expectations. The expansive manicured lawn with the stylish landscaping surrounded the red brick colonial structure. It was a majestic house of worship. There were four huge white pillars that shot up from the ground to hold the roof over the huge covered canopy across the front of the church. At first sight WCC had all the pomp and circumstance of the presidential White House.

The WCC youth had experienced some unpleasant issues in recent months with the previous youth pastor having moral failure that spilled over into inappropriate behavior with some of the young ladies in the youth group. The church was still reeling from this shocker. What was needed now was a youth minister who knew how to mold and shape these hurting and confused souls. The senior pastor was looking for a replacement with excitement, passion, and a solid personal relationship with the Lord Jesus Christ. The fact that Rey had a beautiful wife and they were newly married and passionately in love certainly didn't hurt his case. After just an hour talking with church leadership it was unanimous; Pastor Rey Douglas was the man.

"Indescribable excitement" that was how Callan and Rey felt three months after graduation from seminary when they received the invitation to fill the position of Pastor of Youth Ministries at WCC. This would check a few boxes off their long-term goals. The list had been changed and rearranged through the years but basically the top three remained the same. 1. Senior Pastor of an established church with a membership of 500-1,000. 2. Earn a salary of $100,000 per year. 3. Complete 1 and 2 by the time he turned 30 years old. This new youth pastor position didn't check-off any of the top three, but put him in good standing for all to be filled, if they were patient.

Rey and Callan sat quietly in their car looking at the jumbo sign that flashed the words one at a time World-For-Christ-Church. Rey reached over and took the hand of his bride. He leaned close to her and whispered, "This will hopefully be our one and only place of ministry."

"I hope it's true. I know I will be very happy here." A satisfied smile formed on Callan lips and her eyes twinkled like it was Christmas morning.

They drove slowly around the massive building. Callan let out a squeal of excitement when she looked at the church playground. It looked more like a city park. They drove back to the front of the building and got out of the car.

It was their first Sunday as staff members at WCC. They arrived early to greet people and be seen. Callan wanted to put her best foot forward. Today they would be introduced to the congregation. They confidently walked into the church looking the picture of success. This day they would lay claim to the position they were born to fill. The church welcomed the Douglas family like royalty.

They were ready to showcase their personal talents. There was seldom an issue that Pastor Rey could not handle. His people skills were impeccable. He held the complete trust of the youth as well as their parents.

Early in their ministry at WCC, Pastor Rey realized this youth group preferred games, parties, and fellowship to Bible study, witnessing, and prayer. The thing missing from all gatherings was any challenge to seek a committed relationship with Jesus Christ. As long as the youth were happy, the parents were happy. The youth were coming back to church so there was little to no accountability for Pastor Rey.

He had a great base to start his ministry. There were 75 youth with varying levels of spiritual interest. The job of the youth pastor was to keep them entertained and out of trouble. Rey knew only too well the discord that could be circulated by unhappy teens. He had heard stories from other youth pastors of the problems that disgruntled parents could cause.

"My Chad doesn't fit in. What are you going to do about that?"

"Emma doesn't want to come to church any more. She thinks the sermons you give are boring."

"Jason said that the music is lame."

"Brendon feels like you don't like him."

Pastor Rey felt the conflict between being a party planner and being a Shepherd that led his flock to water. There was still a passion within him to see this youth group really understand and know God. The dream to mold young hearts into a concrete relationship with Jesus had to be set aside. Instead he chose amusement parks like Six Flags, canoe trips, baseball games, scavenger hunts, talent shows, white elephant exchanges, and did a yearly missions' trip to the inner city that tended to be more sightseeing than life changing. The pizza, hot dogs, tacos, and sub sandwiches devoured by these kids could feed a small nation. At Pastor Rey's urging the church ordered a soda machine and cappuccino maker. On any given Wednesday night or weekend the WCC Teen Center was alive with kids hopped up on sugary, caffeine, and carbonated beverages.

Callan met with a select group of teen girls each week at her house. The topic was "Growing Up To Be Women of God." But seldom did they open the Bible or the study guide. It was more like a gossip session about the girls who were not there and Callan loved it. She was one of the gang. The acceptance of these girls fanned the flame that fed her personal insecurities. The critical spirit that her parents had nurtured in her found a happy home in ministry. It wasn't long before Callan was reproducing herself in troubled girls who looked to her for guidance.

Pastor Rey and Callan Douglas rejoiced in the birth of their two sons during their six year tenure of ministering at WCC. Zander Wade was born during their second year of ministry and Ty James came two years later. The future was looking rosy for the Douglas family. Rey estimated in 5-7 years, Pastor Stanford would be ready to retire. He would be the natural choice to step in.

Rey was accumulating a diverse library of sermons. When the call came to be a senior pastor he would be ready. He prepared three Biblical character studies on the life of Joseph, Abraham, and Paul. Each of these series could take up to eight weeks. Also, there were four short series ready to go: the Great Battles in the Bible, The Seven Days of Creation, The Miracles of Christ, and Everything You Ever Wanted to Know About Heaven. An expositional study of the book of Galatians would take months to go through in a verse-by-verse study.

Rey was 28-years old had a wife, two kids, and a growing repertoire of sermons. Rey could hear the control tower calling, "You are cleared for your final approach." He envisioned his name on the door of the senior pastor's office. He would bide his time. Then everything changed.

Pastor Rey sat in his office at WCC looking over his calendar for the next six months. He felt anxious in his spirit. He wasn't sure how much longer he could continue in this never-ending cycle of youth—fun and games. Over the six years he had been youth pastor he tried to raise the bar and was met with opposition from his youth leaders and the youth. Callan too had been a strong voice to maintain the delicate eco system they had created in the youth group.

The phone intercom buzzed. Pastor Rey answered with a tone that sounded more like a sassy mouthed child saying "What do you want now?" than the actual greeting he gave, "Hello."

"Oh. Sorry Pastor Rey. Hope I didn't get you at a bad time. It's Lisa. You have a call on Line 2. It's a Mr. James Fields from Michigan.

I think that's what he said. He said it was a personal matter. I hope it's not a sales call, but I didn't want to pry since he said it was personal. Sorry, if I let another one slip through. These sales guys are slick. Mr. Fields wasn't giving me much information."

"Don't worry, Lisa. If it's a sales call, I can handle it fast enough. My favorite line is…I'd love to know more. Could you send me an email?" Lisa laughed and put the call through.

"Hello, this is Pastor Rey."

"Is this the Pastor Rey Douglas that graduated from Calvary Seminary?" The distinguished voice on the other end of the phone asked.

"Yes. I graduated from Calvary. Is this about the alumni donations?" Pastor Rey asked, wishing his secretary had asked a few more questions now.

"Oh. No. I'm sorry this is James Fields from Community Outreach Church in Hillbrooke, Michigan. I was calling because the position of senior pastor has opened at our church and I would like to invite you to come and interview with our church board."

There was an awkward pause, "Mr. Fields, I'm sorry, but I think someone is playing a joke on you. I did not send out my resume for this position. My family and I are very content at WCC. How did you get my name?"

"Pastor, I was in attendance at the commencement exercises the year you graduated from seminary. I remember the stirring and thought provoking message you preached about not being afraid of change and conquering fear as you pursued God's will for your future. Also, how change and fear can be roads to success when placed in God's hands." A smile formed on Pastor Rey's lips. Mr. Fields words stirred up happy memories of days past. He was flattered that after six years someone else could quote the fundamental truth of that message. This man had Pastor Rey's ear.

"Really? That's amazing that you could remember that after all these years." Pastor Rey baited Mr. Fields for a few more compliments.

"Please call me James. I will never forget that message. When you shared that word I was personally going through a dark time in my own life with a rebellious son. Your message encouraged me to accept the necessary changes that were happening in my life without fear," he lied. The message had neither inspired him or helped him with the unresolved conflict with his estranged son, Carl.

"James, I am totally blindsided by this invitation. We have been very happy in our position at World for Christ and within five years the senior pastor will be retiring. We would be the most likely choice to fill that position. We have been at this church since graduating from seminary." Rey boasted.

"All I ask is let me send you an email with our church information. Some statistics about the community, the church and the pay package. Then you can think it over and talk to your wife. I'll give you a call back in a few days."

"Well, it can't hurt to look at the email. My email address is on the church website. You probably already have that though. Right?" Rey said with confidence.

"Yes, I already prepared the email and I just hit the send button. You should receive it in a few minutes. We'll be in touch." The phone call ended.

Rey immediately opened his email account and there it was an email from James Fields.

He clicked on the attachment to open it. Then scrolled down to the pay package. "Wow!" followed by a whistle. His thoughts went in different directions. There must be money in Michigan. That is generous. The winds of change were blowing and Pastor Rey liked what he felt. Then he remembered Callan. She would be the hard sell.

Rey was tempted to call Callan about a dozen times during the day to blurt out the news, but he knew his wife well enough to know she didn't handle change well and especially not in a phone call. No. This was a face to face conversation.

When Rey arrived home that night his excitement got the better of him. He walked into the house with gusto and bear hugged Callan. He swung her around in a circle. Her feet lifting off the floor and water dripping from her hands.

Callan yelled, "Have you lost your mind?" Her tone implied that she was not impressed by this demonstration of affection. When Rey released her, she folded her arms across her chest and furrowed her brow. He knew this look all too well. He may have over played his cards.

"Callan, I had the most incredible call today at work." Rey went on to give Callan a blow by blow of the conversation. Then finished with "Okay, let's keep an open mind. Don't completely rule it out, yet."

"Rey." Callan spoke with the firmness of a mother to a child. "We have a plan and going to another church isn't part of it. We have invested six years into building and establishing our place in this community and church. I can't stand the thought of doing that over again somewhere else." Callan walked over to the kitchen table and dramatically collapsed into a chair.

"How about if we look at it like a free vacation to Michigan. There is no harm in talking and looking. After all this may be the Lord's will for this time in our lives. We should be open to that. Let's just go and see. Where's the harm?"

Rey watched his wife process the information. She seemed unpersuaded. "Well, a trip to Michigan in the summer without the boys does sound nice and all our expenses would be paid?"

Rey touched the screen on his smart phone a few times and handed his phone to Callan. "Here is the email from the church in Michigan.

There is information about the church, the community, and the pay package. It's almost double what we are making now." Callan's head turned with a jerk in Rey's direction and she grabbed for the phone. "Are you kidding me? Really? Let's get packing!" She was beaming from ear to ear. "Almost double?" Callan laughed and then added, "People love me. I have no problem making new friends."

CHAPTER 6

He's Not Coming Home (six years earlier)

I cry out loudly to God, loudly I plead with God for mercy.
I spill out all my complaints before him, and spell out my
troubles in detail:

Psalm 142:1-2 The Message Bible (MSG)

he sound of the back door creaking open brought Marilyn's hopeful eyes squarely to the door. It was Emily. She poked her head around the door looking to see if the coast was clear. "Is he home?" Emily asked her mother. Marilyn replied, "Do you mean your brother or your father?"

"Either"

"No. Neither. Dad will be home in about five hours. I'm so worried about Carl."

Emily was fourteen, a great kid, quiet and unassuming. She had learned well from her mother. Many of the girls her age had been going out with boys for years, with or without their parents' permission, but Emily wasn't interested in breaking the rules. She was respectful, thoughtful, helpful, and did well in school. She was active in the church youth group and loved to sing on the youth worship team called The Challenge.

Emily was not the simple beauty that her mother was. She was shorter and easily 20 pounds over her ideal weight. Her shoulder length brown hair was curly but not the cute kind of curly. It was more of a problem. She wasn't the most stylish girl in town but she always looked nice. Her face was round with deep dimples on both cheeks and freckles peppered her whole body. Emily did not have a showy confidence but she was comfortable with who she was. Carl and Emily were direct opposites like night and day, The Prodigal Son and The Good Samaritan.

Emily walked tentatively across the room towards her mother. Marilyn looked at her and opened her arms. Emily sat down on her mother's lap and Marilyn allowed her to fill up the emptiness in her heart. She held her girl without thought of time.

"Mom, I'm so sorry you are hurting." Marilyn's arms tightened around her daughter, but she couldn't speak. Her emotions were raw. There were a few moments of silence.

Then Emily began to pray out loud with an authority Marilyn had never heard before, "Dear heavenly Father, help my family. We are in need of Your divine guidance. We can't continue on as if nothing is wrong. Heal the divide between each of us, Mother and father and father and son. I invite You to come into this situation and bring Your healing touch. Make us a family that puts You first above all else and heal the hurts and pains of the past. In the name of Jesus, I pray."

Marilyn moved her daughter away holding her at arm's length. She looked directly into Emily's face examining her as if she were a stranger. Then she asked, "Where did you learn to pray like that?"

Emily smiled. She stood up and leaned over to kiss her mom on the top of the head. "Mom, you are my example. I hear you praying." Emily turned to go up the stairs to her bedroom. She wished it was within her power to stop her mother's pain, but that would take divine intervention.

Walking into her room Emily recalled the last time Carl spoke to her. She had looked up from her bed where she was reading to see her brother standing in the doorway. His voice was low, nearly inaudible. "Hey, sis, I'm leaving. I just wanted to say goodbye." Carl wasn't the secretive type but he continued to speak so softly that Emily felt herself leaning forward to hear. "I just want you to know that I love you."

"Carl, what's going on? Why the whispering?"

"Ems, Dad tried to pit us against each other, but it didn't work. He will never be able to do that. You are my little sister and I've got your back. Remember that!"

"Carl, what are you doing? Are you leaving?"

"It's time. I can't take it anymore."

With emotion in her voice, Emily pleaded softly following Carl's lead. "Please don't do it Carl. Don't go. You only have one year until college. Things will be better. I'm sure. Please, don't go." She was thinking of their mother's loss and not just hers, if he left permanently.

"I'm going down to tell them my plans right now. I have a friend whose parents will let me crash at their place. The house is small and pretty humble. They have a houseful of kids, grandkids, and in spite of tough times they love each other. Dad would call them, "white trash", not his kind of people, but I feel love in their home. No matter how much their kids mess up, my friend's parents just keep loving them and accepting them."

"Carl, you know Mom and Dad love you. Dad harps on you because he wants the best for you."

"Emily, you don't really believe that. He doesn't want the best for me. He wants the best for himself. I've felt for a long time that he's in competition with me. Each time I fail at something he can't wait to rub my nose in it. I think he does it to make himself feel better about his miserable life. I'm just taking myself out of his game." Carl crossed into his sister's room from the door way to give her a farewell hug. Emily leaped from the bed and ran into Carl's arms giving him a bear hug that nearly cut off his air supply. He hugged her back, kissed her wet cheek, and left before he changed his mind. On his way out he turned and said, "You stay up here. I'm not sure if I'll be in touch with you for a while. I don't want you to be in a position to lie for me."

Emily felt the finality of his words. He wasn't coming back to this house ever again. She felt it deep inside of her. She could never rob her mother of the hope that he would return.

Emily had not known her father's wrath like her brother. She seemed to do no wrong in his eyes. She knew he cherished her and thought she was, without prejudice, the best thing since apple pie. Emily couldn't imagine how difficult Carl's life had been seeing all their father's love lavished on her. She knew there was good in Carl because he never was jealous, lashed out at her or blamed her. He loved her too.

Marilyn heard the back door open at 9:50 p.m. on the dot. It was James. He was always true to his word. He said five hours and it was five hours almost to the minute. James has always been a stickler for promptness. That was the beginning of the problems between him and his son. Carl was a free spirit. Clocks, schedules, and responsibility were never a part of this young man's life. It seemed a cruel twist of nature to match such a father with such a son.

James Carl Fields was the only child of Jonathan and Martha Fields. They lavished him with every possible luxury. He was their pride and joy. James grew up without restraint. He was pampered and privileged. When his parents died unexpectedly in a traffic accident he was not prepared for the cruel twist of fate that awaited him.

James went to live with his paternal grandparents in accordance with the will of his parents. Grandpa and Nana were kind and caring but seemed a bit too religious for his taste. The whole church thing was new to him but it was important to his grandparents. He resigned himself to follow their rules. But all the while, there was a slow boiling resentment when he was disciplined. A life with restrictions was an unpleasant and unfamiliar existence.

James's parents had left him a comfortable inheritance that would leave him in good financial standing for the rest of his life. The family business would pass to him when he turned twenty-one. James would bide his time for 10 years and then he would be his own man. He received a degree in business and took over the Field's Insurance Company on the day he turned twenty-one.

A few years later James's grandparents would die within six months of each other. James plunged himself into his business and the church. The church that once had been a form of unwelcomed discipline now became his obsession. The Community Outreach Church in Hillbrooke, Michigan had become his country club. He was a member in good standing and his large contributions to the church soon gave him the title of "youngest person to ever serve on the church board."

James was twenty-five and Marilyn almost twenty when they moved into their present home. Marilyn immediately became the wife and hostess James had dreamed she would be. They were married only two years when Carl was born. If Marilyn could mark the day that things changed, it would probably be the day they brought their son home from the hospital. When Marilyn's time began to be divided like slices of a pie, James could not handle his piece being sliced thinner. He wanted a nanny for the baby but Marilyn's dream of motherhood left no room for someone else to rob her of the joy of nurturing her own child. It may have been the only time in their marriage she didn't do what James told her to do.

As the Fields' family grew and welcomed baby Emily they seemed to settle into a typical family. Marilyn did the homeroom mother stint, hosted 4th of July & Christmas parties for the Insurance Company at their home. She became the go-to-person at church, and volunteered for any committee in the community that she could fit into her schedule.

As the years rushed by, Marilyn's hunger for the Lord intensified and she knew there was more to church than social activities and the Sunday morning service. She attended a community Bible study where the Bible was called the Word and Christians were called Believers. These Bible studies reminded her of how she felt immediately following her prayer of salvation. The Word seemed like healing oil poured on her. Yet, she felt as if, she stood at the doorway unable to cross over the threshold. There was more. She knew it and she wanted it!

As Marilyn's knowledge of the Lord grew she felt her home life disintegrating around her. The word divorce was never mentioned. Instead there was a constant verbal assault on her as a person. She had found a new place of solace that no one could penetrate. She had found prayer. Marilyn began to rise early in the morning before her family and would spend 20 minutes in prayer. It became her refuge, her hiding place. It was during these times she recharged her spiritual battery to face each day.

CHAPTER 7

The Playground Isn't Just for Playing. Kota Edwards—meet Carl Fields/Zac Parker

[18] *But GOD's not finished. He's waiting around to be gracious to you.*
He's gathering strength to show mercy to you.
GOD takes the time to do everything right—everything.
Those who wait around for him are the lucky ones.

Isaiah 30:18 The Message (MSG)

Hillbrooke wasn't a big town but it was big enough that Carl Fields could crash at his friend Kota's home without his parents finding him. That is if they were even looking. Kota lived in an area of Hillbrooke far from the sprawling lawns and brick homes of the Fields' family. Hillbrooke was an up and coming town. However, there were areas where the Fields' family would never go. In fact Carl had never been near the area where Kota lived until they became friends about a year ago.

Carl's first encounter with Kota was at the park on Washington Street, cleverly named Washington Park by the creative founding fathers of Hillbrooke. Carl and his father had another verbal blow up over one or maybe two of Carl's usual failures. Lately, he had a hard time keeping track of the many things that set his father off like bad grades, unexplained absences and tardiness at school. There was also the usual father vs. son transgressions like mowing the grass, taking out the garbage, and cleaning your room. However, the most recent issues between James and the young Mr. Fields were more criminal in nature like coming home drunk and the marijuana his mom found in his pants pocket. It was the latter two that had caused the most recent blow up.

Washington Park seemed like a choice location for stewing. The children's play area had a random swing or two still intact and the old cannon was tagged by would be artists. A few years ago at this park rival gangs clashed leaving three teenagers dead and one permanently in a wheelchair.

That day Carl looked around at the vacant park and was actually hoping someone would pick a fight with him. He had so much pent up anger towards his father he figured it was best for everyone if he were dead. He had contemplated killing himself on a few occasions, but he couldn't bear the thought of his mom or Emily being the ones to find his body. They had both suffered enough. This seemed like the best alternative. Hang out here until some low life started questioning him about being in their hood and then he would play the tough guy. Carl sat pondering all the possible scenarios, but what he hadn't considered was Kota.

Kota walked up to Carl with one hand in his pocket and asked, "Ya sell'n?"

"What?"

"You sell'n or buy'n?" Kota asked.

"What ya got?" Carl played along.

"I have pills, bags, and...." Kota listed his inventory.

Carl reached in his pocket and pulled out some cash. They made an exchange and began meeting weekly, then a few times a week, then daily. Kota didn't care who Carl was or where he came from. Carl never told Kota his whole story. Most people he tried to talk to about his life, just looked at him in disbelief and accused Carl of being some kind of crazy person for not being happy living in the lap of luxury. Carl knew. His sister, Emily knew. And their mom knew the truth. Only his father was oblivious to the suffocating, emotional vacuum and spiritual poverty where they actually lived.

Kota's home was a deep contrast to Carl's home. It was a small city lot on the corner near the old downtown area. Kota lived in a three bedroom house with a wooden exterior that was desperately in need of paint. The misshaped house had obviously been added on to many times—without pulling permits from the City Hall. Those who lived in the suburbs of Hillbrooke would be afraid to stop in this neighborhood.

The yard was overgrown and filled with broken toys, bikes with missing wheels, and garbage bags torn open by dogs; the contents scattered around. The inside of the house was full of people and looked more like borderline hoarders lived there. The aroma of stale smoke lingered in the air. Even with the windows open and the early summer breezes blowing through the house the smell was nauseating. That musty, smell had permeated every carpet, every piece of furniture, and article of clothing. The dwellers inside seemed to not smell the odor anymore, but it had attached itself to all who entered. Then it encompassed its host like a stinky aura.

Kota's parents, Bill & Mary Edwards, were simple and happy folk. In the mist of the clutter, some would have called it filth; there was peacefulness, acceptance, and patience in this home. These were things that Carl Fields could not remember experiencing in his beautiful, expensive, perfectly decorated brick home.

Bill Edwards was a gentle man with a small frame. His voice was soft spoken and his deep set blue eyes always seemed a little bit moist when he looked at his children. This father's love and pride were easy to see. It didn't matter if one of his four offspring did poorly in school, had a brush with the law, or shared the news, "I'm pregnant." These were his children and he loved them all unconditionally.

Mr. Edwards was on disability. He rolled an oxygen tank behind him everywhere he went. His favorite thing to do each day was to sit on his covered porch and watch the cars and people go by. Sitting in his lawn chair on the porch, Bill always had one hand free to wave at all who passed by whether they looked his way or not. The best part of his solitude was sipping his black coffee and sneaking a cigarette. The porch that was once totally screened in had only one remaining screen in place. The rest had been punched out by rambunctious children and grandchildren. No one seemed to care that the damaged screens, still partly attached, draped down from the window frames covering the foliage around the porch.

The day Carl moved in was no exception. "Hey, Pop, this is my friend Carl. He's gonna be staying with us for a while." Mr. Edwards waved in Carl's direction, took a sip of coffee, reached back and turned his oxygen off and lit up a cigarette. There were no questions like, "Is it okay with your parents? Does your mom know where you are?" Nope. Not one question about who Carl was or where he came from or why he was staying. Just…Welcome.

When Kota engaged his father in conversation he had his father's full attention. Mr. Edwards didn't have any favorites among his four children. They each could approach him without rebuke. It was as if Mr. Edwards found more pleasure in the company of his children than in any vice the world had to offer.

Mary Edwards, Kota's mother, had an uncanny sense of humor. She had a husky voice from years of smoking and when she would begin to laugh it often turned into a coughing fit. She was almost a perfect square at five foot nothing tall and almost the same wide. She was comfortable with her size. She never asked, "Does this make me look fat?" She wore whatever she wanted and usually the tighter the better.

Kota's parents were not the questioning type. It seemed their door was open to whosoever will.

"Hey, you kids. Get out of this kitchen." Mary Edwards yelled. "I'm fry'n chicken for dinner. Now out of here." She love tapped one on the back of the head as he scurried by, but no one seemed to be mad or angry.

Looking in Carl's direction Mary asked, "Are you stay'n for dinner?" She was handling the raw chicken in the kitchen sink and hot oil was popping in the electric frying pan on the counter.

"If that's okay? I don't really have any place to go." Carl replied. "I can do something to help out, if you'd like."

"I got no problem with you stay'n as long as you need, but I ain't got no room in this kitchen for a boy." She threw her head back and began to laugh. Then started coughing out of control.

"Well, if you do think of anything. I'll be happy to help pay my way." Carl replied.

"Who pays their way around here? Nobody, that's who, I can get you hooked up on some assistance. I know the ropes at the aid office and I have people down there I know by name. You got a job or income?" Mary asked.

"I have a bit of income with Kota, but not the kind you report." Carl smiled.

Mary laughed again until she was doubled over in a coughing fit. When she regained her composure she responded. "Well, we don't really talk about that as income. Do you work at McDonald's or bag groceries or anything else like that? I don't care if you're not working. I just don't want to get to the aid office and hav'm run your number and find out you got a full-time job somewhere."

Carl wasn't sure how this was going to work with his family income and him still being a minor. "I'm gonna have to get back with you on this Mrs. Edwards. I still have a few things I have to work out. Can I have about a week to take care of some things?"

"Sure, take your time and I'm not tell'n ya again, you call me Mary." Mary turned and without warning yelled at the top of her voice. "Somebody get that junk off the table." Little people came running from every corner to obey.

Carl saw the words **Public Defender/Legal Aid** painted on the old glass top wooden door. He had never had an occasion in his short life to darken the door of a lawyer's office. He was in unchartered waters. When he opened the door a loud bell announced his arrival. He wondered if this was one of the original buildings in Hillbrooke. There were some pretty amazing old structures in this area of town near the college and the court house. However, it was hit and miss which ones had been lovingly cared for, and which ones needed a bulldozer. The jury was still out on this building.

The receptionist greeted him. "May I help you?"

The desk where she sat was massive, Carl thought, they must have built the building around it. The kind older woman smiled at him. Maybe everything was going to be okay. Carl hoped.

He used the most mature voice he could muster and replied. "I need to speak with a lawyer about a personal matter."

"Sure, just take a seat and we'll be right with you." She pointed in the direction of an old, wooden bench with a dirty, green vinyl top. It was so holey it looked like Swiss cheese with dirty padding oozing out of every hole. Carl looked for a place on the bench that was still intact and sat down to wait.

A few minutes later a young lawyer stepped out of the office with khaki pants, a navy blue sweater with a button down collared shirt and brown loafers. He would have been the dream son of Carl's father, James Fields. He reached out his hand. Introducing himself then motioned for Carl to follow him back into his office.

Once inside the office they sat down. He turned to Carl and asked, "Okay, What can I do for you?"

Carl blurted out in one rehearsed breath, "I want to become emancipated from my parents, and then change my name. Can you help me with that?"

"Are you 17?" Mr. Lawyer-man asked.

"Yes, I'll be 18 in about five months."

"I think we can work this out. Is there any physical issue like abuse that is related to this request?" He looked up from his desk making eye contact with Carl. Mr. Lawyer-man searched his face. Then added, "I have to ask for legal reasons."

"No! Well, maybe, if you count emotional and verbal as abuse. Then yes. But I would rather not involve my parents at all. I don't want them to know where I am or what my name is being changed to. I need them out of my life completely and totally. I don't have much money but I can come up with some to help the process along. You just tell me what I need to do, and I'll do it." The desperation in Carl's voice was evident.

The lawyer stood up, went to his filing cabinet and pulled out two packets. He handed them to Carl and said, "You do this paperwork. Then come back in a few days, and we'll get the ball rolling. Have you thought about what you would like your new name to be?"

"I like the sound of Zac Parker. Will that work? And before you ask—I don't want a middle name!" Carl answered.

"It was very nice to meet you, Zac; I'll see you in a few days." Mr. Lawyer-man stood up and shook hands with Zac and at that moment Carl ceased to exist.

CHAPTER 8

The Interview

"I don't think the way you think. The way you work isn't the way I work." —God—

Isaiah 55:9 The Message Bible (MSG)

*T*he plan had always been to wait for the senior pastor position to open at World for Christ Church (WCC). Callan and Rey were buying their home, the kids were happy—everything was good. They were well liked and respected in the community, but in ministry, plans have a way of quickly changing.

Callan and Rey each were lost in their own thoughts as they drove under the huge road sign welcoming them to *Pure Michigan*. A rush of excitement coursed through Rey's whole body—followed by an awareness of all the things that could go wrong in a new place of ministry.

Callan broke the silence, "Rey, I hope they like us. It's been awhile since we've had to prove ourselves to anyone."

Rey tried to reassure his wife, "We'll be fine. We've talked this thing to death. Let's just give it a rest. Just be you. What's not to love?"

Callan rolled her eyes and sighed. "Yea, right! I'm not that same girl I was six years ago. I have two kids now and I'm a busy housewife. It will certainly be interesting to see what this church's expectations are for me. We are in a comfortable place at WCC." Callan paused and then added, "Change has never been easy for me." She turned her head slowly to look at her handsome husband. The corner of his mouth was slowly forming a smile. He glanced quickly in her direction. They both laughed. No one would ever accuse Callan of rolling with the punches.

Callan gave Rey an air punch in the arm stopping just short of hitting his shoulder.

Rey tried to encourage her even though he was laughing. "They will love us both. Cheer up. Don't forget the pay package. At the very least—we get a three day vacation in Michigan. All expenses paid and even if they do ask us to come—it doesn't mean we have to. We are in control of our own destiny."

"This is true!" Callan drifted off into her thoughts for a moment then blurted out. "I don't mind doing a fun little Bible study once a week or singing when needed in the service. What I'm not going to be is one of those senior pastor's wives who is expected to organize everything. I won't be giving the opening prayer at every ladies function, and be at the church every time the doors are open. I have a family to take care of. Please make sure this is clear to the board when we talk to them! They aren't hiring me." Callan pointed at herself for clarification. "They're hiring you! I already have a job." Callan reclined her seat and rested her head on a pillow she brought. She plugged in her headphones and listened to Taylor Swift's latest album. Rey turned the talk radio on and became riveted by the crazy callers doing verbal combat with the guest host over immigration, healthcare, and the latest politician to throw his hat in the ring for president. It was all highly entertaining.

The church in Hillbrooke, Michigan occupied a choice piece of real estate in an upper scale area of town. The 25 acres of church property had a two-acre stocked pond; fifteen of the acres were wooded. It was impressive, but it wasn't the new slick ten-million dollar building the World for Christ church had in the suburbs. The drive into Hillbrooke also revealed areas of the town that were definitely low-income. That was the word Callan used to describe these types of neighborhoods. She felt safe in the car passing by on the expressway pointing in the direction of the obviously shabby area.

Pulling up to the church property the Community Outreach Church looked more like something between an "old money" exclusive country-club and a mountain ski lodge. The impressive three story front to the church was made of stone and glass with rugged timber inlays, but there was no cross or steeple in sight to identify the place as a church. The sign that held the church name was also engulfed with huge rocks that it gave one the feeling of entering a mountain resort more than a place of worship.

The Douglas's turned into the church grounds passing the massive entrance sign. They followed the two lane road around the building until they came to the entrance for the church office. A green canopy covered the walkway. The ground slopped down at the side of the building. The side parking lot looked out on an expansive area for parking that backed up to a woody area. There was another green canopy that covered a staircase to the second level at the side of the building. A sign was attached to the timber staircase that said, PASTOR'S PRIVATE ENTRANCE. The letters were bold and black.

Rey pointed at the door, "Look Callan, these people know how to treat a pastor." Callan's nonverbal communication shouted clearly to Rey that she was not impressed.

Rey parked in one of the visitor parking spaces, and Callan took a moment to freshen up her make-up before going in to meet the church board. Rey walked around the car to opened Callan's door. Just in case someone from inside the church may be watching. Callan stepped out looking every bit the beautiful and confident woman she was—on the outside.

Callan gripped Rey's hand and crossed over into the unknown. "I'm feeling nervous, Rey."

"It's going to be fine. You've got this." Rey opened the door to a beautiful reception area that continued the lodge theme. Behind the welcome counter there were a few ladies typing at computers. An attractive lady in her late thirties or early forties was the first to respond by opening the false countertop to reveal a pass through area. She approached the Douglas's with a welcoming smile.

"Hello, you must be Pastor Rey and Callan Douglas. I'm Heidi (Hogan) Alden the office administrator. I am thrilled to meet you. We have all been looking forward to your arrival. I emailed you the info about the hotel, but here is a hard copy." Heidi handed the page to Rey. He passed it on to Callan. Heidi continued, "Have you checked in at the hotel yet?"

Rey responded, "No, we decided to come here first."

"Oh, that's great. The hotel is located just down the street. It's the nicest one in Hillbrooke." Rey could hear the pride in her voice. "I think you will be very comfortable there."

Pastor Rey extended his hand to Heidi. She pushed it away and went in for a full frontal hug.

Callan's expression showed her surprise. Then without warning Heidi turned her affections to Callan who received an identical embrace. She felt her personal space had been invaded by this overly excited office worker. Callan's family didn't do the hugging thing, and she felt extremely uncomfortable when strangers took such liberties.

Heidi, who was not good at picking up on non-verbal cues, continued with her overly cheerful voice and directed the couple to the conference room down a hallway of offices. Heidi opened the door to a large room with a wood burning fireplace. The massive reclaimed wood mantel was inlayed with huge stones all the way up the wall to the tongue and groove knotty pine cathedral ceiling. Facing the fireplace were two overstuffed, leather, wingback chairs. Between the chairs was a log end table with a lamp made out of deer antlers. Rey eyed the wooden conference table that took up half the room with eight more overstuffed leather chairs on caster wheels. He hoped his mouth wasn't hanging open. This was the best looking conference room he had ever seen. The décor was a perfect fit with his style.

The conference room was peppered with people some seated and some standing. The tallest man in the room approached Rey with his hand extended. "Welcome, Pastor Rey!" He grabbed Rey's hand and firmly gave it a shake.

"I'm James Fields. We spoke on the phone a few times. Let me introduce you to the rest of the board. This is John Alden. You already met his wife, Heidi. We call her the hugger." Heidi threw her head back and laughed awkwardly loud. "Heidi and John both have been attending Community Outreach for years. You could say we all grew up together." Walking around the room Rey and Callan were introduced to no less than ten people.

One by one James handled the introductions. There was the eldest couple in the room Harold and Esther Smith, they looked to be in their seventies. They were grandparently with gentle voices. Rey believed the Smith's probably had a wealth of stories to share with anyone who had an ear to listen.

John and Heidi Alden were in the late 30's, early 40's range, happy, laughing a lot, maybe too much. They seemed along for the ride. They both looked to James for cues, and it was easy to see they admired him.

Peter and Katherine Carver were obviously money people; the hair, the clothes, the jewelry, and the posture. They had it all in spades. They looked very unimpressed by the whole dog and pony show. But they would never give up their front row seats.

Drs. Henry and Dorothy Samson were in their fifties. Henry had distinguished gray at the temples, and Dorothy had that patch in the front that looked like a skunk's stripe. They both were professors at the state universities in town. They radiated the aura of a strong work ethic, expecting the same from others. They looked very intellectual and boring.

Then there was the chairman of the board, James Fields and his wife Marilyn. James was definitely a successful businessman. He walked around the room with the authority of a born leader. Most of those present followed his lead. Marilyn was the exception and the most puzzling one in the group. The jury was still out on her. There was a confidence in her that was sincere. She wasn't showy or loud. There was something different about her. She seemed most comfortable when she was with the older couple, the Smiths.

Rey couldn't quite put his finger on it, but there was something about the Smiths and Marilyn that he liked.

Introductions were over and the group headed out to a nice restaurant for a meal together. There was lots of table talk, and some of the women took the opportunity to grill Callan. More than once Rey was kicked under the table by his wife when a question was too personal. Following the meal the wives said goodbye, except Heidi. She would be available, if needed during the interview process. Rey and Callan followed the group back to the church for the official interview with the board.

James Fields gave the Douglas's the VIP tour of the church. They heard the history of the purchasing of the property and the different building phases. They looked at every nursery, children's classroom, bathroom, office, and adult lecture room. The kitchen was equipped with commercial grade appliances. They looked at the gymnasium-fellowship hall and exercise room. Each had state of the art equipment. The 1,000 seat auditorium with a balcony that covered a fourth of the main floor was beautiful with timber walls stained in the natural color of the pine. The pastor's office was about half the size of the conference room but had all the same amenities; wood burning fireplace, lodge décor and furnishings. The office also had the cathedral ceiling with tongue and groove knotty pine. Of course, James pointed out the private entrance to the parking lot. There was a picture window behind the seating area that allowed natural light into the office. The view from the window was the side parking. The woods boarded the parking lot. It was picturesque.

Following the tour they returned to the conference room where most board members were seated around the table sipping wine. Rey was stunned by the open display of wine being consumed inside the church. He had purposed long ago that he would not partake of alcohol in any form. This was a shocking development to his conservative upbringing. Callan had been raised around social drinking and she was neutral when it came to Christians drinking.

James directed Rey and Callan to their seats at the table, "Pastor Rey, Callan—would you care for a beverage before we begin the meeting?"

Thoughts raced through Rey's mind. Do I want something to drink or don't I? Will I offend them, if I refuse? Maybe it's time I grow up and face the changing times? He answered. "I'd like a bottled water, if you have one." Rey squeezed Callan's hand and asked, "Callan, do you want anything?" He looked at Callan not sure how she would answer.

"Do you have any coffee?" Callan asked. She seemed oblivious to Rey's concerns.

"Sure! We'll get that for you. Cream or sugar?" James asked.

"Just cream."

James hit the intercom button on the phone and asked Heidi to make coffee.

James cleared his throat and officially opened the meeting. "Harold, would you open in prayer." Harold Smith, the eldest on the board was rarely called on for much of anything except to open and close in prayer. He seemed to be the only one who was readily willing to accept this task.

The next hour was filled with questions posed to the candidate couple from James Fields. He asked them about how they came to know the Lord, how they met, their philosophy of ministry, church growth expectations and they reviewed the pay package, vacation plans and health insurance coverage. Rey handled each question with ease. He was a great communicator and could think quickly on his feet. Rey assessed the room with each question he answered and could see the group relax. Some even leaned back showing they were entering another level of comfort—their body language indicated approval.

The interview portion of their weekend was over. Rey drove to the hotel feeling pretty pleased with his professionalism and polished answers. "Callan, how did I do?"

"That wasn't nearly as bad as I thought it would be. In fact, I don't even know why I needed to be there. This is really all about you—and you blew it out of the water!" Callan smiled at her husband. She was proud of his abilities.

Rey returned the smile. He loved Callan's approval. One might say it was his *"Turkish Delight"* or his *"kryptonite."* He could never get enough of it like Turkish Delight and it rendered him helpless to her powers like kryptonite. When they pulled into the hotel for the night they were both happy that portion of the weekend was over.

Saturday morning following the interview, Rey and Callan explored the four square blocks of downtown Hillbrooke. There were a number of cute little store fronts; antiques, home décor, fudge and candle shops. A trendy clothes outlet caught Callan's eye. She disappeared inside on a mission. Rey spotted a soup and sandwich shop with specialty coffees. He strolled down the street and picked up a coffee and donut for each of them. Rey took a seat on the bench outside and answered emails while his wife shopped.

Rey glanced up from his phone to see Callan walk in his direction with two shopping bags and a big smile. "I got you a coffee and donut. I was going to eat it, if you were one minute longer."

"The prices are amazing. They were practically giving this stuff away."

"There's a farmers' market at the end of the street. Do you want to go walk through and see if they have any free samples?"

"Sure. I'm looking for one of those sweet Michigan tee shirts or a hooded sweatshirts. Anything that says Michigan on it will do." More shopping—Callan was giddy.

The remainder of the day was filled with sightseeing and then dinner at the home of James and Marilyn Fields.

The usual Sunday morning attendance of 500 was up to 600. Every person who ever signed a membership card was there to get a peek at the new pastoral candidate. Rey filled the place behind the pulpit with ease. He was impressive and took authority as he preached a well-rehearsed message of exactly 40 minutes. Callan beamed with pride through the whole service. Rey was eloquent and handsome standing behind the sacred desk. He looked great in the spotlight.

Following the service Rey and Callan stayed for a dinner prepared by ladies in the church for a select group of the congregation. There were about 100 people in attendance and Rey and Callan felt like the bride and groom at their wedding reception. The gymnasium was decorated beautifully for the meal. They felt important and honored.

Following the dinner, James walked with them to the car. "James, we had a wonderful time with you and Marilyn last night. Community Outreach is a welcoming place. We felt right at home. Thank you for allowing us to come. We have a long drive ahead of us and two little boys we are anxious to see."

James shook Rey's hand one more time then handed him an envelope, "Here is a thank you from the church for coming. The membership will be meeting tonight at 7 P.M. for the vote. I'll give you a call on Monday morning. You did a wonderful job, just as I thought you would." James smiled and touched Rey's shoulder in a fatherly manor. Then he turned to Callan and gave her a quick side hug. His big arm swallowed her. Rey opened Callan's car door and waited for her to get in then gently closed the door. This was a gesture performed only when he deemed it necessary.

Rey and Callan left the church parking lot and headed for the interstate. Hillbrooke was behind them. It was going to be hard to get their feet back on the ground after the royal treatment they received the past three days.

"Callan, here's the check. Before you open it lets guess how much it's for."

Callan held the sealed envelope and tapped it on the palm of her hand. "I'm going to guess $1,500. What do you think?"

"I think it will be $3,000."

"Are you kidding me? That's ridiculous. I should keep the whole check for me, if I'm closer."

"Well, what if I'm closer?"

Callan jerked her head in Rey's direction and smiled sweetly. "Then I still keep it all for me." Callan ripped the envelope open and screamed, "Its $5,000 dollars. Who gives that much money for an honorarium? We could make a profession of trying out for churches."

"I'm speechless. I believe they must have liked us." Rey and Callan sat quiet for a time. Then the ultimate discussion began. The pros and cons of accepting the pastoral position were deliberated for about five minutes of their seven hour trip. They were both ready to say, YES, if the invitation came.

Monday morning Rey decided to stay home from work. He was having a difficult time getting the events of the weekend out of his mind. It was 10 A.M. when his cell phone rang. The number was from out of state.

He answered. His tone a bit more professional than usual, "Hello, this is Rey Douglas."

"Hi Pastor Rey, this is James Fields from Community Outreach in Hillbrooke. Do you have a minute to talk?"

"Yes, what can I do for you?"

"I have been asked by the church to extend an official invitation to you to join the staff of Community Outreach as our senior pastor. I'm sure you'll want to take a few days to consider the invitation, and that's fine. Could you get back to me within the week with your decision?"

"James, please express our thanks to the board and the congregation at Community Outreach. Callan and I have already discussed and prayed about it on the seven hour drive home yesterday. We both felt right at home in Hillbrooke, and particularly at the church. We feel it will be a perfect fit for us. We believe the Lord has great things in store for us personally and the church. We are looking forward to joining the team at Community Outreach."

"I'm thrilled to hear that, Pastor Rey. I'll let the board know. We'll be in touch with a time frame for your arrival. I will have Heidi send a check to advance you for your moving expenses. We can hash that all out later. Do you have a family photo you could send me?"

"I have a nice one at the office. I'll send it by email tomorrow." The call ended with the typical goodbyes. Both men expressed their excitement about the future.

When Rey hung up the phone the excitement was replaced with an uncomfortable feeling in the pit of his stomach. He pushed the emotion aside, dismissing it as nerves and began making a mental list of all the things he needed to accomplish in the next four weeks.

CHAPTER 9

Welcome To Hillbrooke

"Then he chose David, his servant, handpicked him from his
work in the sheep pens.
One day he was caring for the ewes and their lambs, the
next day
God had him shepherding Jacob, his people Israel, his
prize possession.
His good heart made him a good shepherd; he guided the
people wisely and well."

Psalm 78:70-72 The Message Bible

om and Jean Brown arrived in Hillbrooke one week before
Tom began his new job at Superior Solar Energy Plant. The
company had a fully furnished corporate home on Deer Lake that was
available to them as long as they needed. Tom turned the car down the
winding driveway towards their new home. Blue spruce trees lined
the long drive that finally opened up to a two story log cabin with large
picture windows in the front and back. This permitted a view straight
through the house to the lake. It was an impressive sight, with only one
other house visible on the semi-private lake.

Tom and Jean stepped up to the massive log door and slipped the
key into the lock. Tom swung the door open, took Jean's hand and

together they crossed the threshold into the massive entry. Before unpacking one box or carrying even one item into their new home, the Browns held hands and Tom prayed, "Lord, we dedicate this home to you. May it be a place where the hurting come for restoration, the sick come for healing, hopeless come to find hope and those who are looking for living water will come and be filled."

Jean began to pray, "Lord, speak to us. We ask for Your direction. Guide us in every detail of our lives from where to shop, the doctor we will go to, and the church we will attend. Direct us as we start a small group in our home. Lead us to the people You want us to minister to, and begin to prepare their hearts." Jean paused.

Tom started back up, "Lord, we know you have a plan for our lives, and we surrender to You in everything. Help us have ears to hear what the Spirit says. Help us be sensitive to His gentle guidance. We love you Lord. It is because of You that we live and move and have our being. In Jesus name we pray…" Together they said, "Amen!"

And so it began!

It was moving day for Rey and Callan. Summer in Michigan was perfection with a warm breeze that felt refreshing after the long—long snowy Illinois winter. The yellow moving truck slowly backed into the driveway of the Community Outreach Church parsonage at 1329 Lancaster Drive. The yard was a horticulturist's dream with bright colors everywhere you looked. The purple irises along with orange and yellow day lilies encircled the four well-positioned maple trees on the ample front lawn. The parsonage was a stately white, brick ranch with gray shutters. The red French doors made a grand entrance to the 3,000 square foot home. There were four bedrooms, three and a half bathrooms, a fully finished walkout basement, an attached three-car garage, a remodeled chef's kitchen, a family room with a stone fireplace, and a pastor's office with a private entrance. Rey and Callan had never lived in a lovelier home than this one.

Callan opened the passenger side of their white jeep and stepped out. A proud smile formed on her lips as she took in the beauty of their new home. She had taken a quick tour of the parsonage when they were in town for the interview, but now it was a done deal. She felt a sense of pride well up within her. She thought of the day her parents would come to visit. It would be a triumphant victory for her. She would not need to lower herself to say, "I told you so." She would see the envy on her parents face and that would be victory enough for her.

Rey stepped out of the jeep and opened the back door of the car to release the prisoners, Zander and Ty. The boys had been cramped up for a few hours since their last stop. They bolted out of the jeep running across the yard. Dropping to the ground, the boys rolled in the grass and giggled. Rey watched his boys with a smile.

He turned back to speak to Callan. "Can you believe this is our home? Let's pray and thank the Lord for such a beautiful place."

"Oh, sure, we should definitely do that. Just let me be sure that truck doesn't back into the..." Callan screamed, "No, stop." She ran towards the moving truck with her arms waving in protest. The driver of the moving truck had backed up onto the meticulous lawn leaving a tire track.

Rey collected the boys and unlocked the parsonage door. The last thing he saw before going into the house was Callan reaming out the moving truck driver. Her finger pointed at the rut in the lawn. Then she pointed at the driver. The other hand never left her hip. Rey had seen that look before. He actually felt a little sorry for the poor guy.

The Douglas family settled into the parsonage. It had been a long week of hard work unpacking and getting acclimated to their new surroundings, but they knew they were home. Callan stepped outside to retrieve the newspaper. Someone had tossed it carelessly into the front yard. She made a mental note to find out who that person was and correct the problem. Walking back to the porch, she removed the rubber band that held the small newspaper together with the advertisements. She glanced at the headlines on the front page.

An audible gasp escaped her lips. On the front page of the newspaper looking back at her was that terrible family photo they had taken a year ago. The one where she realized bangs were never a good idea. How could Rey give the church this picture? Why didn't he talk to me? If she knew the church wanted a family photo she would have insisted a new one be taken. Oh, the damage was done now. Everyone in Hillbrooke had received the newspaper with her picture plastered all over the front page and with bangs to boot!

Callan stepped back into the house with the newspaper tightly gripped in her hand. She was ready for battle. Rey sat peacefully at the breakfast table looking out the bay window into the backyard. His Bible lay open on the table in front of him. He lifted his coffee cup to his lips at the same time as the surprise attack. Bamm! The newspaper hit the table with a thud. He jerked—the coffee sloshed back and forth in his cup then over the rim leaving brown blotches on his white shirt.

Rey responded abruptly, "Callan, what is the matter with you?"

"Look." She opened the wrinkled paper and pointed at her picture on the front page. "Just look at me."

Rey took the newspaper and looked at the photo—then at her. "What's the problem? It's our family picture from a few years ago." Then it hit him. "Our picture is on the front page of the newspaper. That's amazing." He looked again at the newspaper and examined the full article.

Callan was quiet, maybe a little too quiet.

"It's our introduction to the community. James asked me for a family photo while we were still in Illinois. I copied the one I had in my office and sent it to him by email. I didn't know it was for the newspaper. I thought it might be for the church bulletin or something." He hoped his words would appease her.

They didn't.

He quickly added. "You look beautiful, honey. I've always loved this picture of us."

Callan didn't take the bait. "Really! Do you think I want this to be Hillbrooke's first impression of me?" Before Ray could speak, Callan said one more word and her disgust was evident. "Bangs!" She grabbed the paper from Rey and put it under her arm.

"Oh come on, Callan. No one is going to be looking at your bangs. They will be looking at your beautiful face!" Rey pushed his chair back from the table and stood up, "Hey, as much as I love the direction this conversation is going, it's my first day of work and I need to change my shirt. I'll call you later to fill you in on how things are going." He turned to go down the hallway towards the bedroom, then stopped and walked back. He reached for Callan's hand, "Let's pray together and ask the Lord to bless the day."

Callan kept cleaning. "You go ahead and go to work. I'll pray for you later when I have time." She stopped to give him a peck on the cheek and went back to cleaning up the spilled coffee.

Rey never saw that newspaper again.

Rey pulled up to the church ready to face his first day as senior pastor. Now he had to decide which door to enter. Would he use the main entrance to the office like the common folk or would he go directly into his private study? Since he had not received keys to the building yet, he chose the office entrance and felt like a boy on his first day at a new school reporting to the office for his class schedule. He had met the whole staff when he came for his interview six weeks ago. They were all friendly and happy to meet him that day, but upon entering the office things seemed a bit chilly. And, it wasn't the air conditioner.

The staff at Community Outreach Church knew each of their jobs were in jeopardy. All church staff served at the pastor's discretion. The secretaries—Grace and Tiffany, the office manager—Heidi Alden, the youth pastor—Dusty Anderson, the children's pastor—Matthew Lewis and the Music and Fine Arts Director—Eldon Chambers would each go through a screening time with Rey. He could let them go immediately or give them a six month trial period. They were all at Pastor Rey's mercy.

One by one the staff members met with Rey in his office. He told them that he would like to have six months to see them in action. Following this trial period, they would meet again and reevaluate. He gave all staff members a book on leadership to read and report back to him in a week. Then he prayed with each one before sending them back to work. This took half the day.

Once alone in his office, Pastor Rey leaned back in his chair. He crossed his hands behind his head and took in the visual beauty of the rustic room. He immediately felt at home and began to unpack his books along with some personal effects making this office, his office. The family picture of Callan with bangs was at the top of the box he was unpacking. He put it in his desk drawer. He'd have to get a picture of just the boys or a new family picture, but for now he better not display *this* one.

He put a new legal pad on his desk, a set of colored pens and his Bible. He arranged them neatly. Then he opened his desk calendar and looked at the sermon schedule he had planned for the year. He felt a bit like God did when He looked at each day of creation and said, "It is good." A satisfied smile formed on his lips, and he closed the calendar.

His first Sunday sermon would be an introduction to the series, "The Foundations of Our Faith." This would give Rey an opportunity to lay a foundation of the fundamentals of what he believed. He opened his Bible to the text and began reading Scriptures on the Triune God— The Trinity. Something seemed different. He felt anxiousness in his chest. He closed his eyes, lowered his head, and rested it on the open Bible.

He silently prayed, Lord, help me. I believe You directed my steps to Hillbrooke. I ask for Your guidance to shepherd this flock. I can't do this without You, nor do I want to.

Pastor Rey lifted his head and looked out the window across the room from his desk. His view was a mixture of trees that surrounded the parking lot. He continued his prayer speaking out loud. "Help me love each person You bring through the doors of this church—no matter who they may be."

A wave of emotion washed over him. Rey stopped praying. He was not prepared for the tears that followed. This was not like him. He explained it away as exhaustion from the move and the stress of interviewing the staff.

There was a box of tissues across the room on the end table. He pushed back from his desk and retrieved the box. Taking an ample handful of tissues he wiped his eyes, blew his nose, cleared his throat and took a sip of water from the water bottle someone had put on his desk.

Regaining his composure, he still had one more thing he needed to accomplish before he went home. He needed to set up his email account that was linked to the church website. He turned on the computer and logged in with the previous pastor's password. Rey said out loud, "I guess I need to do two things. First, change password. Second, set up email."   When he opened the internet, the home page the previous pastor has chosen was a website that showed a passage of Scripture for the day. His eyes focused on the verses, and he began to read the words out loud.

> "Take a good look at my servant.
> I'm backing him to the hilt.
> He's the one I chose,
> and I couldn't be more pleased with him.
> I've bathed him with my Spirit, my *life.*
> He'll set everything right among the nations.
> He won't call attention to what he does
> with loud speeches or gaudy parades.
> He won't brush aside the bruised and the hurt
> and he won't disregard the small and insignificant,
> but he'll steadily and firmly set things right.
> He won't tire out and quit. He won't be stopped..."
> Isaiah 42:1-4 Message Bible

A wave of peace and contentment washed over Rey and his eyes once again filled with tears. The words on the screen were no longer visible. The Word of the Lord was like an arrow in the hand of a skilled archer. It hit its mark—and so it began.

CHAPTER 10

Everybody Oughta Go To Sunday School

*When they said, "Let's go to the house of God," my heart
leaped for joy.*

Psalm 122:1 The Message Bible (MSG)

om and Jean Brown had been in Hillbrooke for six weeks.
That was six Sundays of visiting six different churches. Most
of the churches were filled with friendly people. They were greeted
with warmth, interest and solid Bible based teaching from the pastor.
Following each visit, they prayed for the church, the pastor and even
some of the people. So far the peace of the Lord had not settled on
them.

Tom arrived home from work and collapsed into the comfy recliner
in the family room. He looked out the wall of windows at a perfectly
framed view of Deer Lake. The water was calm with a row boat sitting perfectly still near the center of the lake. There was one adult and
one child fishing. The tranquil image caused an audible sigh to escape
Tom's lips.

He reached over and picked up the newspaper from the end table. His
eyes settled on the front page headline; COMMUNITY OUTREACH
WELCOMES NEW PASTOR. The photo that accompanied the article

had a young married couple with two small boys. The couple looked to be maybe in their late twenties or early thirties.

Tom read the article then rested the newspaper in his lap. He removed his reading glasses and rubbed his eyes. Tom had learned a long time ago not to fight the urge to pray. In obedience, he placed his hand on the picture in the newspaper. He prayed as the Holy Spirit led him.

Jean Brown arrived home. Coming in through the garage door she called out, "Tom, I got Chinese takeout. Hope you're hungry." There was no answer. Jean set the bags on the kitchen island and headed towards the family room. "Tom, are you home?"

"In here. Sorry I didn't answer before." Tom looked up, his eyes moist from his prayer time.

Jean glanced at Tom then at the newspaper that he held sandwiched between his hands. Smiling she said, "I see you found the newspaper. It had the same effect on me this morning."

"What do you think, Jean, should we try this Community Outreach Church on Sunday?" They laughed. But they felt a sense of urgency. They had just received their marching orders and war was imminent.

Six years had passed since James and Marilyn Field's son left home. There had been plenty of rumors around town about where their son might be or what he might be doing. One story reported Carl had hopped a train going to California. Another rumor had him living on a fishing boat in Alaska. The fishing boat report was one Marilyn sometimes day-dreamed about. Thinking of Carl reeling in the catch of the day with his fishing buddies occasionally gave her hope that he was alive and well. Unfortunately, most of the stories she heard about her son were not good. The worst gossip regarding Carl was the story of him being in prison for murder!

Sweet Emily kept trying to reassure her mom that Carl had good in him. They both held out hope believing one day they would be reunited as a family. Marilyn desperately wanted to hire a private investigator to find her son. But James forbad it.

James held firm to the position of tough love. This allowed him to shut the door on any memory of his son. He ordered all pictures of Carl be removed from his sight. Marilyn and Emily were banned from speaking Carl's name within ear shot of James. Marilyn believed it was from guilt and pain that James acted with such callous indifference. Perhaps, the only way he could clear his conscience and remove the pain of his loss was to pretend Carl never existed. Any person who entered the life of James and Marilyn Fields in the past six years would have never guessed this family once had a son named Carl. Was he dead or alive, well or sick, hurting or healthy? No one talked about him.

Marilyn felt so helpless to fight against her husband's firm and unflinching resolve. However, there was one thing James could not control—her prayers.

Marilyn glanced at her watch, it was 2 P.M. She walked up the stairs, opened the first door on the right and peered in cautiously, as if she would be interrupting someone.

Carl's bedroom was undisturbed. It had been undisturbed for six long years. There was a white, armless rocker that looked very odd in this otherwise boyish room. Years ago, Marilyn had moved the rocker into Carl's room, along with a small end table. This was for her own comfort when she prayed. On the table, a 5 x 7 picture frame held a picture of Carl when he was sixteen. He was slimming down from his pre-adolescent chubbiness and coming into puberty full force. His face was peppered with acne, but to Marilyn he was her cherished son.

Marilyn kept her favorite Bible, a journal, pen and a box of tissue on the table by the treasured photo. She had spent many precious hours alone with the Lord in this room. It had become a haven of peace and solitude in her otherwise stressful world.

Marilyn entered the room, and picked up her Bible as she walked toward Carl's bed. The wooden plantation shutters were closed, but the afternoon sun caused beams of light to filter in through the horizontal slats. This cast lines of light across the flannel comforter. She knelt down and laid her Bible on the bed. She moved her hand across the top of the bed remembering the place her child slept. She smoothed out the non-existent wrinkles and buried her face in the softness of the mattress.

Her voice was barely detectable. A moan escaped her lips followed by another and another as she began to intercede. "Jesus, Jesus, Jesus" and at the mention of that name, Carl's bedroom changed from a hopeless reminder of her lost son to a throne room where she had the ear of Almighty God, the Creator of the universe.

> *"Lord Jesus, wherever he is, please spare his life. Protect him, I pray. Open his eyes, open his ears, and make his heart ready to hear. Make a way for him to come back to You. Bring the right person into his life at the right time when his heart is ready to hear.*
>
> *Lord, I ask that You would release the power of your Spirit into the life of my…"* Marilyn paused, and swallowed a dry gulp of air. Rephrasing her prayer she began again with a new found brokenness, *"…Your son, Lord. I release Carl James Fields to You, to Your care. I can't make this thing right only You can, Lord. In the name of Jesus I pray for the salvation of Carl. Amen."*

Marilyn pushed herself up from the floor and returned her Bible to the end table. She picked up Carl's picture, and ran her finger over his face. She took her index finger, touched it to her lips and pressed it against the glass that protected the picture. This was her daily ritual. She had rarely missed a day over the past six years. She certainly had felt the ups and downs of her commitment to pray for her wayward son. One might say she had prayed her way through the seven stages of grief, but she knew the Lord heard her prayers. He heard the deep cries of her heart and was able to glean the wheat from the tares.

Marilyn sensed something was different; there was a desire to stay, to linger, to allow the Lord, the Comforter time to wrap His arms of love around her. The desire to wait in His presence was compelling.

She placed Carl's photo back on the table. Taking a step towards the door a permeating peace washed over her. The words formed on her lips and she spoke them out loud, "I have hope. I have *a* hope."

She wept freely. This was a brand new experience she had never felt before, an awakening. It felt wonderful, alive and empowering. She didn't want this time of prayer to stop. She lifted her hands in complete surrender to the Lord. Praise and adoration filled Carl's bedroom. Then suddenly another language poured fluidly from Marilyn's lips.

Marilyn surrendered to the wooing of the Holy Spirit and dropped to her knees. She rested her moist face on the soft flannel that covered Carl's bed. Marilyn marked this day, in her heart, as the one where she entered into a new place of intimacy with her Savior. He had given her an unknown tongue, a heavenly language. She was able to "pray in the Spirit!" This opened up a brand new level of worship and understanding between God and her.

The word vision was not a part of Marilyn's everyday vocabulary, or the other nice Christian terms like "mental picture or visual impression." Yet, Marilyn knew she saw something while she prayed, and it was real.

She relaxed in the rocking chair, picked up her journal and penned these words.

I was walking in a field, and there was nothing as far as my eyes could see. In the middle of the open space there was a yard with a broken split-rail fence defining the property line. There was only one way into the yard. It was a path that was so filled with junk, it was impassable. At the end of the blocked path was an apple tree with a few apples. I thought what a total waste. No one can get to those apples. That tree is worthless. No one could get past all this junk.

I turned to walk away. Then I stopped to look one last time, and I saw a man walk into the cluttered, junk-filled yard. He began picking up one thing at a time, and carried it away. I watched thinking what a waste of time. Then slowly the path began to open up. Before long it was passable. The man walked over to the apple tree. He touched it, and immediately blooms burst forth on every branch.

I couldn't believe what I was seeing. Then I knew. God was telling me don't give up on Carl. The apple tree represented him. God saw value in my son even when his father and I did not. I believe God is sending someone into Carl's life, wherever he is. I believe that person is going to open the way for him. I believe it Lord. Let it be so.

A peace filled her heart. She closed her journal and whispered, "Thank you, Jesus. I have hope."

One month ago, Kota Edwards was released from prison. Lucky for him he was the driver, and not holding the drugs. That would have added an additional year to his four year sentence. He was settling into life on the outside and living with his parents, Bill and Mary Edwards.

The whole Edwards clan, all four kids and no less than nine grand-kids of varying ages sat abnormally quiet in the living room. A silent dread hung in the air. On the coffee table in the center of the large cluttered living room lay Bill Edwards' cell phone. To anyone outside this room it would have been insignificant, yet to this group it was the focus of interest.

The family made feeble attempts at conversation, while stealing glances at the silent phone. Then an annoying little jingle began to play a 50's style song that once made everyone in the family smile and want to sing along. Not today. The whole family sat motionless, frozen in place, afraid to breathe while the phone danced to the music.

"I'll get it." Mary stood and reached for the phone.

"No! They'll want to talk to me." Bill said. Mary reluctantly handed the phone to her husband of 35 years.

"Hello, this is Bill Edwards."

The room was quiet. Everyone listening intently trying to make sense of the one sided conversation.

"Okay. I'll take the first appointment you have available."

There were a few more "yeses" and "noes" and an occasional "okay." Then the ending, "Thank-you Doctor, I'll call back tomorrow to confirm that time."

The room was quiet.

Tears began to form in Bill's eyes. How could he tell them? Mary stood by his side rubbing his shoulders and choking back sobs trying desperately to be the strong one. No more words were spoken among them. They knew. The test confirmed the worst. Bill had very little time left in this world.

The newspaper laid open on Bill's lap with the story about the young pastor who was new in town. Moments before the paper had been a simple distraction while Bill waited for the phone call from the doctor.

Bill held the paper up and declared, "Mary, I think this family should all go to church on Sunday. It will be just what we need." Bill looked around the room at the faces of his beloved, misguided and grieving family. He felt like the best loved man in the world.

Then with a bit of forced happiness he blurted out, "Are you all in? Will you come to church with me on Sunday?"

The group began to nod in the affirmative one by one because no one was able to utter a word.

Sunday morning arrived in the Douglas home, and they were ready for their first service at Community Outreach Church.

Rey walked into the bathroom where his wife was finishing up her makeup. The boys were fighting loudly in the next room. "This is it, Callan. It's been an amazing time in the ministry with you at my side. I believe the Lord has great things in store for us in Hillbrooke."

"Are you seriously trying to have a conversation with me right now? Really?" Callan let out a sigh of frustration. "I'm getting two little boys, and *myself* ready for church."

"Sorry." Rey started to walk away, but turned to add, "I feel such a closeness to the Lord like I haven't felt since high school."

Callan rolled her eyes. "Honestly, you're not going to talk about that standing in warm water thing again are you? We can't be late. I want to be sure everyone knows I don't look like that ugly picture that was in the newspaper."

Rey felt shot down and sadness touched his heart.

Callan continued her rant oblivious to her husband's pain. "Also, don't forget to introduce me to people when *you* know them and I don't. That is so awkward for me. It's like I have no value at all! When they say," Callan used a mocking voice, "and who's this lovely lady?" Then she returned to her normal voice, "It's like I'm an afterthought—nameless. I am not going to be known as *the pastor's wife*. I have a name!"

Rey thought about driving separately to church. His pastor friends had warned him that the Sunday morning car ride to church with the family in tow can be the most volatile time between a pastor and his wife. The advisors also said that the devil likes to mess with the pastor's head before he gets up to preach. Pastors must protect themselves from such negative distractions.

Rey wanted to defend himself. Instead he chose to take the high road. "Just stay close to me, my dear. I would be proud to let the whole world know you're my wife, and your name is Callan and your bangs have grown out to an attractive length."

He leaned in for a kiss.

She snapped, "Watch my lipstick!" Then turned her face and pointed to her cheek.

Rejection crept in again. Rey pushed those feelings down and gave his well-groomed wife a little peck on the cheek. He retreated to the family room to wait.

Community Outreach Church had one Sunday service. It began at 11 A.M. and ended no later than noon. Years ago the church decided to forgo Sunday School or any kind of adult Bible education. They opted instead for a Sunday night program for kids and teens only. This gave Rey a light speaking schedule. He spoke once a week.

Rey looked out the window of his office at a nearly full parking lot. He wasn't sure if this was the normal attendance or if attendance was up. He figured there would be some who came just to see the new show in town. Surely someone would let him know by Monday, if he hit the ball out of the park, or if it was status quo.

James Fields was in the grand lobby of the church welcoming people as they arrived.

Pastor Rey was happy to see a familiar face. "Good morning, James. I didn't know you were a greeter."

"No—I'm not! I'm normally not even in the lobby before service, but I was wondering if the newspaper article might bring in some new families. I wanted to be available to welcome them."

The music changed signaling the service was beginning. Eldon Chambers, the music director, opened the service with a peppy song and people slowly began standing. Some people even clapped to the beat of the music.

"Pastor Rey, I met one new family who came because of the newspaper article." James pointed in the direction of a nice looking couple in their 50's. "That is Tom Brown. He is a VP at the new Solar Energy Plant. They have money. Be sure and meet them after the service. Invite them out for a meal. I'll have some others do the same. We need to set the hook, while they are looking. They are *Community Outreach's kind of people*."

The words, '*Community Outreach's kind of people*' hit Rey like a gut-punch. He turned towards James to make a remark and saw an expression of shock on James' face. Rey followed his line of vision to a large group of people walking into the church.

Pastor Rey walked over to welcome the senior member of the group. "Hi. I'm Pastor Rey Douglas. I don't believe we've met."

The newcomer was wearing velcro tennis shoes with white tube socks and black dress pants about two sizes too big. His checkered shirt resembled a tablecloth. He was dragging a portable oxygen tank behind him. There was a distinct odor in the air of stale smoke and musty mildew that engulfed the family.

Pastor Rey extended his hand. The man of simple means accepted giving it a friendly squeeze.

With a raspy voice the man said, "Reverend, my name is Bill Edwards and this is my wife, Mary and this is most of our family." Bill waved his hand at the group of 10 people standing around him.   He smiled a toothless smile at Pastor Rey.

Mary had a tight curly perm that was half grown out which gave her head that flat look on the top and bushy on the sides.   It was bleached light brown with about an inch of gray roots.   She wore a dress that was snug and left very little to the imagination.

"Welcome Edwards' family.   This is my first Sunday so I don't know if you are long time attenders or new like me."

"It's our first time, Reverend!"

"Wonderful.   I hope we can talk again after the service."   Pastor Rey turned to pick up his conversation with James, but he was long gone.

He looked back at the Edwards family who were looking very out of place.   He watched Mary's eyes dart around from one well-dressed couple to another, hoping for just one pair of friendly eyes to throw them a lifeline.   But there were NONE.   They took seats in the back row.

CHAPTER 11

Church is over Life Begins

*"Don't hide your light! Let it shine for all; let your good
deeds glow for all to see,
so that they will praise your heavenly Father."*

Matthew 5:16 Living Bible (TLB)

*P*astor Rey closed the service by having the congregation read together the doxology from the gray hymnal.

Praise God, from Whom all blessings flow;
Praise Him, all creatures here below;
Praise Him above, ye heavenly host;
Praise Father, Son, and Holy Ghost

Following the reading, Rey gave a dignified, "Amen." Week one at Community Outreach Church was history. He stepped down from the platform feeling accomplished and proud. He grabbed Callan's hand. They hurried to the back of the church to greet people as they left.

Bill and Mary Edwards were some of the first people to shake Pastor Rey's hand. Their large family had already exited the church during the doxology. Bill wasn't going anywhere until he had a moment to speak to Pastor Rey. Bill's hoarse voice still carried volume. He could be heard all the way across the lobby.

Rey looked up to meet James Fields' disapproving scowl.

"Reverend, that was a wonderful sharing you did. I was happy to be here with my whole family." Bill paused to catch his breath leaning on the tall handle of his oxygen tank. "I have something small I'd like to ask you, Reverend. Not sure if this is allowed or what the preacher does, but I'd like to have a private talk with you at my house. Is that possible?" Bill reached into his pocket and pulled out a tithing envelope. A pencil sketch of the church was prominently positioned on the front of the envelope. "I wrote out my address and my phone number there on the card. Bring your wife too and any little ones. Me and Mary love kids. We always have a bunch underfoot. Love to have yous stop by. It's very important." Bill stopped talking. He leaned heavily on his wife.

Picking up where Bill left off, Mary spoke with unmistakable concern in her voice. "Well, we better get going. Others are waiting to greet you and your wife."

Mary leaned in to give Callan a hug following the example of others. Callan tightened up and offered a limp hand. Mary took it and smiled. "Nice to meet you Mrs. Reverend."

She took her husband's arm. They walked slowly to the parking lot where their son, Kota, waited to drive them home.

Again Pastor Rey saw James watching him from a distance. Then James was gone.

After he and Callan had said goodbye to the last parishioner, Pastor Rey headed to his office to drop off his sermon notes. Callan stayed in the grand lobby to chat with Heidi and Tiffany from the church office. Ty and Zander ran up and down the aisles in the sanctuary pulling tithing envelopes out of the pew pockets. They laughed as they laid waste to everything in their path. Callan glanced at her playful boys, but said nothing.

Rey opened the door to his office. Right on his heels was James Fields.

Surprised—Rey gasped, "Oh, James, you startled me. How did you like the service?" Rey asked this before he had actually looked into James's face.

"The service was fine." The harsh tone in his voice caused Rey to stop what he was doing and look directly at James. Both men stood over six feet tall. To an innocent onlooker it may have appeared these two were ready to square off.

"I saw that man with the oxygen tank invite you to his home. You surely aren't going? Right?" He waited a moment. Rey didn't respond. James added. "Let me rephrase that. As chairman of the church board, I would like you *NOT* to go. We don't want to encourage people like *them* to feel welcome."

Rey was speechless.

"There are many churches closer to where *they* live that would work for them. They would feel more at home there. Having them here would certainly make *me* uncomfortable wondering if my car is being broken into during church on Sunday. They are just not our target crowd. You understand? Do you want them to come back and bring more like them?"

"I didn't know you felt that way, James." Rey wanted to say so much more like I don't feel comfortable excluding groups of people from a church. That is far from anything I've ever read in the Bible. Jesus wanted sinners, poor, rich, young and old to all come to him. But Rey kept his thoughts and was ashamed for not speaking up.

"I knew you would see things my way. You didn't come here just by chance. I have watched you through the years, and followed your ministry. I knew you were *our kind of people*. The Doxology was a perfect closing to the service. We should do that every Sunday." James slapped Rey on the back, "Goodbye, Pastor." He turned and left Rey's office.

There was a distinct chill that remained in the air. This conversation took Rey by surprise. He wondered what James meant when he said that he had *followed his ministry.*

Wednesday morning started out the same as Monday and Tuesday. Rey was on his way to the church office promptly at 8:45 A.M. While waiting at the red light a mile from his house Rey glanced down and saw the edge of a tithing envelope between the seats. He worked his fingers between the seat cushion and the beverage holder. Finally, he was able to pull the envelope out.

The name Bill and Mary Edwards was written across the top of the envelope with the address to their house and a phone number. Rey pulled into the gas station a few blocks from the church. He typed the address into the GPS on his phone.

The Edwards family lived five miles away. The roundtrip would take about 12 minutes. He was just a little curious that's all. Rey thought about being late for work and pushed the thought aside. He touched start on the GPS and followed the directions to the home of Bill and Mary Edwards.

Rey had not been in this part of Hillbrooke. He knew that Callan would never have gotten out of the car, if he had brought her. He drove slowly down the Edwards's street. There were no mail boxes. Very few homes had numbers visible.

That must be the house he thought. He parked across the street far enough away to not be noticed. A few moments passed and Bill Edwards stepped out of the house dragging his oxygen tank. He plopped onto a folding chair on the covered porch.

Pastor Rey sat straight up in his car like he had been caught doing something wrong.

Bill waved at each car that passed by. Some people tapped their horns and waved back, most just passed by without giving Bill a thought.

Rey felt a wave of emotion sweep over him, much like that first day at the office. He thought. I hope I'm not going to start crying again. He fought it. He stayed and watched Bill a few more minutes. Then he put his car in reverse backing into a driveway with a huge pot hole. The car jerked back and forth. He glanced in Bill's direction. Bill was busy smiling at a pedestrian walking by. Rey put the car in drive, pushed gently on the pedal to avoid attention and headed down the street in the opposite direction.

He hated that he didn't take the time to meet with Bill Edwards. He remembered his words, "It's important!" Why didn't he stop?

A few minutes later he was safe at the church looking out his office window at the view of the woods. He took a deep cleansing breath and sat down in his leather office chair. Pastor Rey tried to push the picture out of his mind of the kind man sitting on his porch waving at people as they passed. He wondered what Bill and Mary needed to talk about. He hoped they would find a good church with a pastor who would give them the attention they needed—and deserved. James was probably right. They really didn't fit in at Community Outreach. He pulled the tithing envelope from his pants pocket and crumbled it up tossing it in the waste basket under his desk.

A voice booming through the intercom interrupted his thoughts. "Pastor Rey, it's Heidi. You have a call from a new couple who visited on Sunday. They wanted to talk to you. Can you take the call?"

Alarmed he asked, "Did they give a name?"

"Oh. Sorry. Yes, he said his name was Tom Brown from Superior Solar Energy." Heidi gave a nervous laugh. "I guess I should have started with that little bit of information. Should I put the call through?"

"Yes, Heidi. Thank you." Rey wondered which previous pastor hired Heidi as office manager and why. So far she had not impressed him with her office skills. She busted into his office the first week without knocking while he was praying. When he wasn't in his office she took the liberty to come in and move things around on his desk with the guise of straightening things up. She often forgot to ask who was calling, or like this time she had the information and didn't pass it on. Rey wanted to give her the benefit of the doubt, but she was making it difficult. There was also the loud laughing that had grown from annoying to intolerable.

Rey's phone buzzed when Heidi put the call through. "Hello, this is Pastor Rey."

"Hi Pastor Rey, this is Tom Brown. My wife and I visited your church on Sunday, and I wanted to call since we were not able to meet you following the service. Jean and I enjoyed the service, especially the message. We felt very much at home. We moved here about six weeks ago and have been looking for a church this whole time. I was wondering, if you and your wife would be free for dessert at our house on Friday evening say about 7 P.M. I can email you the address. Should I use the email listed on the church website?"

"Yes, that would work. It is the email for the pastor not the church office. I'll still need to check with my wife to be sure that will work with her. Can we bring anything?"

"No. It's our treat. We want to get to know you both and see how we can best serve the church and you in the future. I won't keep you on the phone. I know you are a busy man. I'll wait to hear from you." Tom ended the call. Rey felt a little better about abandoning Bill Edwards.

Callan had googled the Brown's before she consented to go to their house. She didn't want to be blindsided by some ghetto stink-fest. The winding drive leading to the Brown's home left Callan's mouth gapping open.

"Oh, my God, this is gorgeous." They pulled into the adjacent parking area with a perfect view of the sparkling water of Deer Lake. The evening sun cascaded on the lake making it look like twinkling diamonds.

They walked with confidence to the front door, hand in hand, ready to seal the deal for them and Community Outreach.

Tom and Jean opened the door and welcomed the Douglas family into their home.

"Pastor Rey, come see the beautiful view off the deck." Tom motioned for Rey to follow him.

"Callan, would you like to come to the kitchen with me while I finish making coffee?"

"Sure. Your home is lovely, Jean. That pie looks delicious."

"It's my favorite go-to company dessert. It's Key Lime Pie. It's the one that is fluffy and tart with a graham cracker crust. Do you like to bake?"

"I do. We plan to begin entertaining soon. Right now we are still living out of boxes. It's only been two weeks."

Jean walked out on the deck where the two men were enjoying the view and the summer breeze off the water. She motioned for them to join her inside. "Tom, let's have our pie and visit inside."

Jean served the pie and coffee. There was plenty of small talk between bites of pie and sips of coffee. There were stories of how each couple met, a bit about the children, funny stories of some embarrassing moments and then how each one came to know the Lord as their Savior.

Callan went first. Her testimony was concise and to the point. She told about her summer camp salvation. Callan had always held that as the time when she first believed. Then later at Bible College she revisited her childish prayer with an adult conversion. This time, she prayed a prayer of salvation during a special meeting her freshman year. Callan was uncomfortable talking about personal life experiences with strangers. However, the discussion did stir up some memories of that remarkable evening that she hadn't thought about in years.

Rey shared next about being raised in a wonderful home with amazing God-fearing parents. He accepted Christ as his Savior, praying with his parents, one night before bed. He was five years old. He decided to be baptized in water as a young teenager. He felt comfortable enough to share with the Browns about the experience he had as a teen in youth group, while Callan squirmed in her seat. She was sure the Browns would think they were some kind of crazy Holy Roller religious fanatics now.

Tom and Jean shared about accepting the Lord after they were married, and how salvation was the best life decision they ever made. After the Browns finished their story, Callan thought she may be the only sane one in the bunch. She looked at Rey who was totally taken in by their story of God's love, provision, mercy, healing and how they had an intimate relationship with Him. In fact, they freely talked about *Him* in a way Callan had only heard during her years at Christian College. It was all getting weird. Very weird and she was uncomfortable with this kind of discussion.

Her cell phone pinged signaling a delivered text message. It was from the babysitter. Callan scanned the message quickly. *I forgot what time to put the boys to bed. Sorry to bother you.*

Callan thought, thank God. "Well, it's from the babysitter and I think she is in over her head with our two rambunctious boys. We'd better call it a night. Thank you, Jean and Tom for your wonderful hospitality. You have a lovely home, and I do want that recipe when you get a chance."

Rey reluctantly stood to say goodbye. The conversation had been refreshing water to his thirsty soul. He was especially interested in the intercessory prayer and small group the Browns had been involved in at their last church. Rey had always called prayer—prayer. He always thought it was one of those words that didn't need any description. Listening to Jean and Tom talk was stirring something up within him. It gave him both a full and hungry feeling all at once.

Before Callan could escape to the car Jean took her hand. Callan was freaking out on the inside. *Why is this woman holding my hand?*

Jean asked, "Would it be alright with you both, if we prayed before you left?"

Callan's eyes went into saucer mode.

Rey oblivious to his wife's nonverbal communication blurted out, "Yes, we'd love that."

Tom took his wife's hand, reached out for Pastor Rey's hand. Then Rey took Callan's other hand completing the circle. Jean and Tom closed their eyes and lowered their heads. Callan caught Rey's eye and rolled hers. She used her head to point at the Browns. She mouthed the words, CRAZY PEOPLE. With that Rey closed his eyes and lowered his head.

Tom led out in prayer, "Dear Heavenly Father, it is with a happy heart that I come to You rejoicing for the new friends you have brought into our lives. We lift this family up to You asking for the Holy Spirit to guide, protect and speak into their lives as they do the work of the ministry. Lord, I ask in the name of Jesus that Rey and Callan would come together and be a powerhouse for You. May they be strong in Your name and in the power of Your might. Pour out Your Spirit—renewing and refreshing them. When the troubles and trials come, may they be reminded that You are ever present with Your ears open and Your arms extended to them. Bless this family as they do the work You have called them to do in Hillbrooke. Lord, grant them favor with everyone they meet as You develop and mold this man of God into the image of Your Son. I ask this in the name of Jesus, Amen." Tom brushed away a stray tear. He was such a softy as Jean jokingly called him.

Jean gave her husband a loving hug while saying, "He can't even give thanks for the food without getting a little emotional."

Rey was fighting back tears too. He didn't want a repeat of that first day in the office when he was surprised by a sudden display of emotion. The same feelings were rushing in right now. He could feel the reins slipping from his grip. Something inside of him wanted to cry out to the Lord. He took a deep breath and was able to keep it under control.

CHAPTER 12

Things They Are A Changen

*'You trained me well. You broke me, a wild yearling horse,
to the saddle.
Now put me, trained and obedient, to use. You are my God.
After those years of running loose, I repented.
After you trained me to obedience, I was ashamed of my past,
my wild, unruly past...'*

Jeremiah 31:19 The Message (MSG)

E mily Fields was no longer the chubby freckled fourteen-year-old who begged her brother, Carl, not to leave. She stood in her undisturbed bedroom; nothing had changed in the six years since her brother left. Unlike most girls who go away to college, Emily didn't gain the freshmen fifteen, but rather lost twenty pounds. Her hair was longer. The natural curls that once were unruly now framed her face with style. She had grown into a beautiful swan on the outside, but on the inside she still felt the ugly duckling.

Emily was one month into her summer break from college when she broke the news to her parents that she would not be returning to classes in the fall. She had completed her Associates Degree and passed the state Paralegal Certification. Her father tried to convince her to continue in her education to a Law Degree. However, Emily wanted to take at least one year off and work in the law profession to be sure this was the right career path for her. There was one other reason for staying home a year. She could feel her mother slipping away, growing distant and sitting for hours in Carl's bedroom alone. She thought it might be within her power to be the bridge between her parents disintegrating relationship.

At college Emily had been a serious student not allowing herself time for a social life. A few young men showed an interest in her but none turned her head. Guys were not on her radar right now. She had secured a job at the Legal Aid office in the old part of downtown Hillbrooke that looked very promising. This gave her the opportunity to do the type of legal work that interested her. What she didn't want was the "get rich quick" kind of legal work or sitting at a desk pushing papers.

Legal Aid provided her the kind of law that helped people who would otherwise be buried in the system. She treated each young person that walked through the door like it was Carl. She felt closer to her brother whenever she helped troubled teens or young adults.

Emily arrived home the same week that Pastor Rey and Callan Douglas came to town to candidate for the church. She liked them and felt they would be a breath of fresh air compared to the old regime. Before Pastor Rey and Callan came; the familiar stench of death was in the air. The services were lifeless, dry, old and routine.

Emily saw the changes. In a matter of months, Rey breathed life back into the church. New families were attending. The music was upbeat and alive. But most of all, the messages were applicable to life and actually interesting. Community Outreach Church was alive and powerful.

Two months had passed since Pastor Rey preached his first message. Things were not what he had expected when he consented to come to Hillbrooke.

James Fields scheduled a weekly meeting with Pastor Rey to discuss church issues without the other board members present. He came through the Pastor's private entrance and without knocking walked into Pastor Rey's office. James plopped down in the wingback chair across from Pastor Rey's desk and opened his leather portfolio.

He glanced down at the writing on his legal pad. The weekly reprimand always began the same way. "Pastor, I noticed a few things this week that you will need to work on." He paused and looked up at Pastor Rey. "The complaints I've heard lately have to do with the fact that you are too emotional in the pulpit. People don't mind a bit of timely anger in a message to keep the sheep in line, but crying? I think you should lose that all together."

Rey sat at his desk quietly and listened. A slow boil simmered.

"And some feel your messages make them feel bad about their lives. Maybe you could tone that down a bit. We're all struggling to live a good life here. No need to make us feel any worse about things. I look at it like this. They came to church so don't make them feel bad about it."

Rey couldn't hold his tongue any longer, "Would you like to look at my sermon schedule?" The sarcasm was lost on James.

"If you think my opinion would help, I'd be happy to do that." James smiled and leaned back in the chair.

Rey fought the urge to roll his eyes like a child. He kept his thoughts to himself.

"Also, if you want to keep the ladies and men's prayer meetings you started that's fine. I won't be attending again. I found it very uncomfortable when you called all the board members present to come to the front—singling us out. Then you asked the other men to form a circle around us and put their hands on our shoulders. That was totally unnecessary and an invasion of my personal space." Rey watched James tense up. His voice was taut with a hint of anger.

"James, I do want to be respectful to you." Rey paused forming the next part in his mind before he spoke. "But, I also must follow the leading of the Lord."

James stood up. His tall frame casting a long shadow across Pastor Rey's desk, "Don't make me regret bringing you to Hillbrooke."

Before Rey could speak, James was gone.

There was so much more he wanted to tell James. There were good reports coming into the church office on a daily basis; reports of answered prayer, salvations and those telling of growing deeper in their relationship with the Lord. Also, James must know that the church income was up. One of the best things that had happened personally for Rey was the small group he started with Tom and Jean Brown. That had exceeded all his expectations, but he was reasonably sure James was not interested in that.

Rey didn't get to share any of this with James. In the past, when he tried to share the positive things happening—James accused him of being an optimist. His feelings were dismissed with James' usual reply.

"New people are here today and gone tomorrow! They lack commitment to Community Outreach. As soon as a new show comes to town they will all be swaying to the beat of the music in another church."

Rey had heard it many times over the past few months.

"They are the kind of people who lack the commitment to put roots down and stay at a church long term."

Rey knew there was an element of truth to what James said.

The new small group meeting at Tom and Jean Brown's home was eight weeks old. The members were diverse, but blended together like butter and sugar, a great base for many wonderful recipes. The Browns led the group. Pastor Rey attended, but Callan chose to stay home and watch the boys. She said that she didn't want them to be parentless another night of the week. Rey reminded her it was the only scheduled week night meeting they had, but Callan wouldn't budge.

Two couples from the board attended, Harold and Esther Smith, the older couple in their 70's and Henry and Dorothy Samson, the PHDs. Pastor Rey knew that James wouldn't come but felt led to invite Marilyn and Emily Fields. That brought the number to nine. The group met on Thursday nights. Jean provided dessert and coffee each week. Tom led a short devotional. Then anyone who wanted could share how the Lord was moving in their personal lives.

The first week things were awkwardly quiet as this new concept was presented to the group. They closed each meeting with a prayer time. Whatever the needs, they prayed. Marilyn was immediately comfortable with this style of praying. She closed her eyes and felt like she was sitting in the rocker in Carl's bedroom. She had never experienced this outside the four walls of that room.

The group was like a tiny seed being planted in fertile soil. Each week it was watered and nourished. Then the first blade of green started poking out of the ground. With each week that followed, it grew taller and stronger. The nine members grew close as they shared, prayed and fellowshipped together. It wasn't an oak tree, but it was definitely a sapling full of potential, promise and life.

Pastor Rey had a hunger and passion to dive deeper into God's Word. He was spending two hours a day on Bible study, and it never quenched his hunger. He wanted more. He could sense this was the beginning of something life altering. God had a beautiful plan for his life. He knew it. He felt it. He was ready for whatever wonderful thing God was going to do next.

He pushed out from his desk. Leaning back in his swivel chair he cupped his hands behind his head. He gazed up at the wood ceiling for a moment. Then he began to pray.

"Lord, I feel it. You are doing a new thing in this church and in me. I invite You to invade my life and use me as You see fit. Help me stand against the tide, because I feel it is turning. Things have been easy for us in the ministry, but I know You have more. So much more is coming. I need You to prepare me. Make me strong, bold and brave for Your glory. LordY I ask this in your wonderful name. Amen."

The intercom buzzed. Rey opened his eyes. Heidi's annoying voice filled the peaceful office. "Pastor Rey, it's the funeral home on Main Street. Can you take the call? Did someone die? Do you know who? I haven't heard anything."

"Put the call through, Heidi. I'll see what they want."

Pastor Rey greeted the caller and waited for the reply.

"Hi Reverend, this is Kyle Mills from Mills Brother's Funeral Home. We have not met yet. Sooner or later I meet all the ministers in town. We had a request for you to do a funeral for a Mr. William Edwards. His wife Mary said that you were the only minister they knew."

"Bill? Bill Edwards died?"

"Yes. I believe they did call him Bill. The family selected Thursday at 1 P.M. for the funeral with the burial at the Hillbrooke Cemetery about one mile north of town. The viewing will be on Wednesday from 1-8 P.M. and again on the morning of the funeral from 9 A.M.—1 P.M. The family would like a funeral dinner. Would you and your church be able to accommodate the family? They are expecting about 70 people."

Rey thought of the prayer he prayed just moments ago. He had to be brave, even though he had never done a funeral. Strong, even though he felt ashamed beyond words that he put this poor family out of his mind and now Bill was gone. He would never have an opportunity to speak to that man again. Bold, since his church may not look kindly on him doing this funeral or providing a dinner for the family.

Lord help me! He prayed.

"Mr. Mills, I'm sorry to hear of Bill's passing. Yes, I will do the funeral and the church will be happy to provide a dinner for the family. Do you have a phone number for Mary? I need to talk with the family as soon as possible."

After information was exchanged, Pastor Rey hung up the phone.

As soon as his intercom light went off, Heidi beeped in. "Pastor, did someone die? Are we doing the funeral? Do I need to get the team together for the funeral dinner?"

Pastor Rey answered her questions one at a time. "Bill Edwards who visited here my first Sunday passed. I will be doing the funeral and we will host the family and friends for a dinner following the burial here at the church."

The phone was quiet. Then sheepishly Heidi asked, "Bill who?"

"He was the man with the large family who sat in the back. He had an oxygen tank."

"Oh. I do remember them. Why are we doing *that* funeral? Do you personally know them?"

Pastor Rey didn't want to get into a discussion with Heidi, but he answered her questions. "They asked for me to do the funeral, and it's my honor to serve them in their time of grief."

Rey couldn't see Heidi, but her attitude emitted through her silence. He continued. "Since I'm not sure how things are done here, I'm giving you the responsibility of the funeral dinner. The funeral begins at 1 P.M. on Thursday. With the service, cemetery and travel time we should be back at the church by 2:30 P.M. Plan on 70 guests for the dinner." The other end of the line was abnormally quiet. Pastor Rey ended the conversation before the questions resumed.

Heidi sat at her desk stunned. What was she going to do now? How would she ever find people to help with a dinner for *those* people? No one even knew who they were. It will take a week to get rid of that smell. Last time that family was here the smell lingered in the grand lobby for a week. I really hate this part of my job, Heidi thought. I hate calling people and begging them to help. It's so easy to recruit help when someone important dies. Who the heck was Bill Edwards? Well, that just added hours to my work load this week.

Then Heidi thought of that wonderful thing that office managers get to do—delegate. She called Tiffany and Grace over to her desk conveniently passing the buck.

"You two work together to get this thing done. Pastor Rey said to expect 70, but let's plan on 40 for lunch. Also, you will need servers available and a clean-up crew. Just make it an easy meal like ham sandwiches, chips and cookies. We can turn on the pop machine and serve coffee. We don't need to cover the tables or put up any decorations. That will work best. Then we won't have to bother our ladies to bring food. We will need to be sure and have all the windows cracked open a bit even if the weather turns cold. If you have any questions don't wait until the last minute to ask for help." Heidi used the back of her hand to shoo the girls back to their desks.

Pastor Rey dreaded making the call to Mary Edwards. The shame of not stopping to see that sweet man after he asked him so kindly was consuming him with guilt. Bill said that he had something important to talk to him about. Maybe Bill knew that he was dying. Pastor Rey chided himself. Why had he turned tail and run? Whatever possessed him to value his job, home and money above the spiritual life of a human being? Pastor Rey's shame was epic. He knew the wrong he had done to this man and his family.

The regrets were mounting as he wondered if Bill knew the Lord. Maybe that was the important thing Bill wanted to discuss with him. Maybe he wanted to make things right before he died. Rey just couldn't stop his brain from heaping guilt by the bucket full into his soul.

He prayed silently. Lord, forgive me for my pride. Help me to love this family in their time of need without prejudice.

Rey dialed the number and waited for the hello. "Hi Mary, this is Pastor Rey. I am sorry to hear of Bill's passing."

A moment of silence seemed like eternity as Mary tried to form her words through her sorrow. "Reverend, thank you. Thank you for doing this for our family."

"Mary, I'd like to stop over as soon as possible to talk with you and any other family members that are available about the funeral arrangements."

"Can you come now? We need someone. We are…" the words stopped again and Mary yielded to the tears. "…so lost without him. Please come. Do you need our address?"

"No Mary, I know where you live. I'll be there in about fifteen minutes."

"Thank you, Reverend. Thank…." Mary was cut off again by her grief. The pain of her loss traveled through the airwaves from her humble home to Rey's affluent office. He said goodbye and hung up the phone.

Pastor Rey could not stop the waves of emotion that washed over him. The shame of not visiting Bill in his home hit him first. Then the thought of the repercussions from some in the church for accepting the funeral attacked him.

Rey was angry at himself for allowing someone other than God to control him. Still, what stung the most was the missed opportunity to share the love of the Lord with Bill. This could not be undone. This was all wrapped up together in one big box of regret. Rey cried out to the Lord again. "Father, forgive me!"

Then he thought, What about James? He is going to have a coronary when he finds out I'm doing this funeral and Callan will be horrified.

These turned out to be understatements. James was red with anger and spoke more about the reputation of the church in the community than about the loss of a life. Callan pleaded with Rey through many tears to decline doing the eulogy for this stranger. She said that they could tell the funeral home there was a family emergency. They could say they were called out of town for a few days. Don't funeral homes have ministers on retainer? Why did Rey have to be the sacrificial lamb? She could feel her world unraveling. Callan pleaded with Rey—but to no avail.

CHAPTER 13

Oh Be Careful Little Mouth What You Say

God is sheer mercy and grace; not easily angered,
he's rich in love.
He doesn't endlessly nag and scold, nor hold grudges forever.
He doesn't treat us as our sins deserve, nor pay us back in
full for our wrongs.
As high as heaven is over the earth, so strong is his love to
those who fear him.
And as far as sunrise is from sunset, he has separated us
from our sins.

Psalm 103:8-12 Message Bible (MSG)

The Train Depot Café in downtown Hillbrooke was a quaint little restaurant with 50's style chrome tables with matching chairs. Around the outer walls of the small café were red vinyl covered booths. Each table had a juke box attached to the wall that accepted quarters. The atmosphere was alive with the golden oldies. Above the eating area there was a miniature train that circled the room on the rafters. The train whistle sounded at 15 minute intervals delighting the customers, young and old.

Most Wednesday mornings, James Fields and Peter Carver, from the church board, met privately at the Train Depot Café for breakfast. This was their time to go over any church issues that needed tweaking. James arrived ready to unload his wrath on a friendly ear.

"That preacher is becoming a problem. He has gone and accepted a funeral of a no account bum. Why is our church doing vagrant funerals? The dead man visited once! Once and we are doing his funeral! He didn't have to accept! I'm sure it was just out of guilt because I forbid him from visiting that family. This is not the direction I want our church to go."

James stopped long enough to wave his hand in the air to get the waitress's attention. She looked his way and he pointed at his coffee cup and mouthed the word "CREAM." The waitress nodded and hurried over smiling with a small stainless steel pitcher of half and half. James was a big tipper. This allotted him a certain amount of favor with the waitstaff.

Peter Carver never said much at these breakfasts, just listened and agreed. He liked being in the know of all the objectionable things that were happening at the church and in the community. He didn't care about any of the people or their sad stories, but he enjoyed sharing it verbatim when he got home with Katherine. The Carvers led boring and sheltered lives. When they rubbed shoulders with the working class through gossip, it made them feel they had somehow done their duty to the poor.

James continued. "I am literally sickened by this whole thing. Plus, we are doing the funeral dinner to boot...at the church...for a bunch of low lives. Why he agreed to take this funeral is beyond my reasoning. He should have said, 'NO.' We don't need to impress anyone at Mill Brother's Funeral Home."

"Who died?" Peter asked.

James said his name as though it were a swear word being cursed at someone across the room, "Bill Edwards."

The waitress arrived at the table carrying two ample plates of food. She sat the platters down in front of each man. The men turned their attention to breakfast.

In the booth directly behind James Fields sat a young man. His usual friendly face replaced with one full of hate and anger. He could feel the blood pumping through his veins at an increased rate. His fists were so tightly formed that it caused his arms to tremble. His leg started bouncing with pent up energy. Taking a deep breath, he turned to look at the occupants of the booth behind him. He vaguely remembered the one who sat directly behind him from the time his family visited the Community Outreach Church.

The waitress came to his table. "Kota, are you ready to order? I was sorry to hear about your dad. He was a true gentleman."

The men at the table behind him were getting up to leave. The waitress touched Kota on the shoulder and said, "I'll be right back."

"Mr. Fields let me get your check for you."

Kota watched James Fields leave the restaurant and get in his car. On the side was one of those magnetic signs that said *Fields Insurance Agency, life, home, auto, and travel*. He grabbed a napkin and wrote down the name of the company. He would google it later for all the info he needed. This wasn't over, but first he would bury his father.

Mills Brother's Funeral Home was the inner city funeral home of choice. It had once been the only show in town until Bonnett's Funeral

Home and Crematory built a fancy place about two miles south of Hillbrooke near an expressway exit—situated along a river with exquisite landscaping. Bonnett's was regal in appearance. The portico that extended out with grand pillars gave the appearance of a southern mansion more than a funeral home. The entry doors were flanked by bronze statues of children holding hands with flowers scattered around their bare feet. This type of beauty didn't come cheap. Thus the two funeral homes in Hillbrooke became known as the *haves* and the *have nots*.

The Edwards' family was firmly established in the *have nots*. Mills Brother's was their funeral home. They offered a variety of packages with credit plans. Mary Edwards took the cheapest package available and set up a payment plan acceptable to the funeral home.

Pastor Rey arrived at Mills Brother's about ten minutes before the family went in for their private viewing. The first viewing of the loved one in the casket is a reality that few people are prepared for. The funeral home director called everyone together. Pastor Rey joined the family.

Mary was encircled by her children as well as a herd of little ones of every shape and size. Pastor Rey stayed at the back of the room to allow the family time alone near Bill's casket. A pastor is prepared for the worst, even expecting it, but this family shocked him. There were soft sobs and lots of hugging. There was no screaming or falling on the floor in despair. They may have looked the part of a family without hope, but they acted like a family of faith.

Pastor Rey gathered Bill's family together before the doors opened to the public. He shared a short devotional and closed in prayer. Then the parade of people came in to greet the family and give their condolences.

Pastor Rey stood to the side and watched. He was shocked when one hour into the viewing time James, Marilyn and Emily Fields arrive.

Marilyn approached Mary and introduced herself as the person from Community Outreach who would handle the funeral dinner.

"I never meet your husband, but I can see your family loved him very much. Please let me know, if there is anything I can do to help you over the next few days. I'd love to come and visit you when things settle down." Marilyn slipped a small business card into Mary's hand. It had her home and cell phones along with her address.

Emily stood at her mother's side and quietly observed. Her mom had a compassion and boldness that she had not seen in her before.

James stood at the back of the funeral parlor with his arms folded firmly across his chest. He saw Pastor Rey and motioned for him. Rey followed James into the hallway.

Tucked away in a quiet corner, James reprimanded Pastor Rey, "This is a travesty that our church is connected with this man's funeral. Look at these people. I can't believe you would want them in the church. They could steal things, destroy the building and that smell…."

Rey held his hand up to stop James from saying another word—he wished he would have stopped the spew sooner, "This is neither the place nor the time." Rey spoke with authority. He wasn't quite sure where his strength came from at that moment. He had never had the courage to stand up to James until now. He was shaking on the inside, but on the outside he held his shoulders back. With resolve he turned and headed back to the Edwards' family.

On the way back, Rey noticed Kota standing alone. He was around the corner from where James and he were speaking just moments ago. Kota's back was to Pastor Rey, but there was no question that this young man was Kota Edwards. His exposed tattooed arms were as good as a name plastered on the back of a football jersey. Pastor Rey placed his hand on Kota's shoulder. Kota turned. His eyes were red, but it wasn't sadness Rey saw. It was anger.

"Kota, if you want to talk some time. I'm here for you and your family."

"Sure Reverend, like you were for my Dad."

Rey was unprepared for the sharpness he heard in Kota's voice. Kota met Rey's eyes. He dropped his hand from Kota's shoulder. This was not the same young man he had talked to just a few days ago when they met to discuss the funeral.

"My mom needs you right now so I got no problem with you. But I know your type, and I know you don't care about me or my family. This is all a show. We both know all about your type of God." Kota kept his eyes fixed directly on Rey while he spoke. "No matter. When this is over I'm done with you and your stuck-up church." Kota pushed past Rey and returned to the back of the funeral parlor. A few friends were waiting to talk to him.

Reminded again of his failure, Pastor Rey stood frozen with shame, alone in the small alcove. Then he heard the words whispered behind him. "This isn't over. Not by a long shot." Rey turned towards the familiar voice. James Fields met him with a scowl. His tone quickly changed when he saw his daughter, Emily, and his wife walking towards him. "Ladies, are you finished?"

James extended his arm around his daughter's shoulders pulling her in for a quick hug. Emily slipped her hand inside her father's arm as they walked to the parking lot.

Kota watched from the doorway feeding a hatred for this man. At that moment, Kota felt an intense loathing that was stronger than any he had previously experienced. When he was in prison he had listened to the stories from hardcore inmates who felt vindicated in their crimes against others. These stories finally made sense to him. The *murderous* hatred, the *get even* hatred, the *eye for an eye* hatred—all aimed at making someone pay for a wrong that was done. Kota began to form a plan that would teach James Fields a lesson he would *never* forget.

After Heidi assigned the funeral dinner duty's to Tiffany and Grace, she took her phone into the hallway and dialed the first number on the list. "Hi. Meg, can you start the Prayer Chain?"

"Sure, what is it?"

"It's a troubling state of affairs. Let me just tell you the situation, and then you can word it however you like. I know I can trust you," and with that the sordid story of Pastor Rey, the Edwards family and the plans for the funeral luncheon spread through the church like a malignant cancer. The script read something like this; Hero—James Fields who's greatest concern was for the well-being of the church and community. The Antagonist/Villain—Pastor Rey who is selfish and uncaring arrives in the peaceful town of Hillbrooke to wreak havoc on its trusting people. The Setting—A lovely church about to be destroyed—by the evil outlaw gang the Edwards Clan.

Heidi closed out the prayer request with, "Just pray as you feel led." She ended the call with a satisfied smile on her lips accomplishing what she intended.

Jean and Tom Brown felt led to stop by the parsonage. Pastor Rey sat alone on the front porch in a white rocking chair. He was staring out into space unaware that the Browns had pulled into the driveway.

Tom opened his car door and yelled, "Hey Pastor, everything okay?"

Rey looked startled. He jumped up from the rocker.

"Tom. Jean. You're a breath of fresh air. Come on in." They all stepped into the house.

Callan, unprepared for guests made her excuses and hurried the boys to another room.

The Browns and Rey sat down in the family room. No words were spoken; Rey dropped his head into his hands and began to cry. Tom moved from his seat on the sofa to his Pastor's side, placing one hand on his back, Tom began to pray over Rey in a way that Rey had never experienced before.

Callan quickly changed her clothes and touched up her makeup. Hurrying down the hallway she stopped short of the family room. An unfamiliar language was being spoken in her home. She was unprepared for the feelings of fear that came over her. But at the same time something was drawing her to go in. Callan knew she needed to be part of whatever was happening, but she hesitated. Then she retreated back down the hallway to the solitude of her bedroom.

Seminary did not prepare Pastor Rey for such an occasion as *this* first funeral. He had taken the practical course required by all pastoral students called homiletics. In this class they each prepared and preached a number of different types of sermons. They even performed mock weddings, baby dedications, water baptisms and funerals.

The week they worked on funerals, the professor had put a variety of funeral types into a bag and each student drew one out. Rey, fortunately, got an elderly Christian woman who died peacefully. It was easy and routine. He performed well getting one of the highest grades in the class. Others were not so fortunate. One girl in his class had to do a mock funeral for a stillborn baby. Rey's roommate got the one for a teen killed while texting and driving.

Behind the scenes, this class of ministers-in-training often joked without considering they would one day need all these skills as they navigated families through real funerals. Comforting those who mourned and whose hearts were broken from grief. Unaware they would be working with a plethora of personalities, problems and issues.

The funeral of Bill Edwards opened with a rendition of *Amazing Grace* sung by Elvis Presley. When the music faded, Pastor Rey stood behind the rickety podium. His first words into the attached microphone caused an ear piercing sound to fill the room. The small group of about 50 people covered their ears and flinched in pain. The funeral director standing at the back of the room ran to unplug the sound system. He made apologies to those in attendance. Then he nodded to Rey to continue speaking without the benefit of amplification. Rey cleared his throat and began again with the reading of the obituary. Then he opened in prayer.

Looking around the room, Rey spotted some friendlies. Everyone from the small group at the Brown's home were in attendance except Marilyn and Emily who were back at the church making sure everything was readied for the funeral dinner. There were also some unfriendlies. Kota wore a scowl on his face that was mirrored by James Fields. Pastor Rey was the lucky recipient of these unwelcoming glares.

The prayers of the Browns from the previous night continued to encourage Pastor Rey as he shared. "Bill loved to sit on his front porch and wave at anyone passing by. Whether in a car or by foot, he never missed an opportunity to wave his greeting. He was a happy and kind man even as he was facing death. There was no bitterness or anger in him. After he passed, Mary, his wife, found a small New Testament with the books of Psalm and Proverbs tucked under his chair cushion on the porch. While flipping through the pages, Mary found many verses that Bill had taken the time to underline. Psalm 23 was completely underlined and I'm going to read that chapter now from Bill's Bible."

Pastor Rey held a small green New Testament in his hands and began to read. "The Lord is my Shepherd. I shall not want..." Pastor Rey looked up between verses and saw that Kota's face had softened as he listened to the personal stories about his father. The funeral ended with a fun Johnny Cash song, *I've Been Everywhere, Man.* The humor of this song was that Bill had rarely traveled anywhere in his fifty plus years. Following the song, the final goodbyes were made at the funeral home, and the family proceeded to the cemetery. Pastor Rey read the committal service at the burial site; the funeral director concluded the service with an invitation for family and friends to proceed to Community Outreach Church for a dinner.

CHAPTER 14

Did He Know The Lord?

He does not crush the weak, Or quench the smallest hope;
He will end all conflict with his final victory...

Matthew 12:20 The Living Bible (TLB)

*T*he afternoon sun cast the right amount of natural light into
the church fellowship hall giving a cheery atmosphere to
the somber occasion. Marilyn had chosen *not* to take the counsel
of the girls from the church office; neither in menu choices or decorations. She did not cut any corners to simply fulfill an obligation.
The seven round tables were covered with yellow linens. In the
center of each table there were live plants tastefully tied with light
blue ribbons. Each table had a few thoughtfully placed photos of Bill
Edwards.

Marilyn made homemade lasagna, antipasto salad with Italian
dressing, garlic bread and a variety of homemade pies. Three other
ladies stepped up from the church to volunteer in the kitchen.

Marilyn had to quash conversation more than once during the
preparations steering the ladies back to edifying topics. It still caught
Marilyn off guard, when people who claimed to be Christians—fol-
lowers of Jesus, fell so short of reflecting Christ to the world.

Marilyn was humbled to serve anyone the Lord brought into her life. It didn't matter if they were rich or poor, saved or unsaved, clean or dirty. More than once she had been chastised for doing things beneath her position as the wife of a wealthy businessman. It didn't matter to Marilyn; she loved helping others especially in their time of loss. Marilyn personally understood loss. She wanted to be an instrument that brought comfort and peace to others. She believed this, *"To whom much is given, much is required...what you do to the least of these you do unto me."*

The ladies in the church kitchen peered through the serving window and watched the doors to the fellowship hall open. The first guests through were Kota and his mom, Mary. She was holding tightly to her son's arm looking unsure if they were in the right room. Kota looked more like the leader of a motorcycle gang than the eldest son of the deceased arriving from a funeral.

Marilyn and Emily hurried out from the kitchen to welcome the family, pointing out the locations of the bathrooms and giving instructions.

Marilyn tried to help ease the hesitant guests. "Welcome. Please, take a seat anywhere you wish. When Pastor Rey arrives he will pray over the dinner. Then we will serve the food." Marilyn gestured pointing at the tables. The Edwards' family looked humbled and expressed it with words of appreciation.

Marilyn noticed Kota who escorted his mother in. He appeared to be carrying the weight of the world on his shoulders.

Following the prayer, the family of Bill Edwards went quietly through the food line and returned to their tables. The conversation sounded like a soft hum, not the usual loud talking and garish laugher of the Edwards family. Marilyn could see the family was reacting to their uncomfortable surroundings.

The church volunteers refused to come out from the kitchen leaving Marilyn and Emily to serve and refill the food tables as needed. They hoped the Edwards family wouldn't sense the lack of hospitality radiating from the kitchen. Marilyn and Emily resolved to work all the harder to extend kindness to this family. Once everyone was served, they visited with each table expressing their condolences.

When Kota saw Emily approach his table he invited her to sit for a moment.

She accepted. "Hi. I'm Emily Fields." She pointed in the direction of her mother who was sitting at the next table talking to Mary Edwards and said, "And that's my mom, Marilyn. We are both sorry for your family's loss. I have never lost a parent. I can only imagine how difficult this must be for you and your family."

On the inside Kota felt his blood reach the boiling point. This was the daughter and wife of the cruel man he had overheard talking about his father in the restaurant just days ago. Timing was everything, he thought. He made small talk with Emily finding out where she worked, where she had gone to high school, college and some of her likes and dislikes. Kota thanked her for the dinner and all that her church had done for his family. Even as the words exited his mouth he could taste the gall of his own lies.

At the end of the luncheon, Kota wanted to walk out and leave the mess behind him. But, he was compelled by the memory of his father. He approached Marilyn and asked, "What can our family do to help with the clean up?"

Marilyn touched the tattooed arm of the young man. She guessed him to be about the age of her own son, Carl. "We have a team coming in later to take care of things. It was thoughtful of you to offer. Let us serve *you* today. You go and be with your family. Remember all the good times with your father. It has been our privilege to serve you."

Kota thought, yep, privilege to serve...I'm not the only liar in town.

The windows from the church kitchen opened towards the parking lot. The conversation of the workers easily drifted out into the afternoon air.

"I can't believe Marilyn and Emily were out there making small talk with *those* people. Who do *they* think they are anyways?"

"Marilyn's always been a bit *holier than thou* for my taste."

"That stale tobacco odor is stinking up the whole fellowship hall!"

"And did you *smell* that suffocating odor of moth balls and mildew?"

"It's a good thing we opened the windows or we'd all be choking right now."

"Thank God they're finally leaving."

"Now we can clean up and put this thing behind us."

"Heidi said that Pastor Rey opened Pandora's Box. I hope that doesn't mean he'll be doing every degenerate's funeral in Hillbrooke now."

Kota stood outside the church building, leaning against the log exterior, smoking a cigarette. He threw the half smoked cigarette near the open kitchen window and watched the smoke drift into the kitchen. He thought to himself; hope you ladies enjoy the rest of that cigarette. He wished he'd had a joint to light up and give them a real party.

Kota reached in his pocket and pulled out his car keys. He held them in his hand and smiled. Extending the longest key from the chain he held it level with his hip. He walked through the church parking lot dragging his keys along the sides of no less than five cars. He really didn't care whose cars they were. In his opinion, there were *none* inno-cent in this church. No—not one!

Pastor Rey opened the door to his study. He stepped just inside the threshold and closed the door behind him. Leaning back against the closed door he allowed the pent up tears to flow. Without taking another step, he dropped to his knees. Falling forward, he buried his face in the carpet surrendering to his sorrow.

There had been no peace for him at the close of Bill's funeral. The questions that had haunted him for days were still pointing fingers of accusation at him. Was Bill saved? Did someone tell him? Had he found the peace and mercy of the Lord? Did he die in his sins without the forgiveness of a Savior?

Only heaven held the answers to these questions. For the rest of his natural life, Pastor Rey would live with the consequence of his decision to follow the voice of man and not the voice of the Lord. How could I care so little for another human life? Chastised by his own thoughts, he was overcome with remorse.

Following the kitchen clean-up, Emily and Marilyn walked out to the parking lot together. They began noticing the deep scrapes on various cars. Emily's little sports car was one of the marred vehicles. Marilyn dreaded breaking this news to James. It would only confirm to him that he was right. There was damage after the Edwards' family left the church, just as he had predicted.

There was no point in putting it off. Marilyn made the call. James's company insured both the church along with most of the people who attended. This was not going away, and there was no way this was going to go well for her or Pastor Rey. James called the police. He met them at the church. By now the other kitchen help had exited the building. All their cars but one had been vandalized.

The police took the statements of each car owner, along with James, who *did* turn out to be the insurance agent for all parties. Accusations were flying with all fingers pointing at the Edwards family.

The police officer said, "The church does not have surveillance cameras, so nothing could be proven. But we do know that Kota Edwards is a known criminal. Still without an eye witness there is nothing we can do." The officer entered Kota's name into his laptop. Then he looked up from his computer screen at James and continued, "He's on probation, one misstep and he'll be back in prison. We'll be keeping a close eye on him."

James looked sternly at his wife. "Now do you understand? We are not playing with high school pranksters. This is a felon, and he has been inside our church!"

Marilyn didn't argue with James assessment of the situation. She also didn't believe Kota was a danger. She felt there was good in him. She saw the same hurt in his eyes that she remembered seeing in Carl's.

Emily excused herself from all the *mean spirited,* hen-talk from the church ladies and went to sit in her car. She turned on worship music and checked her emails. Her phone signaled an incoming message from her FaceBook account. It was a friend request from—Kota Edwards. Had she heard the information shared by the police regarding him, she would not have readily accepted his friend request.

Emily opened his FB page, scrolled through some of his photos and read a few recent comments. They were mostly words of comfort for the loss of his father. The photos were mainly family members laughing together, playing cards and Kota sitting by a campfire. There was a nice picture of Kota and his dad sitting side by side on the porch. It captured a sweet, natural affection between the two men. Emily smiled when she looked at it.

Then she did something she had never done before. She sent Kota a private message that said, *It was nice talking with you today. I hope we will have a chance to talk again sometime.* She paused. Then she hit the backspace button on her phone and deleted the last phrase; *I hope we have a chance to talk again sometime.* She left the part; *It was nice talking with you today.* She hit send and immediately felt uncomfortable.

The police finally left the church. Still standing in the parking lot, James looked in the direction of the pastor's office window. Pastor Rey looked out from his palace of solitude. James glared at him from the parking lot. It sent chills through Rey's body.

James said out loud to no one in particular, "I've got bigger fish to fry." He turned away from Marilyn without saying goodbye and walked towards his car.

Once inside his car, he scrolled through his favorites list on his cell phone and called each church board member starting with his known allies first. Peter Carver, his breakfast buddy, was able to meet for the emergency board meeting. Then he called John Alden, Heidi's husband, who only knew one word whenever James called, "YES." Henry Samson said that it would depend on his teaching schedule. He and his wife were in the first semester of teaching college.

He made his last call. The phone rang. "Hello. This is Harold Smith."

James wondered why he always answered the phone like that—does he think I don't know who I called? He was already feeling annoyed with the man. "Harold, I am calling a special meeting of the board for tomorrow night at my house. We've had a few recent issues with Pastor Rey that we need to discuss. It's best if Pastor Rey is *not* present at this meeting. I want everyone to have the freedom to share without restraint. We need to be sure that Pastor Rey is taking the church in the direction that is best for the future of Community Outreach."

"James, I want to go on the record now and say that I am not in favor of a meeting without our pastor in attendance. I support Pastor, and I like the direction our church is going. However, I will be at the meeting. See you tomorrow." Harold got ready to hang up but James continued.

"I know you're in thick with the Pastor and with the Brown family too. I know all about your *small group* and the spiritual manipulation going on. You, of all people, should know better than to get religion and emotionalism mixed up together. That is like mixing fire and gasoline. That kind of combination will only bring destruction." James's voice had changed from a savvy businessman to an angry teenager, "I have my sources. This type of hyper spiritualism is not the image we want to project for Community Outreach and *believe me*—this is one of the items on the agenda for tomorrow night. Just so you know, HAROLD..." James spit more than spoke his name. "You are outnumbered on the board and your days are numbered along with Pastor Rey's!" Click!

James was a bully, but Harold wasn't intimidated by him. He had served on the church board with him for many years. Harold had always been outnumbered. This was nothing new, but now he felt strength of spirit. He had a hope that he hadn't felt in over twenty years. Come to think of it, the last time he felt this way was before James joined the church board.

James knew that Harold would call Pastor Rey as soon as they hung up. He needed a plan that would either bring Rey back into the fold or banish him and Harold for good.

James looked down at his cell phone again and searched for the parsonage phone number. Once he found it he touched the CALL button. The phone rang at Pastor Rey and Callan's house.

"Hello, this is Callan Douglas."

"Hi Callan, this is James Fields. I was wondering if you had a few minutes to talk. I'm at the church, and I want to stop over and talk privately with you. Would that be okay?"

"Is Marilyn coming?"

"No. She isn't available. I just need to run a few things by you, but if you are uncomfortable we can meet outside."

"Could we talk on the phone?"

"No. I think this needs to be done face to face."

Callan never felt she was a person who was sensitive to the Lord's leading, but something in her was yelling, NO, NO, NO, but out of her mouth she heard the words, "Sure. See you soon."

CHAPTER 15

Can We Talk Privately?

I was hungry and you fed me,
I was thirsty and you gave me a drink,
I was homeless and you gave me a room,
I was shivering and you gave me clothes,
I was sick and you stopped to visit,
I was in prison and you came to me.'

Matthew 25:35-36 The Message Bible (MSG)

$\mathcal{T}$he worship music filled the air at the Brown's home. Jean worked in the kitchen preparing food for a business dinner she and Tom were hosting later that day. The atmosphere went from sunshine and happy thoughts to darkness. The sun literally went behind a cloud. The once bright kitchen was now covered with a foreboding gloom. The warmth of the sun on Jean's skin was replaced with a cold chill. It crept into the room banishing the afternoon sunlight.

Jean's spirit was in tune with the wooing of the Lord. She began to pray, first with her own words, followed by unknown words. Then she began groaning as the Spirit of the Lord led her to intercede in prayer. For what—she didn't know. She obeyed and prayed as the Spirit of the Lord directed.

The phone rang interrupting Jean's prayer time. She pulled herself up from the kitchen floor and walked over to the counter to answer her cell phone.

"Jean, this is Esther Smith. Harold just called me. There is going to be an emergency board meeting tomorrow night at James Fields' house to discuss possibly firing Pastor Rey. We have to pray. Should I call the other members of the group?" Esther was the sweetest of grandmotherly types. She had a gentle voice that matched her spirit. Whenever she told a story, whether it happened in her childhood or yesterday, her eyes would pool with tears. If the Lord had named Esther, he would have called her, Compassion.

"We'll call the others, but first *we* will pray." Jean poured out her thoughts in prayer to the Lord, only this time, Esther stood in agreement with her.

Callan nervously stood on the front porch of the parsonage. Any minute James's car would pull into the driveway. She paced back and forth across the porch. Why did he want to talk to me? She wondered. Why not Rey? It makes me uncomfortable. This can't be good. She was sure about that. She sat down on the rocker and stared across the front lawn. Her leg began to nervously bounce. She laid her hand on her knee to stop the movement.

Callan's thoughts turned to her husband. Why can't he just pastor this church the way the people want? Why does he have to push the envelope? The Browns! This is *all* their fault. They put this nonsense in Rey's head. That small group meeting has stirred things up. I knew from that first meeting that the Browns were trouble. Why do people have to be so emotional about their religion?

Callan's thoughts were interrupted by a car door slamming. It was James. She thought it was a bit much that he found it necessary to slam his car door like an attention seeking preschooler.

James walked resolutely up the porch steps and took a seat in the other porch rocker. Callan's face showed her fear. James knew he could work with that. She diverted her eyes to the fall colors in the front yard.

"Callan, I want to start out by saying I know you are a good woman. I have watched you try to keep your husband on the right path. Rey would not be the man of God he is without you at home keeping him grounded. That is why I felt it necessary that we speak privately." James allowed his words to soak in.

Callan's face softened at the flattery. "I do manage things for Rey allowing him the freedom to Pastor without worrying about issues at home."

Callan met James eyes. He didn't speak.

Then she added. "He would be lost without me. I'm certain of that."

James kept eye contact with Callan and continued. "Callan, this is the problem. Rey accepted that funeral and allowed the dinner to take place at the church. I warned everyone. If we open our church doors to *those kind* of people then we would surely feel the repercussions."

Callan shook her head in agreement.

"Your husband refused to listen and now—five cars have been vandalized at the church following the dinner. Most of the cars belonged to people who volunteered to serve the funeral dinner. They were there to show kindness and look how they were treated."

Callan shook her head this time in disbelief.

"The fellowship hall reeked and had to be aired out. Everything had to be sanitized following the dinner."

Callan made that clicking sound in the side of her cheek—the sound that you make when you really want to emphasize your disgust.

Callan moved her rocker to face James. Now he knew she was giving him her full attention.

Callan asked. "Did you talk to Rey about this?"

"I've tried on a few occasions. I wanted to steer him in the right direction, but he seems bent on going his own way, which brings me to my visit. I wanted to see if you and I might be able to work together to get Rey back on track." James waited to see, if he could read Callan's body language. "Do we have the same agenda?" He watched to see if she would be easily led or if she held the same opinions as her husband.

A welcoming smile crept across Callan's lips, "I respect you and know you have the best interest of our family in mind. I'm blessed beyond words for the love and care this church has shown us. All our needs and wants have been met. What more could I ask for?"

James reached out and patted the top of Callan's hand. It was the hand still steadying her bouncing knee. Callan jerked when he touched her.

James continued. "I thought you might feel that way. Here is what I would like from you." James unfolded his plan. "First, put pressure on Rey from within the home. Second, make him accountable. Don't give him everything he asked for. If he's not willing to consider your needs, then don't consider his. Third, you and the boys should be the most important thing in his life. Make sure you remind him of that frequently. Have some key phases and comebacks ready. Use them to fight your battles. If all else fails don't be afraid to resort to tears."

Callan listened.

To an outsider looking in the situation resembled a fruit tree, a serpent and a woman deceived. And so James skillfully spoke into Callan's heart—poisonous venom.

Pastor Rey watched James's car pull out of the church parking lot. He returned to his desk and opened his Bible. His sermon notes for Sunday were spread out across the desk. He tried to collect his thoughts enough to study, but it was futile. He opened his Bible to reread his text for Sunday, but the words blurred on the page. Taking a deep breath, Rey purposed to push through this.

"Lord, help me." He prayed out loud with his eyes wide open. "I can't do this without You. I need *Your* strength."

Then he heard it. A voice said, *"Go home."*

Rey turned thinking Heidi had walked into his office again unannounced, but there was no one there.

Then he heard it again, *"Go home."*

He thought he was losing it for sure now.

He slammed his open hand on the desk to clear his mind. Again he heard the words, *"Go home!"*

Rey picked up his phone and punched in the intercom numbers for Heidi's desk. "Did you just call me?" He asked.

"No. Pastor, is there anything you need?" Heidi dutifully responded.

"I'm going home for the rest of the day. I'll be in at nine tomorrow." Rey hung up the phone. He packed up his briefcase, collected his study books, his notes and his Bible. Then he left through his private entrance.

James' phone buzzed notifying him of an incoming text message. He quickly glanced at it, not wanting to lose his momentum with Callan. It was from Heidi. HE'S ON HIS WAY HOME!

"Callan, your family's future at Community Outreach is *now* in your hands. We'll talk again, soon." He gave her shoulder a squeeze as he passed by and hurried to his car.

Callan was filled with uneasiness as she watched James back out of the driveway.

Rey stopped at the four way intersection and waited his turn. An uncomfortable sensation ran through his body as James Fields' car sped past him. He wondered why James was in his neighborhood. He turned his car into the driveway and saw Callan on the porch deep in thought. The afternoon sun shined on her worried face. He opened the garage door, pulled in and parked his car. He entered the house through the kitchen door.

Callan came in the house to greet Rey, "We need to talk. Let's sit in the family room."

With concern in his voice Rey asked. "Was James just here?"

"Yes, he was and that's why we need to talk."

"Callan, I don't want him at this house, when I'm not home."

"We sat outside and he's at least 15 years older than me. I'm sure you don't have anything to worry about concerning either one of *us*."

The emphasis on "us" was easy to read. Rey knew she felt there was a problem with him. "That's not the point, Callan. It's how it looks. Besides that I don't trust him. He is a dangerous man."

Callan sat in a comfy chair. Rey took a seat on the sofa directly across from his wife. A large ottoman divided them.

Callan began, "Rey, I told you. *I told you.* You've got to think about what you're doing. James knows the situation here. He told you not to do *that* funeral. Why didn't you listen?"

Rey had been looking down at the ottoman. When Callan stopped talking he looked up at his wife—written across her forehead in big, bold letters was the word; COVETOUSNESS. He closed his eyes and shook his head trying to clear the image from his mind. As quickly as that word disappeared another came. This time it was written across Callan's heart. It said, JEALOUSY. Callan's lips were moving, but Rey couldn't hear a word she said. She reached for his hand across the ottoman. When she touched him, written on top of Callan's hand was the word; GREED.

Rey jumped to his feet. This was over the top for him. Even with everything that had been happening the past months. Seeing his beautiful wife tattooed with these horrible, cruel words was shocking. How could this be? Callan sat back in her chair watching her husband.

"Rey, what's the matter with you. You look possessed."

Rey looked again at Callan and the words were gone. He sat back down not sure what was happening to them. The words burned in his mind. Then it became clear to him. The Lord revealed that his precious wife, whom he loved dearly, was being plagued by; greed, jealousy, and covetousness. They had become her motivation for all her life choices. How had he missed it? He knew it had gotten worse since coming to Hillbrooke. He had dismissed it to her busy life as a wife, mother and partner in ministry.

"Callan, will you pray with me?" Rey looked into his wife's eyes. He realized they had not prayed together in months. The woman who looked back at him was a person he barely recognized.

"Rey, this is not the time. Didn't you hear what I said? If *you* don't change, we are going to be without a job and without a home."

The board met and the decision was made to wait and see if things turned around for the better. Everyone continued limping along for a few months. On the outside things seemed to be peaceful. Rey could feel the lines being drawn. Sides were being taken even with the prayer covering of the Brown's small group. The group prayed for the church, the pastor, his wife and the lost in the community. This was a new concept to Community Outreach. They prayed for the heathen in faraway lands, but never in their own neighborhood.

Following the funeral of Bill Edwards, Rey decided to begin an outreach ministry to the local prison through the church. The only other person willing to participate in this ministry was Harold Smith. Neither one of them had ever stepped foot inside a police station—let alone a prison. The two men gladly completed the training jumping through all the hoops.

Two months of prison visitation made Pastor Rey and Harold veterans. They went twice a week spending one hour at a time with the inmates. This ministry was mainly to the inmates who were serving short sentences like 2-6 years for non-violent offences like burglary, dealing drugs and personal drug offenses. In the past eight weeks Pastor Rey and Harold had experienced threatening glares, verbal mocking and language that would make a sailor blush. They refused to give up.

One inmate had become Rey's special project. His name was Snake. At first, Pastor Rey had a difficult time calling another human being Snake. After a while, it became his name—the same as if his name was George or John.

He had a tattoo of a snake coiled around his neck with the long body draped over his shoulder, hanging down his right arm, ending just before his elbow. On the left side of his face the snake's head poked up with its forked tongue hissing out in a striking position just under his eye. It was actually quite a sight to behold.

Snake had a mean streak in him. He stood an imposing 6'5, with long hair, pulled tightly into a pony tail. His eyes were empty of life. Rey wondered what had happened to this man. Rey and Harold had purposed never to ask anyone about the crime(s) that landed them in prison. Rather they would wait for the inmate to offer that information when and if they felt comfortable to share.

Each week the meetings grew more civil. Rey did a half hour of Bible teaching. Afterwards, the men discussed the topic and asked questions. There seemed to be an interest budding among the inmates to know more. Snake was the exception. Rey wondered why he even came with his hateful questions and bitterness towards God.

Following one of their meetings, Snake stayed to speak with Pastor Rey. "I'm up for parole in a few months. I know you don't know me, but I'd like you to come to my hearing when the time comes. You don't have to say anything for me, just come."

"Snake, I'd be happy to do that. Just get me the information. I'm available to talk with you anytime."

"I know 'bout religion, and I got no place for it in my life."

"We're praying you have a change of heart. I don't know what turned you off of God. Not all Christians are like the people who failed you. God can still redeem your life and use it for good. You're not beyond repair. None of us are."

"Pastor, you're crazy. You don't know anything about me. I don't need *your* God's forgiveness or pardon! I chose my own way. I'm pay'n my own way—nobody but me."

"I'm happy someone paid my way. His name is Jesus. He has the marks in His body to prove it. His forgiveness is not just a pardon. He wiped the slate clean. The wrong is gone. The Bible says it is cast into a sea of forgetfulness. I won't lie to you. My life has been pretty squeaky clean in comparison to yours. But, I'm still a sinner in need of a Savior. Right now the only difference between us is—I accepted the gift of forgiveness through Jesus Christ, you haven't."

"Like I said, been there and that was death to me. Maybe, if we could have met five or ten years ago, but not now. I'm in control and I like it that way." Snake headed to gate where the guard stood. He turned and said, "See you next time Pastor." He passed through the barred door into a world that Rey knew nothing about.

CHAPTER 16

It's Going To Be Okay

Can two walk together, unless they are agreed?

Amos 3:3 New King James Version (NKJV)

Emily headed for work the next day. Down the passenger side of her car was a deep key mark like a racing stripe. She had heard her parents fighting last night, but retreated to the safety of her bedroom turning up her music to drown out the gritty details.

Emily passed the legal aid office and turned into the parking area. She noticed a man leaning up against the building near the entrance. He balanced on one foot with the other foot resting against the bricks behind him. He looked like he was posed for a blue jean's advertisement.

Emily parked her car. She grabbed her briefcase out of the passenger seat and walked towards the office entrance. The man in the blue jeans turned towards her. He was Kota Edwards.

"Hi. Kota. What brings you here?" Her voice was warm and friendly. She was unaware of Kota's past. "I hope you're not having any legal troubles?" She laughed.

Kota smiled back and thought; she is friendly to a fault. This will be easier than I expected. "I remembered you worked here. You and your mother made my family feel so welcome at your church yesterday. My mom was comforted by the meal. She felt your church went above and beyond our expectations. My family couldn't stop talking about it last night."

"There's no need to thank us anymore. We wanted to do it. I'm happy your family appreciated the dinner. It was done out of love." Emily was pleased their efforts were appreciated. She smiled at Kota. He liked the way it made him feel.

The cruel words of the kitchen ladies rolled through Kota's mind. This kept his vengeful anger in focus; degenerate, smelly, criminals, poor, no account. He was back.

"Could I say thank you by taking you out for lunch today?" Kota looked less menacing in the morning light dressed in blue jeans with a light-weight jacket. His face was clean shaven.

"I guess that would be okay. I usually eat lunch at this little coffee shop by the college. It's within walking distance from here. Do you know the place?" Emily felt sorry for Kota's loss, but there was an apprehension that she couldn't shake. Surely, he didn't have any expectations. She dismissed the uneasiness, after all Kota's father was buried yesterday. He wasn't flirting with her.

Kota nodded. "I know the place well. How about we meet at noon? Will that work for you?" She was drawn to him for some unknown reason. She never thought she was the good girl who liked the bad boy, but maybe she was.

"I'll try to be there on time. My work schedule can be unpredictable. I may be a few minutes late."

"Okay then, it's a date." Kota turned and walked down the street in the direction of the coffee shop.

Emily watched Kota walk away wondering if he thought this was a date/date. She hoped he understood she was just being friendly. She opened the door to the legal aid building feeling a little worried. Again, she ignored the feeling she had just made a huge mistake. Walking to her desk she prepared to meet her first client. She decided she was over analyzing the situation.

Emily looked at the clock. It was 12:15 P.M. She hated being late for her lunch appointment. Her job was not a factory job where you punched a clock. You serve people when they need help. Emily told the receptionist she was leaving for lunch and would be back in 45 minutes.

The walk to the coffee shop was refreshing after being cooped up in a small stuffy office all morning.

The coffee shop was busy with students from the nearby university. Emily opened the door and walked in scanning the seating area for Kota. She spotted him near the back with a group of students gathered around him. They were laughing and talking. He was clearly a regular.

Kota looked up from the crowd. Emily caught his attention with a wave of her hand. Kota whispered something to the group, and the students walked away in different directions. Emily walked the short distance from the door to the table. With each step uneasiness crept in. Her thoughts felt like a warning. You don't know anything about him except his father died. Is he a student? Does he have a job, or a family of his own? He could be married for all you know. Does he have any understanding of spiritual things?

When Emily reached the table Kota was standing by a chair he had pulled out for her. The gesture seemed a bit grand for a college coffee shop. She sat and he scooted her chair snugly up to the table. He was a bit older than her, but not by much.

Kota broke the silence. "I know you eat here often, but have you tried the chicken wrap? It's one of my favorites."

"I do eat here, but not really that much. My schedule is unpredictable so I brown-bag-it a lot. By the way, I'm sorry for being late. This is a perfect example of my work day. Somedays I have to grab a bit of food in the copy room while I'm running off papers for a client." Emily felt nervous. She knew she was talking too fast about nothing.

"If you don't mind can I order for you? I know the perfect sandwich."

Emily liked his confidence. "Sure. It would be nice to have a break from decision making for a few minutes."

Kota went to the counter and ordered. He was friendly with the salesgirl at the cash register. Emily couldn't hear the conversation, but they both glanced in her direction and smiled. She returned the smile, feeling a bit on display.

Kota returned to the table carrying a tray with two specialty coffees and sandwiches wrapped up in wax paper. He placed the tray in front of Emily. "Hope you like the Michigan Cherry Chicken Wrap?"

"I've never had one, but I love the salad. I imagine it's the same." Emily picked up the wrap and selected one of the coffees. She bowed her head and laid one hand on top of her wrapped lunch. Her lips moved silently. When Emily looked back up, Kota was watching her.

She blurted out. "I've prayed for my food ever since I was a child. It's a habit. I think it's a good way to remember to be thankful."

He said. "That's fine. I like watching."

Emily felt a warm feeling when Kota looked at her. She knew she had that puppy rescuer syndrome. She needed to be careful.

"Thanks for meeting with me. I know it must be awkward seeing that you barely know me."

Emily gave Kota a friendly smile. "Well, we did meet at church." Then she laughed and relaxed. The conversation took a natural flow asking all the first date questions. Even though Emily kept telling herself that she was just being kind to someone who had experienced a recent loss. However, she was relieved there were no romantic overtures made during the meal.

Kota was a nice guy she determined. If he wanted her friendship, she would give it to him.

"I need to get back to the office. Lunch was great."

"Can I walk you back?"

"That would be nice." Kota stood to pull out Emily's chair. He was a good conversationalist. Once the oddities of the first few minutes had passed, Emily enjoyed her time with him very much.

Their conversation was friendly and casual on the walk back to Emily's office.

When Kota opened the door he asked. "Could we do this again sometime?"

"Sure. You can contact me on FB." …and that's how it began.

Back at her desk, Emily felt like a teenager sitting in history class daydreaming about the boy she met in the hallway. Kota was a stark contrast to those youthful crushes. He was the first guy she had gone out with in over a year. Of course they were just friends—barely acquaintances. She tried in vain to deny her heart was opening to this bad boy who seemed good.

Kota felt proud as he strolled back towards the college campus. He knew how to ask all the right questions, look friendly, not pushy and how to be polite. He knew how to make a lady feel special. He could tell this first date had gone according to plan. He would continue to dangle the hook while she nibbled. When the time was right, with one big jerk, he would set the hook and begin to reel in his trophy.

In the months that passed, Kota knew he had Emily right where he wanted her. He could tell she was falling hard for him. The best part, he thought, was how confident she was that he was the one making all the changes. He was the one moving over to her side of the line. He smirked. That's never gonna happen. This moving slow, dropping crumbs, lost in my grief stuff was working perfectly on *daddy's little girl*. Just a bit more tweaking and my plan for Emily and James Fields will be complete. Kota could taste the sweetness of his revenge.

Life in the parsonage had become problematic over the past few months. James Fields would have been proud of Callan had he been a fly on the wall. She fought Rey at every turn.

"Don't leave your family for those *misfits* in the prison. Keep this up and your *own* boys will end up criminals. They *need* their father."

"You're going to the Browns again. Those people are *cultish*. You should ask them to leave the church before they infect more people with their kookiness."

"You don't have time for *me* anymore. I feel like our marriage is in trouble. Can't we go out just the two of us? "

"The boys were asking about you last night. They miss their father."

"Skip the small group tonight…I'll make it *worth* your while."

"I heard about this great new family in the community who are considering our church. But, they heard a rumor that the pastor only cares about the poor. You are getting a bad reputation, Rey. This is *not* who you are."

Rey tried to keep the peace, but Callan was bent on magnifying every issue in the church.

Finally, Rey had enough. With passion in his voice he spoke, "Callan, *this* is our life. It's not going to change. I'm never going back to what I was when we came here. I *hate* that person. I will never be status quo again. I will fight for the poor, the hurting and especially the lost. I will do all I can to tell them about Jesus. I want you to be at my side."

The tone of Rey's voice shut Callan's ears. She interpreted his tone as anger vented in her direction. She burst into tears which had become a weekly occurrence.

"I can't take it anymore. I have to get out of here. If the boys and I leave then you will be able to see more clearly what's *really* important."

"Callan, please don't go. We are a family. And, families work out their differences—they don't leave. We've just hit a bump in the road. We can get through this with the Lord's help."

Callan's lip quivered and tears looked inevitable.

Rey suggested. "How about marriage counseling? Would you consider that?"

All the emotion that moments ago were ready to spill out was gone and Callan calmly answered. "Yes, let's do that. James Fields recommended someone to me."

"You can't be serious. We will find someone outside of both our circles. Someone that we can both agree on."

The emotion was back and Callan's voice was loud. "I knew you didn't really want to work it out! The boys and I are going to my parents for a while. You can take this time to make the necessary changes."

At that moment, Rey was considering surrendering to Callan's demands. He wanted his wife back. He wanted peace and harmony to return to their home. He had always thought they were a team. He was willing to do anything to save his marriage. Before he conceded or said another word. He closed his eyes and silently prayed.

Callan looked at him waiting for a response.

The words formed in Rey's mind, *it's going to be okay.* He could not explain the peace that filled him. He opened his mouth to speak.

Callan held up her hand to silence her husband, "That's it. I'm leaving."

The next morning Callan and the boys headed for her parents' home. She visualized the inquisition that awaited her on arrival. She had only offered her parents the watered down explanation that her family was under extreme pressure because of strained relationships between the church board and Rey. She was hoping a few weeks of peace outside the situation would be good for both of them. Knowing her family, Callan was fairly certain she was replacing one storm for another.

The problems in the church had now reached hurricane force. This caused Pastor Rey's anxiety levels to rise. With Callan gone, he felt very alone and helpless. He was concerned how Callan's parents might fuel her negativity. They had never cared for him, his career path or his churchy ways—as they called it.

Rey leaned heavily on the encouraging words the Lord placed in his heart. *Everything is going to be okay.*

Rey continued to pray for his family.

Sunday morning Rey struggled to get through his message. He looked out at his divided congregation. The members who were against him had positioned themselves throughout the sanctuary. Wherever he looked they were glaring back at him. Rey had tried to focus on the faces that were hungry for the Word. Unfortunately, he felt more like evil was triumphing over good. Pastor Rey closed the service with a halfhearted dismissal prayer.

He stood alone at the back of the church to greet people as they left. There was a definite shunning by some who pushed past him without a word. Many did stop to shake his hand and asked about Callan and the boys. It wasn't lying to say they had gone to visit her family. They had not gone anywhere since they arrived in Hillbrooke nearly nine months ago.

After most of the congregation had left the building, Rey noticed Harold and Esther Smith still sitting in the sanctuary. They appeared to be praying. He had nothing left to give. He walked over and sat behind them. He reached up and put his hand on Harold's shoulder.

Harold turned around and saw his Pastor. He stood and walked to the pew behind him taking the seat next to Rey.

Tears burned in his eyes when he felt Harold's arms engulf him. Rey looked at this man as a spiritual father. When Harold released him, Esther handed her husband an envelope. Harold pressed it into Rey's hand. "This is the key to our cabin in Traverse City. It's a place of solitude. Esther and I just call it "The cabin." It's nothing spectacular. We love to go there just to pull away from the pressures of life. It's a hideaway. We thought you might like to go there for a few days to get away and pray. I've enclosed the directions along with step-by-step instructions for getting everything up and running once you get there. You have my phone number if there are any problems."

Rey looked at this precious friend and hugged him. Harold waited a moment, then continued. "Esther and I love the drive up there with the woods and pine trees. There's not a lot around to distract from direct communication with God. If you are struggling with decisions—I can't think of a better place to spend a few nights." Harold smiled at Pastor Rey.

Rey was visibly moved, "Thank you, Harold. It's been a difficult week. Being out of the office may be strategically insane with things heating up with James and some of the other church members."

"Pastor, you do what you need to do—for you. I can keep James Fields in line." Rey could see Harold's shoulders press upwards. He stood a bit taller as he spoke. Rey was comforted by his protective concern.

"I probably should stay home and face the music." Rey looked at the envelope in his hand like it held a free roundtrip ticket to a remote island paradise. Then he remembered Callan and the boys weren't going with him.

"Did I tell you there are 40 wooded acres with walking trails, a stocked pond with trout and bluegills? The pond may still be frozen this time of year, but it may be too dangerous to ice fish. The pond is viewable from the living room window. The sunrises and sunsets are breathtaking." Harold drifted off in thought for a moment. "I can't explain why, but when I'm at the cabin I feel like God is rocking in the chair next to me. And when I pray it's more like a conversation between old friends."

Rey pushed the envelope with the keys into his pocket, "This may be just what I need. It sounds amazing. I'll pray about it when I get home. Then make a decision."

Pastor Rey Douglas drove along the slick two-lane road in absolute silence. Swirling through his mind, like the bitter wind of a winter storm, stinging questions rushed in. How did things go so wrong? If I had stayed the course and stuck to my plan my wife would be at my side right now. My church would not be in turmoil. He slammed both hands onto the steering wheel, "What was I thinking?"

He paused. And again spoke out loud, "What am I doing running off when I should be strategically planning and protecting my pastorate? Am I doing the right thing? The church needed a leader not a puppet."

A car zoomed past drawing him back to the present. He was almost there. He had endured the four-hour drive with his faithful companions, regret and remorse. These two acquaintances had sat one on each shoulder bombarding Rey's thoughts with their relentless sniper attacks for many months. He drove on in silence.

Rey pulled up to the small log cabin. The A-frame shape gave it the look of a teepee. The covered porch had two rockers. A picture flashed in Rey's mind of Harold and God having a good old rock off together on a summer day.

The month of March in the north could be unpredictable. The weather seemed to be holding for now. Rey hoped the wood stove in the cabin would be sufficient to keep him warm. He had already decided he would spend his time at the cabin fasting. There were big decisions to be made. He wanted desperately to partner with God. He needed the mind of Christ to help him navigate through this mess.

Fasting was a new concept for Rey. He had personally never fasted. The church where he was raised never once taught on the topic. It was only mentioned in reference to the 21-day fast of Daniel and the 40-day fast of Jesus in the wilderness. No one at any church he ever went to was interested in doing either one of these. In seminary the Bible stories with fasting were taught, but not applied. The only church he attended after graduating from seminary focused more on *feel good* messages.

The desire to fast was birthed from within. It was strong. He didn't understand it. He made the decision to obediently listen and follow the leadings of the Lord. In the past nine months, he had experienced so many new things. Fasting seemed trivial in comparison to bursting into tears at any given moment or hearing people pray in unknown tongues. Or, seeing unthinkable words supernaturally appear on his wife. Or, the strong impressions he felt from the Lord to do things he never felt capable of—like prison ministry. Going without a meal or two was going to be kid stuff—he imagined.

CHAPTER 17

I'm Drawing You Back

*"...don't you see how God's wooing you from the jaws of danger?
How he's drawing you into wide-open places—inviting
you to feast
at a table laden with blessings?*

Job 36:16 The Message Bible (MSG)

*Z*ander and Ty fought in the van most of the way from Michigan to Southern Illinois. Callan's head was pounding from a lack of caffeine, complaining children and the mounting stress of facing her critical parents. She slowed down and turned into the drive of her childhood home. Waiting on the porch were her parents, Daniel and Naomi Walters. Seeing them standing there; Callan had a momentary feeling of hope. Maybe they were anticipating her arrival. Her smile faded when she saw the expression on her mom's face. It was cold and judgmental. Callan had seen it many times before. Her father turned his head away as she guided the car to a stop. Her heart plummeted back to a harsh reality.

It has been nearly a year since she has visited her parents or they had come to visit her. She stepped out of the car to greet them. They casually strolled down from the porch. The hugs were awkward. The kind of hug you give when you're unsure if the other person was expecting a handshake instead. Both parties followed through with the hug secretly wishing they had chosen to shake hands.

Callan watched her parents' uneasiness continue with their grandsons. They had never been doting parents and seeing this detachment continue into grand-parenting caused a deep sadness in Callan. She felt sorry for them, and all they were missing being a part of these two high-spirited little boy's lives.

Zander and Ty were old enough to spend the night with grandparents, but they never offered to take their grandsons. Callan certainly didn't feel comfortable asking. She thought of Rey's parents. They were always wonderful to her and the boys. They wanted to see them on a moment's notice. Her in-laws had been to their home at least once a month since they arrived in Hillbrooke. She would rather have gone to Rey's parents for a few weeks, but with Rey and her at odds, that would have been awkward. For the boys, it would have been a much better fit.

It was a brisk March afternoon in Illinois with no snow on the ground. Callan sensed her posture change as she followed her parents into the house. She felt like a disobedient teenager soon to receive the lecture of a lifetime.

After being cooped up in the car for hours, Zander and Ty ran around the front yard a few times to unwind, releasing pent up energy. Callan and her parents went to the family room to talk. She knew it was only a matter of minutes before she would hear precisely what those two stern faces were thinking.

The front door slammed shut startling Daniel and Naomi. Callan watched her parents jump and felt a mischievous giggle form inside of her. She didn't dare let it out! This was going to be a long few weeks especially for two very active little boys.

Zander and Ty rushed into the family room full throttle, not sure where to go or what to do. The verbal assault on Callan was imminent.

She felt like one of those tag-team wrestlers who had just been thrown into the main ring. Only she was alone. There was no team member to tag when she was too exhausted to continue. She would be outnumbered two against one. There would be no one on her side when the damaging verbal assault landed her on the mat. Her heart felt a pang of painful longing as she thought of Rey, her champion, who had always been her buffer during difficult times with her parents.

A flood of words poured out of Naomi's mouth. "Callan, what is going on? Are you and Rey getting a divorce? You know how we feel about that. Did he hit you? Is he having an affair? If he is, then that's different. People would understand and even feel sympathy for you."

Callan spoke with a controlled, but firm voice, "Mother!" Then she looked over at her young sons who were wide-eyed and looking at their mother. Zander was old enough to understand something wasn't right. His face was full of confusion.

"We certainly are not getting a divorce and our marriage is fine." Callan jumped up and hurried the boys to the basement family room. There were a few leftover toys from her childhood in the safety of the lower level. All the toys were girl play things of course. Callan found the old Nintendo and video player were still hooked up to the TV. This would entertain them for a little while.

After settling the boys into some safe distractions, Callan returned to her waiting parents who seemed more like children ready to throw tantrums than adults—parents—her parents.

"Mom, Dad, I need a few weeks away from home to sort some things out, but mainly to give Rey time to make the right decision. He needs time without us under foot to learn to better appreciate me."

Callan's mother softened a bit. She understood this type of manipulation. She was suddenly proud of her daughter for wielding her God-given power.

Callan's dad tagged in, "Well, that is all good and fine, but it would be best if you didn't come to church with us while you're home. It would cause too many questions. You are probably all churched out anyway being a pastor's wife. Consider this a vacation, but we won't be your built in babysitters while you're here." He got up and went to the living room to read his newspaper.

There wouldn't be much more dialogue between father and daughter during this visit except a "Good Morning." "Good Evening" and "Can't you keep those boys quiet?"

Now that there was distance between Callan and Rey, it made it difficult for her to remember why she left in the first place. Callan's mother dutifully helped keep that wound raw. She was like the little cartoon devil dressed in red with a pitchfork sitting on the left shoulder of her victim. She'd whisper evil things, however, Callan's mom didn't whisper. She took every opportunity to drop negative thoughts into her daughter's mind.

"It's good for a man not to feel too confident. Make him call you. Don't demean yourself and be the first to surrender. He needs to learn to always listen to you above everyone else. When he doesn't—then you make him *suffer*. Eventually, they learn. It will be so much sweeter when you win."

"Mom, I miss him."

"Really Callan, you have to keep your emotions in check or you will lose all control. Take a stand and refuse to back down. Rey is a man. He'll come around to your way of thinking soon enough. Trust me."

Callan felt sick in her stomach. For the first time, she realized that James Fields and her mother sounded a lot alike. She found herself wishing her good, kind husband would walk through the door and whisk her away from this crazy place.

The days passed with a lot of "Don't touch that." "Can't you control them, Callan?" "Who tracked this dirt in the house?" "No, you can't watch TV in here, go to the basement." With each unkind word spoken to her boys, Callan tried to balance the hurtfulness with extra hugs at bedtime. Zander and Ty really missed their dad. Callan missed him too.

The next day Callan took the boys out for a drive. She was hoping to clear her head. She needed to give the boys, as well as her parents, a break. The unpredictable March weather warmed up enough for them to stop at her favorite park. The boys ran excitedly from toy to toy. They were free to yell, climb and get dirty. Callan sat in the car checking her email and then her Facebook, occasionally glancing up to watch her boys playing.

After finishing her personal communications, she stepped out of the car and called the boys. They were both hanging upside down on the monkey bars swatting at each other then roaring with laughter. She decided to let them play a little longer. What's the rush to get back to prison? She thought.

Spotting a picnic table near the play area, Callan walked in that direction. Sticking out between the wood slats on top of the table was a piece of paper rolled up. It looked like a scroll. Callan eased it out from between the slats and unrolled it.

It said, *Looking for a church? Come see us on Sundays @11A.M. or Wednesdays @7 P.M.* There was an address, telephone number and a website. Callan sat down at the picnic table and looked up the church on her smart phone. Scrolling through the church webpage Callan mulled it over, did she really want to go to church or just stay home and enjoy the quiet house while her parents were gone. She thought about the greeter team waiting to attack her when she walked in the church doors. On the other side, she thought how nice it would be to have anonymity. No one would know her. There would be zero expectations. That sounded wonderful. She decided to give it a try.

On Sunday morning Callan loaded up the boys and headed to the unfamiliar church. While driving, she formed her plan. She would tell people who asked that she was visiting her family for a few weeks. That should put them off her scent quick enough. She's not local. She would be as evasive as possible. Even if she did share her name, and where she was from, no one would know Hillbrooke, Michigan. It's nearly eight hours away.

The church sat in an open field with no landscaping. It was one of those pole barn churches that were thrown up quick and cheap, but she didn't care. She turned off the main road into the church drive.

She parked the car and was able to breeze by the preoccupied greeters without a handshake, bulletin or welcome gift. She felt like a pro maneuvering the unfamiliar building. She followed the parents with kids the same ages as her boys. They were flowing down a hallway to the left. It was an easy kid-drop off with few questions asked. The boys were thrilled to get out and mix with other kids. Now she would have 90 minutes of freedom with no kids, no parents, no husband, no board members, just peace.

Callan followed the crowd into a large multi-purpose sanctuary. She looked up at the ceiling making the connection that this was a gymnasium. The basketball hoops were tucked up in the rafters at both ends of the room. The floors were made of wood with painted foul lines marking the basketball court. Padded blue folding chairs filled the space in the center of the gym/church.

The music began before she found her seat. It echoed loudly off the walls. It was deafening. The crowd size was about 300 people. Just enough to fly under the radar, Callan thought. She chose to sit in a row that was nearly full and near the back, hoping this would give the appearance that she was not alone.

People alone were a target for the overzealous church goer to attack with questions. "Are you new to the community?" "How did you find out about us?" "Have you filled out the visitor card?" Callan thought how she just wanted to be left alone. She cleverly selected her row and found her seat. There was one seat empty between her and an older couple in their fifties. They looked about her parents' age.

This service was much livelier than she expected. There was an abundance of joy as the people sang, clapped and lifted their hands. None of that was unfamiliar to Callan, but the people who went to the altar and stood with their hands lifted during the song service seemed a bit over the top. Some of those altar people were kneeling down on the floor. She was curious and wanted a better look. But there was no way she was moving from the safety of her seat.

The songs were unfamiliar to Callan except one she had heard before—somewhere. She followed the words of the songs on the two large screens on either side of the platform that looked more like a school stage than a church. All in all, it was a pleasant experience mostly because no one knew who she was or the struggles she faced in her personal life.

The music changed from loud and lively to soft and sweet. Many people sang with their eyes closed without the aid of a hymnal or the words on the screen. Callan continued to watch taking in everything.

Then it happened. A soft voice whispered to her, *"I have loved you with an everlasting love and I'm drawing you back."* Callan jerked her head to the left and looked at the older couple who both seemed to be praying. She glanced behind her but the seats were empty. On the other side of her was a mother sitting down holding a sleeping baby. There was a soft mumbling throughout the room as people's prayers filled the church. Then it grew quiet.

There was a hush that filled the room. A man's voice boomed out from the far side of the room near the front. He was speaking in a language that was not English. Callan looked around. The people seemed okay with this outburst. There was a mysterious holy reverence. She sensed it. Something strange was happening—she felt woefully uninformed.

The voice stopped. There was another short silence. A few rows away she heard a woman's voice speaking, *"I haven't forgotten you. Even when you forget me I longed for you. I've waited for you. You have been running, but soon you will run back into my arms."* There was a brief pause. No one moved and no one spoke. Then the lady continued, *"for I have loved you with an everlasting love and I'm drawing you back."* Callan felt faint. She sat down in the folding chair. Those were the words she heard just moments ago. *"I have loved you with an everlasting love and I'm drawing you back."*

The pastor came to the microphone and said, "For those of you visiting with us this morning, that was a Gift of The Spirit found in the book of I Corinthians. These verbal Gifts are an encouragement and edification to the hearer. The Lord is speaking to one or some here today that may have drifted from the safety and protection of the Lord. He wants you to know that he loves you. He's waiting for you. He desires to win you back, and He loves you. His love for you will not cease. He loves you now and forever."

Callan couldn't focus on what the pastor was saying. She felt weird on the inside and shaky on the outside. If she hadn't been trapped in the row by the mother holding the baby she would have bolted out of that church, but she didn't move.

The pastor closed the singing time with a prayer. Then people started greeting each other. Callan quickly reached for something to read from the seat pocket in the chair in front of her. She tried to look very busy taking in all the information on the prayer request card she was holding. She hoped to get through the greeting time without having to talk to anyone. No one interrupted her reading. Soon the announcements were given followed by the offering. Then the pastor stepped forward to preach.

He was older than Rey. He seemed in touch with his congregation. He opened his message with a joke. It went right over Callan's head but most of the people roared with laughter. She thought this must be some inside joke amongst these people. The sermon title and scripture verse popped up on the screens. The pastor delivered a message like she had never heard before.

His text was from Proverbs. The title was **Guarding Your Heart**. He spoke with a voice that went right to Callan's heart. "Our hearts are the wellspring of life, and the conduit by which the Lord speaks to the Believer. We are his treasured possessions, and we need to be careful not to fill our minds and hearts with the trash of this world. Keeping your hearts pure from trash will allow the truth of His word to strengthen you." The pastor then quoted from memory Philippians 4:8. "Finally, brethren, whatever things are true, whatever things *are* noble, whatever things *are* just, whatever things *are* pure, whatever things *are* lovely, whatever things *are* of good report, if *there is* any virtue and if *there is* anything praiseworthy—meditate on these things."

God's Word being quoted from memory and not simply read captured Callan's attention. She felt a passion in the pastor's voice. The

Word seemed infused with life. The Word came from a heart who knew the Author intimately.

At the close of the message, Callan sat motionless. There was a stirring in her. There was an unmistakable tugging at her heart. A tugging she had not felt since that excitement she felt at camp with her school friend, and again her first year at Bible College.

The pastor invited people to come forward to the altar. The closing was not a doxology or some simple prayer of dismissal. He challenged the people in that room to examine their lives, ask forgiveness and allow God to help them make sincere changes.

There were selected people standing across the front of the church waiting to pray with the people who chose to come forward. This was different than anything Callan had ever experienced.

She wasn't afraid. She stayed until the pastor closed the service and released the people. She sat back down to collect her things. When she looked up, the couple sitting next to her was moving in closer to greet her.

She had let her guard down, and now she would have to deflect nosy questions. Callan plastered on her fake smile and readied herself.

The lady extended her hand into Callan's personal space. She knew she had no option but to accept it.

"Hi. I'm Tina and this is my husband Mike. We noticed you were sitting alone and wondered if you were visiting this morning."

Callan knew she had to maneuver these questions with skill or she would open the door to an invasion into her private life. She gave them her rehearsed reply.

"Hi. I'm Callan and I'm in town for a few weeks to visit my parents." This should have sent the snoopers packing, but it didn't and she wasn't prepared for more questions.

"We are happy you chose our church to visit while you are in town. Where *do* you live?" Tina asked.

This was a make-it or break-it question. She could answer truth-fully. Surely, they wouldn't know anyone in Hillbrooke, Michigan. Callan answered, "I'm from here originally, but living in Michigan now."

"Really, where do you live in Michigan?"

Callan could feel the invasion of interest coming. She still answered honestly. "You've probably never heard of it. It's called Hillbrooke." Callan turned to go thinking she had ended the inquisition when she heard a loud squeal.

"Hillbrooke, no kidding, dear friends of ours just moved there. Tom and Jean Brown, but how could you know them." The color drained from Callan's face. She lost her composure for a moment, while thinking about the small group crazies; Tom and Jean. Yikes!

"I'm sorry, I need to pick up my boys since this is our first time vis-iting. I don't want them to be scared." Callan tried to escape as quickly as she could, but Tina was quicker.

"Let me walk with you."

Callan felt trapped.

"Can Mike and I take you and your boys out for lunch today?" The ever smiling woman asked.

"I think we need to get home to my parents, after all we did come to spend time with them." Callan lied.

Tina didn't give up, "If you are still in town on Wednesday nights we have church and the kids would love it. The adults do a Bible study that is interactive, and the group sizes are not intimidating. Maybe, if you are still in town, you could come?" Tina asked.

"That sounds great. I'll need to check and see if our family has any plans." Callan hurried the boys out the church doors.

The boys were chattering nonstop about how much fun they had. They carried an array of glued, glittered and colored papers.

Mike and Tina stood at the church doors waving goodbye. Callan hurriedly pulled out of the church drive putting as much distance as possible between her and anyone who knew Tom and Jean Brown.

Kota hung up the phone. The arrangements were made. His plan for revenge against James Fields was set in motion. Of one thing he was sure, Emily was falling for him. Maybe she wants to rescue me? Kota smirked to himself and thought—who cares. Whatever her reasoning, it works for me.

The one sobering thought was that as hard as he tried to change Emily, he knew she had changed him far more. He was cleaned up, enrolled in college, even passing his classes. He knew for the success of his plot he would need to see a little more movement from Emily in his direction.

Emily constantly invited him to attend her church and some group meeting at a friend's house. Kota thought, that's never gonna happen. He had been working hard over the past months to come between her and the church. So far she had not cracked, but he knew she would. When she did, it would be consensual. It's the only way to ensure his plan would work.

Emily had invited Kota a number of times to meet her parents. Kota asked her to keep their relationship a secret until he had his life in order. Then he would like to meet them.

Emily hated keeping secrets, especially from her mother. Kota wanted the perfect time to spring their relationship on *dear old dad*. He was reasonably sure the right time would be when Emily had an announcement. Kota's plan was to get the cart before the horse. That would be the ultimate payback for this self-righteous Christian.

Kota thought, James Fields doesn't think my family is good enough? He will be destroyed when his dear daughter gives him a grandchild fathered by the son of the *degenerate* Bill Edwards. Then he will be doubly crushed when I desert her soon after. My revenge will be complete.

Kota had plenty of experience with women. Emily had none with men. He could tell that she was getting very close to the point of no return. He was more than ready to lure her over to his side. The sooner the better, he thought.

CHAPTER 18

Pray Now

*"If anyone thirsts, let him come to Me and drink. He who
believes in Me,
as the Scripture has said, out of his heart will flow rivers of
living water."*

John 7:37-38 English Standard Version (ESV)

*S*tepping out of the jeep, Rey looked at the beauty surrounding him. It was a sunny day in spite of the cold. The property was everything Harold Smith had told him it would be. The pond was frozen with a few water spots visible through the snow. The walking paths were barely visible under the undisturbed snow. A sudden gust of wind swirled around Rey sending a shiver through his whole body. He hurried in long strides towards the cabin leaving a path in the snow. The key Harold gave him opened the door with ease. He stepped inside and was pleased to see that the furnace was set on 55 degrees. Turning the thermostat up to 70 gave him time to bring in firewood and build a fire to warm up the small cabin.

Rey unpacked the jeep bringing in the few meager items he had hurriedly packed. He unpacked his sweat suit, hunting socks, a pair of flannel pajamas, a change of clothes and his hiking boots. Once his personal items were put away, he opened his briefcase. He carefully arranged on the kitchen table his Bible, a devotional book, a fresh legal pad and a set of new colored pens. He wasn't sure how the next few days were going to play out. He just wanted to be spiritually ready for whatever the Lord had for him.

An hour had passed since Rey arrived. The fire in the woodstove crackled. He looked at the case of bottled water sitting on the kitchen counter. He was feeling his first pangs of hunger. He took a bottle of water and drank it down in gulps.

He opened a 365-day devotional book flipping through the pages to his birthday. It was titled, *Paul Shipwrecked*, he thought that pretty much summed up *my* life. Then he read the devotionals for his wedding anniversary and the boy's birthdays. He closed the devotional book and returned it to the table.

Digging into his briefcase he brought out the study book he was using for his own personal development. It was called, "*A Life Lead by the Spirit.*" He picked up where he left off a week ago. He read one chapter, underlined a few noteworthy phrases, then he closed the book and placed it back in his briefcase.

He checked his watch. It had been ninety minutes since he arrived at the cabin. From where he sat, he could see the clock on the stove, the clock on the microwave, the wall clock, and the alarm clock next to the bed. He felt taunted by the slow passing of time. Could he really be alone in this cabin for three days without entertainment, food or companionship? One thing he was sure about, bedtime couldn't come soon enough.

Rey filled the next few hours of daylight by splitting fire wood. When he got back inside the cabin, he loaded up the woodstove and grabbed another bottle of water. He guzzled it down without stopping, feeling very manly when he finished. He threw the empty bottle across the room into the waste basket, both arms shot up in the air and he yelled, "Score!" He made a hissing sound like a pretend crowd was cheering his victory point.

Then he looked around the empty room void of cheers, lowered his arms, took his boots off and crawled into the bed to read his Bible. He wasn't exactly sure when he drifted off to sleep.

Sunlight filled the cabin bedroom. Rey forced his eyes open while rolling over to look at the clock. It was 7:30 A.M. One day down and two to go! His hunger, loneliness and sadness returned with a vengeance. He figured he had about 16 hours of daylight before he escaped into sleep again. He swung his feet out of the bed and headed towards the kitchen to make coffee. He realized a few steps to the kitchen that there wasn't any coffee—only bottled water.

He returned to the bed. Climbing back in, he pulled the covers tightly up over his head. He tried to block out the light, his hunger and the world. At 8:15 A.M. he begrudgingly surrendered to the morning light.

Grabbing his Bible from the nightstand, he read a random chapter from Psalms and then some in Proverbs. He closed the Bible, got dressed, put on his hiking boots, winter coat and walked in the woods for a few hours. It was refreshing. He tried his best to pray as he strolled casually down the path through the woods on the Smiths' property.

Returning to the cabin, Rey looked at his watch it was only 10:30 A.M. He felt a wave of depression sweep over him. He decided to drive into town and walk around. Maybe even go to a movie. Driving away from the cabin he said, "One more day. I'll give it one more day and then I'm going home."

It was 3 P.M. when Rey arrived back at the cabin. Still hungry, still feeling shut out by God and missing his wife and boys.

He threw open the cabin door and walked in. This time he yelled. "God, where are you?" It was quiet. Not a sound. Rey knelt down by the bed and tried to pray. He felt alone. His mind was void of words. Giving up, he shuffled out to the porch and sunk into the rocker that faced the semi-frozen pond. He rocked for a while and thought about the complicated mess he still had to face when he returned to Hillbrooke. An old hymn came to mind and Rey started singing.

A mighty fortress is our God,
A bulwark never failing.
Our helper He amid the flood
Of mortal ills prevailing.
For still our ancient foe
Doth seek to work us woe.
His craft and power are great,
And, armed with cruel hate,
On earth is not his equal.

He stopped singing after the first verse. It was all he could remember from his childhood. He was actually surprised he knew all the words to the first verse. He listened to the quiet around him. Then the rumble of Rey's stomach drew his attention back to the here and now.

Rey yelled out loud, "Lord, I'm not giving up! I know You have something for me *and I want it*."

Marilyn sat in the rocking chair in Carl's bedroom. It was two in the afternoon and the light spilled into the hallway from under the door. She felt unusually burdened for her son.

She prayed, "Lord, I see Carl. He is standing at a crossroads. One road is wide and heavily populated. People are cheering and calling for Carl to join them. On the other side the road is narrow. There are only a few people. They too are calling for him to come, but this group is small and their voices can't be heard over the other crowd. Carl is moving towards the wide road." Marilyn paused and the volume of her voice changed, "Lord, stop him."

"Please, Lord. Silence their voices and make a way for him to hear you calling." She pleaded. "Lord, use the most unlikely people in the most unlikely ways to bring Carl to you. Lord, I pray all this in the name of Your Son, Jesus." Marilyn's known words stopped and groaning from deep within took over. It was the sound of one travailing under some great weight.

Marilyn prayed as the Spirit guided. Although her words were unknown to her, she knew she was pleading for the life of her son before the throne of God.

Marilyn picked up her prayer journal and penned this note. Under the direction of the Holy Spirit, she wrote.

> *Dear Carl,*
> *It has been nearly six years since you left us. I have faith-fully prayed for you—for your safety—for your salvation. I will never stop praying for you. I know my tears have not fallen to the ground unnoticed or uncounted. The Lord has heard my prayers and counted my tears. He has not forgotten me, and he has not forgotten you. He loves you. He will find a way to get through to you. You think you are forgotten, but you are loved. As much as I love you, God loves you more. He is calling out to you to come to him. Don't miss his voice. Don't allow anger and hatred to rule your life. You are at a crossroad, and you have the power to choose. Choose life—not death.*
> *Love,*
> *Mom*

Marilyn carefully ripped the page from her journal and folded it in half. She opened her Bible to John 3:16, the verse that she read so many years ago when she accepted the Lord. She pushed the folded note tightly into the binding and closed her favorite Bible. This was the Bible she bought shortly after Carl left. In six years it has never left Carl's room. She had made many notations and underlined every verse that comforted her. She cherished this book above all others.

She returned the Bible to the table, leaving the room she shut off the lights. She would be back tomorrow to pray again.

It was a peaceful Tuesday afternoon at the Community Outreach Church office. Pastor Rey was out of town. The other staff members decided to take advantage of his absence. They called in to say they were running errands outside the office or working from home, which was code for *the cats away so the mice will play.*

Heidi was alone in the office when the phone rang. Checking the caller ID she saw it was from the Fields Insurance Company. She figured it was James checking in.

"Hello, Community Outreach Church, this is Heidi."

"Heidi, this is James. Do you know where Pastor Rey is? I've been calling the parsonage and no one is answering." Heidi could hear the displeasure in his voice. She knew Pastor Rey was going out of town but failed to report this information to James. Her job was to keep him informed of anything regarding Rey or Callan that she knew or found out about.

"Didn't the Douglas's tell you that they were going to be out of town this week?" She quickly put the blame on them.

"Really? Do you know where they went?" James questioned.

Heidi felt like she was tiptoeing through a landmine. If she offered too much information, then James would wonder why she had not kept him abreast of all church office news.

Heidi spoke slower than normal like she was unsure of her facts. "Well, I think Pastor Rey may have gone to Harold Smith's cabin, but I'm not sure. I don't know when he left either. Callan may or may not have gone with him." She tried to stay vague about what she knew and when she knew it.

James grunted. "Hummh!" He hated being out of the loop, and Heidi knew this.

She added, "If Pastor calls in, I can let him know you're looking for him. That is—if you want me to?"

"No thanks. I'll call him on his cell." James ended the call. Sitting alone in his office he wondered why Pastor Rey would go to Harold Smith's remote cabin up north. He personally had never been to the place, but heard from others it was minimalistic at best.

James had programed Pastor Rey's number into his cell phone, but the phone was in his car. It was nearly quitting time. He grabbed his things and headed for his car. With each step, the thought of Rey Douglas caused his jaw to tighten. Since that man's arrival, James felt his tight grip of control on the church weakening. This loss of influence was an unfamiliar and unwelcome emotion. Once in his car, he found Rey's cell number in his favorites list and called him. The phone rang four times then went to voice mail. James didn't leave a message.

He envisioned Pastor Rey sitting somewhere with his phone in his hand, seeing the caller ID and ignoring his phone call. Rey mocking him by hitting the decline call button and going on about his business like James was nobody. His calls didn't matter. James fanned the flames of his indignation. At the thought of Rey Douglas, his face burned with anger.

The next board meeting was scheduled for Sunday evening. James would be ready to take things in hand once and for all. It was within his discretion, as chairman of the board, to call an emergency business meeting—if he deemed it was necessary. James entertained thoughts about how he could use Callan to his advantage, but he realized she had proven herself useless to him.

Rey was relieved to see day two ending. The sun was setting and he was happy to see darkness come. He would have eight hours of sleep for his restless mind. He tried one more time to read his Bible. Within a matter of minutes he closed it. He prayed reminding the Lord that he would not give up. Then he eased into bed hoping sleep would come quickly.

The room was dark; the bed warm and his thoughts were fading when Rey thought, *Is this not the fast I have chosen?*

Then he spoke the words out loud. "Is this not the fast I have chosen?" Rey knew that verse. It was in Isaiah—somewhere. It was going to drive him crazy until he found it. He felt around in the darkness until he found the lamp. Turning on the light he reached for his Bible on the nightstand.

He flipped to the concordance at the back and looked for the word *FAST,* then under that word he found the book of Isaiah. He ran his finger over each verse and stopped on 58:6 *fast that I have chosen.* He hurried and looked up the passage and read.

> *"Is this* not the fast that I have chosen:
> To loose the bonds of wickedness,
> To undo the heavy burdens,
> To let the oppressed go free,

And that you break every yoke?
[7] *Is it* not to share your bread with the hungry,
And that you bring to your house the poor
who are cast out;
When you see the naked, that you cover him,
And not hide yourself from your own flesh?
[8] Then your light shall break forth like the morning,
Your healing shall spring forth speedily,
And your righteousness shall go before you;
The glory of the LORD shall be your rear guard.
[9] Then you shall call, and the LORD will answer;
You shall cry, and He will say, 'Here I *am.*'
"Pray now!" Rey heard the words again, *"Pray now!"*

The past months had been a series of hard lessons for him. The more he obeyed the stronger His directions were. He was learning to follow the leading of the Lord.

Rey searched for his hunting socks under the covers. Finding them he pulled them up over his feet before stepping on the cabin floor. He walked out to the living room and stoked the fire until the embers glowed. He put a few more pieces of split oak in the woodstove. Then he began to walk around the cabin worshiping the Lord. The glow of the fire dimly lit the room. Something was different this time. Rey's worship started out with simple words of adoration. His deep appreciation, gratitude and love for the Lord finally found words. They emptied out of him in praise.

Callan came to his mind and Rey interceded for his wife. "Lord, I love her. I know her heart is good. She has surrendered to the pains and hurts of her childhood. I know she loves You. Open her eyes to Your truth. Soften her heart, help her make good choices. Give her a will to fight against the things that are trying to rob her of all that

You have for her. In the Name of Jesus, I come against her insecurities, inadequacies, jealousies and envy. Let them be replaced with the knowledge of who she is in YOU. Give her a divine revelation of YOUR love. Give her contentment like Paul the Apostle had when he said, in whatsoever state I am, I've learned to be content."

Rey prayed for his wife like he had never prayed for anyone before. He forgot that he had not eaten in two days. He forgot that he was in a cabin in the northern part of Michigan. He forgot that his church was in shambles. He felt great. Rey had heard of people calling prayer— *spiritual warfare*, but this was his first time praying for someone else like this. He used his words to wage war against evil principalities under the guidance of the Holy Spirit.

Rey continued to pray moving on to his sons, Zander and Ty. He called out their names to the Lord, pleading for the Lord to guide their future. He boldly asked God for their protection. He asked for spiritual guidance to help them make God ordained choices for their lives.

He prayed for the pastoral team at Community Outreach. Each time he allowed the Spirit to guide him. He continued to pray under the direction of the Spirit for the church board members who randomly came to his mind.

Then he called out the name of James Fields—his prayer changed. He began groaning and weeping. Rey knew that he was no longer praying from his own understanding. He was praying the mind and heart of the Father for someone in need.

In that moment, he no longer disliked James or feared him. He saw him as a wounded child, a damaged soul in desperate need of healing. When the burden lifted, Rey began to give praise, adoration and worship to Jesus. The words poured from his lips. He withheld nothing, and the tears flowed freely coursing down his cheeks. He willingly lifted his hands in complete surrender.

Then he dropped to his knees unable to stand in the presence of an awesome God. He felt like he was being immersed into a warm vat of oil as the Spirit of the living God flowed through him.

Then it happened.

He began to worship the Lord in an unknown tongue. It poured out from him like a river of living water. He was no longer that teenager who stood ankle deep, afraid of the unknown, afraid to go deeper. He was totally immersed in the satisfying fullness of God the Holy Spirit.

It was Wednesday morning and Rey watched the sunrise over the pine trees. Sometime during the night he found his way to the padded rocking chair facing the picture window. Tears began to flow again as the super-natural presence of the Lord, that engulfed him through the night, cradled him. Rey rested safely in the Lord's embrace.

CHAPTER 19

God Heals The Broken Hearted

When you call on me, when you come and pray to me,
I'll listen.
When you come looking for me, you'll find me. Yes, when
you get serious about finding me and want it more than
anything else, I'll make sure you won't be disappointed.

Jeremiah 29:12-13 The Message (MSG)

James arrived home after a tough day at the office still tormented by his imagination that Pastor Rey rejected his phone call. Walking into the house his mood was dark. He called out to Marilyn. She didn't answer. Looking into the kitchen he spotted a handwritten note on the counter.

> James,
> A family in the church received news that someone dear to them died. I prepared a meal to take to them and will be home about 6 P.M. Your dinner is in the oven.
> Love,
> Marilyn

Marilyn's altruistic nature fueled James's anger. He allowed his thoughts to run wild. Why did she always have time to help everyone

166

except me? Where was she now when he needed to talk to her? He couldn't remember what drove him into her arms all those years ago. Why didn't he leave?

Since their worthless son had left home, Marilyn had changed. She had an inner strength that would not crumble—no matter the mind games James played. Marilyn was moody and emotionally sloppy about her religion. He hated that. He would like to show her what life would be like without him, but he knew why he stayed. There was never a prenuptial agreement between them. He had no one to blame for that but himself. It was his idea to rush off in the heat of passion and marry. Now Marilyn was entitled to half of everything that was his.

He clenched his teeth tightly and slammed his fist on the note.

James left the kitchen and stomped up the stairs. He stopped outside the room of his prodigal son. He had not opened that door in six years, but today he pushed it open and flipped on the light.

He stood just inside the threshold. He scanned the room with a critical eye until his gaze landed on Marilyn's Bible. He walked across the room and grabbed it. Storming out of the bedroom he slammed the door hard enough to cause the picture on the wall outside the bedroom to crash to the floor.

James looked at the picture leaning against the wall. He hated that picture of a sailboat on the open water. He gave the framed art a kick, resisting the urge to smash it to bits. He turned with the Bible under his arm and headed for his car. Opening the passenger door, he slipped the Bible under his briefcase. Tomorrow he would decide what to do with Marilyn's *treasured* Bible.

Emily pulled into the driveway and parked her car. James strolled over to greet his daughter with a smile. When Emily stepped out of her car, James gave his daughter a hug and asked. "How was work today? Are you thinking anymore about going back to college next fall and getting that legal degree? Then you can have people work for you."

Emily smiled. She knew her father wanted a successful daughter to brag about. Legal aid would never be enough for him. "Dad, you know I love the research and talking to clients. Their stories are fascinating." She slipped her arm inside her father's as they walked to the house. "And sometimes my clients are innocent and truly in need of help. When I see the hope on the faces of some of those I've served, it gives me more satisfaction than money ever could." She looked up at her father. "Dad, not everyone who's poor is trying to rip you off or get away with a crime."

"But what about the money? You got'a have money to live like this." Her father gestured as they crossed the threshold into the house.

"Is Mom home?" Emily asked.

Her father's mood turned dark, and his sarcasm could be heard. "No she's out righting all the wrongs of the world." Then he spun his daughter towards him and held her hands. He looked directly at her, "Please don't be like her. You must have a little bit of me in there somewhere." He laughed and gave his daughter a quick hug. Then he released her. Something about Emily was like a healing balm to James's beastly nature. Father and daughter walked into the kitchen together. James forgot why he was so mad at Marilyn for the moment.

Callan couldn't get the church service from Sunday out of her mind. It was creepy to think something in your head one minute then someone across the church, a stranger to her would say that same thing. It was odd. And those people she sat by—what were their names? Tina was her name, but she couldn't remember his name. They knew Tom and Jean Brown. It was all too paranormal.

Callan's thoughts turned to Rey. He would have loved that service with all the spiritual strangeness. He would have been right in his element. If he called, she would not mention any of this to him. She hoped he would call her soon. She missed him.

Callan's phone began vibrating on the end table in her parent's family room. Her parents had asked her to turn off the ringer because the sound bothered them. It wasn't like her phone was ringing all the time. She only received two calls since she arrived; one call from Heidi with way too many probing questions—the other call from Grace, who prayed with her over the phone. That was a bit strange too—praying over the phone.

The caller ID showed it was Rey. They had decided before she left that they would not call each other for a few days. Callan was happy he called her first. She picked up the phone and walked to her bedroom for privacy.

"Hey. How ya doing?" She asked Rey. Inside she wanted to yell, I miss you so much. I want to come home, but she kept her tone even and void of emotion. She would not show her hand first.

"Callan, I hope you're sitting down because the most amazing thing has happened."

Callan could tell by his tone, this was big. She sat down on the edge of her bed. The excitement in his voice was nearly unrecognizable from the Rey she had left a few days ago. "Is everything okay? What's going on? You're kind of scaring me, Rey!"

Rey poured out his whole experience at the cabin without leaving out any detail.

Callan's mouth felt dry. She couldn't find a single word to speak. Fear gripped her heart. Her husband had gone fanatical. She envisioned the life of a single parent with two energetic boys. Tears formed in her eyes. How would she provide for them? She hadn't finished college. Her parents, what would they say? How would she tell them that her husband has become—a Pentecostal?

"Callan, are you there?" But all Rey could hear was soft sobbing. He waited.

Finally, after a few silent minutes, Callan spoke. "Rey, this is a lot for me to process right now. Can I call you back later?"

"Sure, I am heading home in about an hour. I need you Callan. We are a team—a family. I miss you. I love you. I know the Lord has an amazing plan for our lives. Callan, come home. I'm praying for you." Callan cut him off.

"I'll call you back in a while!" She hung up. She fell over on her bed burying her face in her pillow to smother her sobs. Her heart ached. She had big decisions ahead of her. If she fought this, she would destroy her home. If she surrendered—it was just too scary and unknown.

Callan picked up her cell phone to call Rey back, but instead called her sister who lived 30-mintues away. She asked her to keep the boys for the night. In that moment, she decided to attend the midweek service that Tina had told her about. Her plan was to go and see for herself what these people believed. The Browns came from this place, and maybe there was information she could gather on them that would bring her husband back to his senses.

Callan did something she had not done in a very long time. While she was lying across her bed, with her face in her hands—she prayed. "Most Gracious Heavenly Father, I don't want to see my home destroyed by such foolishness. Help me to get the information I need to make the necessary changes."

And the Lord heard her prayer!

Kota showed up at the Legal Aid office to take Emily out for lunch. This had become a daily activity. Kota was taking classes at the University just down the street. Emily was falling for this gentle-man. He was different than any guy she had ever dated before. The picture of Kota and his father that she saw on FaceBook, that first day they met, had moved her more than she could have imagined. Kota's love and adoration for his father was evident. The photo showed Mr. Edwards with his head resting on Kota's shoulder and Kota's head lying against his father's. It was a candid and natural moment that captured their love. Kota, occasionally tried to put on a tough guy, macho persona, but Emily easily saw to the heart of the man.

The stories Kota had shared with Emily about his parents and siblings made her heart long for a home with this kind of love and acceptance. If only he would accept the Lord. She had tried to bring up the subject many times, but he was skilled at redirecting her.

Today was going to be different. She was determined to get Kota to come to church with her this Sunday!

Sitting face to face in a booth at the coffee shop, Emily reached across the table and held Kota's hand. "Kota, I'm sure you know how I feel about you." Kota smiled and nodded. "I have tried a number of times over the past few months to talk to you about something very important to me."

Kota interrupted her, "Emily, I was thinking we could go away for the weekend. I know you want to wait to become intimate, and that's fine with me. We could make it separate rooms. We would have time together for days in a row without any other interruptions. We can talk about anything you want."

Emily imagined them sitting at a campfire holding hands as she unfolded the plan of salvation to Kota. That alarming pressure in her chest returned. It felt like something was squeezing her heart. Her eyes began filling up with tears. "Kota, I can't do that. I can't keep doing this. It's too hard. I care about you a lot, but there is someone I love."

Kota pulled his hand away from hers. "You're seeing someone else?"

She smiled and giggled through her tears. "Yes and no, but not the way you think. I'm talking about my relationship with Jesus. I love Him. He is my Lord, my Savior and I have lived my life trying to please Him. I can't be in a relationship with someone who doesn't feel the same way about Him as I do."

Kota felt a battle within. He had grown more in love—than hate with the daughter of James Fields. She was innocent in his vendetta. Kota let his guard down. "I'll be at church on Sunday. I'll listen and see what this is all about."

Emily's face burst into a smile that was contagious. She reached across the table and embraced Kota. Then she headed back to work and Kota to classes.

James stopped by the church on his way to work Wednesday morning. His mood was still foul from the night before. He pushed the church office door open with force, losing his grip on the handle, the door crashed against the wall with a thud. Startled, Heidi looked up from her desk. James was surprised too by the crash. Heidi jumped up to greet him at the counter.

"James, you should have called. I would have run out to the car to pick up the board agenda."

James held the single piece of paper in his hand barking his orders to Heidi. "Make copies of this, and place one at each board member place in the conference room. The meeting will be Sunday evening, put one copy on Pastor Rey's desk. Once you're sure Pastor Rey has read the agenda, call me. I want to know if he reacts or says anything."

Heidi reached for the paper. James pushed it across the counter sending the paper floating to the floor. When Heidi reached down to retrieve it James added, "I want him to know what's coming on Sunday."

Heidi agreed.

James walked out of the office feeling the victor. He was going to put an end to Pastor Rey's new found freedom. Rey needed to know that he was answerable to the church board. He serves this church at my discretion.

Leaving the church office, James noticed the Bible donation box tucked under the coat rack. He remembered that Marilyn's Bible was in his car.

He smugly walked to his car and retrieved the book. While walking back into the church he opened the Bible to the owner's page. He ripped out the front page where Marilyn had neatly printed her name and the date she purchased the Bible. The date was one week after their son ran away. That was six years ago.

James lingered for a moment and wondered—is Carl still alive? He pushed the thought from his mind. Taking the front page of the Bible, he crumpled it up into a tiny wad and stuffed it into the front pocket of his dress coat. He dropped the Bible into the donation box like it was a piece of trash and walked back to his car feeling vindicated.

Heidi went into the copy room and began to run off the copies of the agenda. The first one through the copier she snatched up and read the agenda with interest. #1. Review the church Statement of Faith. #2. Review approved outreach ministries. #3. Discuss suitability of Rey Douglas to continue as pastor. #4. Revisit the Pastor's pay package.

The list went on with ten points of business in all. Each point leading back to something Pastor Rey did, didn't do or might do in the future.

Heidi thought that Pastor Rey may be back in the office later that afternoon. A mischievous smile formed on her lips. This agenda may just bring on the fireworks James was hoping for. Heidi anticipated the Pastor's arrival. She didn't want to miss one minute of his reaction, and she needed to report back to James.

Heidi walked to the conference room with the stack of papers. She stopped by each staff member's office to let them know what was happening. Her first stop was the youth pastor's office. She knocked. Then eased the door open. "I hope I'm not bothering you. I have some news that I thought you should know." She paused for effect.

The youth pastor looked up at Heidi with a confused look on his face. He didn't speak.

Heidi continued. "A board meeting has been scheduled for Sunday evening. It's possible that Pastor Rey may be fired." She tried to remember to keep a concerned tone in her voice. In her heart she was feeling glee not sadness. "We really need to pray for God's will in this matter—and of course, this is highly confidential."

Heidi reveled in the youth pastor's shocked reactions. This scene played out a total of three times as she stopped by each staff member's office, and told Grace and Tiffany as well. She was proud she threw in the bit about praying. That was the perfect guise to get the information out.

The conference room was her next stop. She placed all but one copy of the agenda in a folder. She placed the folder on the table in front of the seat that James occupied at the board meetings. He had told her to put them on the table in front of each board member's place, but she thought this was better. There may be snooping people pass through the conference room before Sunday.

Then she proceeded to Pastor Rey's office. His door was locked. She returned to the office to retrieve the spare key she kept in her desk. She returned, unlocked his door and placed the agenda dead center on his desk. She looked at a few other personal papers he had lying around, but found nothing of interest. She left Pastor Rey's office locking the door behind her.

There was a bounce in Heidi's step and a smile on her lips. She thought, if Pastor Rey gets fired the next person to go is that sympathizer, Grace. I really can't stand her!

CHAPTER 20

Rivers of Living Water

*Enter into His gates with thanksgiving, And into His courts
with praise.
Be thankful to Him, and bless His name.
For the LORD is good; His mercy is everlasting,
And His truth endures to all generations.*

Psalm 100:4 & 5 New King James Version (NKJV)

*P*astor Rey arrived home late Wednesday morning. He
unpacked the few items he took with him to the cabin, showered and headed to the church. He was keenly aware of the Lord's
presence. Callan was not far from his mind. Rey prayed again for his
family, asking the Lord to use his experience at the cabin to draw him
and Callan together, not drive them apart.

On the car ride home, he felt the Lord breathe a fresh word to him
for the service on Sunday. He needed his computer at the church office
to look up references and information in preparation for his message.

When Rey arrived at the church, he decided not to use his private
entrance. He entered through the front office to greet the staff. The
look on Heidi's face made him feel like a parent who opened the bedroom door to discover a child had colored on the walls and was still
guiltily holding the crayon.

Rey pushed his paranoia aside. "Good Morning ladies, I feel like I've been gone a week instead of a few days."

"Glad you're back, Pastor. Did you have a restful time?" Grace was the first to respond.

"Better than any words could express."

Heidi ducked into the work room and busied herself by putting paper in the copy machine.

"Welcome back Pastor. Did you enjoy the great outdoors?" The youth pastor stood in the hallway leading back to the staff offices.

"It was wonderful. You know, I wasn't able to fish or hunt, but I did walk in the woods, chopped fire wood and prayed. Harold Smith wasn't kidding, though. Their cabin, though humble, was refreshing." Rey chatted with the other team members as he continued down the hallway to his office.

He unlocked his door and closed it behind him. Straightway, he noticed the paper on his desk. He knew he did not leave a single paper, perfectly placed in front of his chair. He sat down and read.

Then he read it over a few more times—reading between the lines. He felt agitated, but instead of reacting in anger, he slammed his open hand on the paper with authority and began to pray. The volume of his prayer carried into the hallway.

Outside the pastor's office, Heidi stood her ground listening. The other staff scurried like mice into their offices. She stepped closer to the door struggling to hear his words. This was not like any prayer she had heard before. A fear gripped her. She moved away from the door and headed for the office workroom.

Heidi walked passed Tiffany and Grace without saying a word. She went into the work area and closed the door behind her. She pulled her cell phone from her pocket, searched for James Fields name and called him.

Heidi exited the workroom. Tiffany looked up and met Heidi's stern gaze. Tiffany's face looked like her whole comfortable world was about to come crashing down around her. Heidi turned her attention to Grace whose head was bowed. She appeared to be praying in a whisper at her desk.

"Get ahold of yourself, Grace. This is a place of business." She scolded. Then she turned to Tiffany, "Don't *you* have some work you could be doing."

Pastor Rey stayed in his office until he saw the last car pull out of the church parking lot. He exited the church building through the front office doors stopping to pick up the donated Bibles. Tomorrow he would pass them out to the inmates. He didn't know how much time he had left as pastor of the Community Outreach Church. But until they asked him to leave, he would use his time to reach out to those who were hurting and encourage Believers.

Callan walked into the gym/church with her Bible tucked under her arm. Tina and Mike Morris spotted her immediately. The crowd was smaller as the Morris's had predicted. There was no place to hide. She was sure by now that Tina had called Jean Brown to get the whole scoop on her. She imagined the two women spending hours on the phone relentlessly gossiping about her.

Callan tried with all her might to stay focused on the Bible study conversation. It was futile. Once in a while she would smile, and then look back down at the open Bible on her lap. Mostly, her mind ran wild throughout the Bible study discussion.

The service closed with prayer. She was unimpressed. These people were crazy over every word written in the Bible. How was it interpreted? Why it was written? To whom it was written? She was thankful for her overactive imagination that got her through the past hour. With the service over she still had nothing new to discredit the Browns or the thing that had happened to her husband.

As she got up to leave, Tina Morris approached her. "Would you like to come to our house for dessert?"

"Oh, I don't know." Callan was close to graciously bowing out of the invite when she remembered she needed more information to discredit these people. "Well, I guess, I could stop over for a little while. My sister has my boys for the night and my parents usually go to bed early."

"Great. I wrote our address down, but you can just follow us. Our house is about five miles from here with just a few turns."

Callan walked to the parking lot with the couple who were virtual strangers to her. She couldn't believe she was really going to do this. She followed their taillights thinking all the while…I'm doing this! I'm really doing this. I can still turn around. Go home. They don't even know my last name. They only know I live in Michigan. It would be easy.

Callan pressed on, drawn to find out more about these people and what they *really* believed.

Tina and Mike Morris pulled up to a two story colonial house. It was dark outside, but the house looked warm and friendly with a single light glowing in each window that looked like a candle burning.

Callan parked her car behind the Morris' and followed them into the house. A peace greeted her when she entered their home. A box of kid toys was tucked under a bench by the door. It stood out to her as a stark contrast to her parent's sterile home. The toys spoke a message to Callan's heart, KIDS ARE WELCOME HERE.

The walls were lined with family photos. The pictures were all of a young couple with a little girl. There were beach photos, snowmen building photos, and campfire shots. Callan wondered if the pictures were of their daughter or granddaughter. A much younger Tina and

Mike were in most of the photos. She concluded that it must be their daughter.

Above the doorway leading into the living room were two giant vinyl words attached to the wall. "I AM". Just *I AM*. They were probably meant to be a conversation starter, but Callan wasn't biting. On the coffee table were piles of books with Christian titles. These two must be avid readers. Callan imagined. Still feeling uneasy she thought, what have I gotten myself into? These people could be crazy fanatics, and no one knows where I am. Lord—help me and with that a peace washed over Callan that she didn't understand.

Callan attempted to make small talk. "Who is that little girl in the pictures?"

"That's our daughter. She died about six months after most of those pictures were taken. She was our only child."

Callan felt her face flush. "I'm so sorry. I had no idea."

Tina touched Callan's arm. "Don't worry about it. She would be twenty-eight now. Her name was Elizabeth. We are at peace with that chapter of our lives. Losing her nearly destroyed us, but God restored us each individually, and then healed our broken marriage."

Callan felt at a loss for words. Showing comfort to the grieving had never been one of her strengths. She liked things to be upbeat, fun and playful. She left helping those who were hurting to Rey. She had lost count how many times over the past four days that she wished Rey had been with her.

Callan heard Mike in the kitchen making coffee. Dishes were rattling around. A wave of emotion was trying to overtake her—stop thinking about Rey she told herself.

Mike came into the living room balancing a tray with coffee cups and chocolate cream pie. "Here you go ladies."

"Thank you. It looks delicious." Callan reached for the pie thankful for the distraction.

"Callan, are you married?" Tina asked.

"Yes. My husband and I have been married a little over six years." Callan could feel the next question looming.

"What does he do for a living?" Mike asked.

Callan decided to redefine her husband's career choice. It wasn't really lying, just using other words to define the pastoral role. "He's a teacher. Sometimes he counsels people too."

Tina looked up from her plate. "Oh, what grade and subject does he teach?"

Callan thought, oh the tangled web... "Let's talk about you two. I'm interested in what your church believes. I had a few questions about the service on Sunday. During the service some people talked from the congregation when it got quiet. Was that planned ahead? Who told them what to say? How do they pick them?" Callan leaned back hoping these questions would take them off the scent of her life.

Between bites of pie and sips of coffee, Tina skillfully answered each one of her questions. Callan actually found the information more helpful than harmful.

"Ladies, I hope you will excuse me. I'm going to take these dishes to the kitchen. Then head upstairs." Mike collected the plates and was gone.

"Wow! Tina, I'm impressed. He is well trained. I like that in a man."

Callan could hear worship music playing upstairs. She thought how funny that Mike wasn't watching some sporting event. He was talking in soft tones. She wondered who he was talking too. What was he doing up there?

Tina and Callan talked casually for a little while. Callan found the conversation with Tina easy. She began to relax and open up to this motherly woman. Then the thing Callan feared most happened.

Tina said, "Callan, can I pray for you?" Normally, Callan would have been better prepared in this kind of situation, but her walls had vanished, crumbled to bits in the presence of this godly woman. Sitting there in Tina's living room she felt safe.

Callan nodded her head in the affirmative. Tina reached over and took Callan's hand.

"Lord, I love you. Thank You for Your kindness. Thank You for Your compassion. You are the One who delivers us from the hand of the enemy. Your kindness to Your children is from everlasting to everlasting. You formed us and created us for a purpose. You are our Rock and Fortress, a Strong Tower and a place of Refuge for us to run to in our time of trouble." Tina spoke these words like the person she was talking too was right there in the room.

Callan knew her Bible enough to know that these were words used to describe God. She had never considered praying Bible verses before. Then something new began stirring inside of her. It felt wonderfully alive.

Callan fought the emotion—without success. She simply couldn't hold back any longer. Tears began to roll down her cheeks.

Tina continued to hold Callan's hand, taking her free hand, she placed it on Callan's head. Tina began to speak in an unknown language. Callan had never felt anything this powerful in her life.

She surrendered.

No longer could she hold back. She fell forward into Tina, resting her head on Tina's shoulder. Tina cradled Callan in her arms much like a loving mother comforts a wounded child. Callan began to release the pain that had been pent up inside her since that day so long ago when a little girl stepped off a bus from summer camp with life changing news and no one cared.

Tina continued to pray as the Spirit led, sometimes in English and sometimes in an unknown tongue. Callan grew quiet, but still clung to Tina and the safety of her arms.

Tina put her lips close to Callan's ear and whispered, "Callan, the Lord wants You to know that he has loved you with an everlasting love, and He is drawing you back. He has never left you. He has been with you since the time you came to him as a child. He has watched over you. He has never stopped tending the flickering flame in your heart. He has a work for you."

Callan thought, how could she know?

"You have tried to control things. You've tried to do things your way, following your own path. You have tried to hide the pain, but the Lord wants you to know when you surrender control to Him you will find more peace and happiness than you ever dreamed possible." Tina paused. Then she invited Callan to praise the Lord with her.

Callan, still holding tightly to Tina, whispered in a broken voice, "Jesus, I need you. I love you. Forgive me. Please take away this pain. You are my life. I want you…" those were the last words Callan spoke with her understanding. Her sweet voice filled the room with songs of praise. It was a melody heaven alone could understand and Tina wept.

The phone in the Community Outreach parsonage startled Pastor Rey. He rolled over in bed to check the time. It was midnight. He fumbled around reaching for the phone. A rush of adrenaline kicked in as his concern for the need on the other end of the phone sent his imagination soaring. Rey whispered a prayer, "Lord help them." He put the phone to his ear. "Hello"

"I woke you. I'm sorry." It was Callan.

Rey fumbled for the light on the nightstand. "Is everything okay? Are the boys okay? Is it your parents?"

Callan interrupted. "Rey, everyone is fine." She laughed. "I got it. It happened to me."

"What? Got what?" Rey glanced at the clock on the dresser. "Callan, it's midnight. What are you doing up?"

"I'm on my why back to my parents."

"You're driving! Where have you been?"

"Rey, let me finish. I went to church tonight and a couple invited me back to their home. They're friends with Tom and Jean Brown. This church I went to—you would love it. It is one of the Spirit-Filled churches. Tina prayed for me. Rey, I got it. I got it!"

"Are you saying what I think you're saying?"

"Yes. It was wonderful, freeing and the Lord is good, loving and forgiving."

"Yep, it sounds to me like you got it bad!" Rey began to laugh. Then cry. "Come home Callan. Come as soon as you can." Rey busted out in prayer, "Lord, protect her and bring my family home."

Callan's voice was broken with emotion, "I'll text you when I get back to my parents. See you tomorrow. I love you. I never stopped loving you. Not for a moment!"

"Callan, I know. I know your heart. I missed you. I might as well get up now. There won't be much sleep for me tonight."

The next morning Callan told her parents. She told them everything. It didn't go well. In spite of unkind words and even some name calling, she was able to hug them goodbye and this time it wasn't awkward for her. Through tears she told them how much she loved them. She thanked them for raising her in a home where she learned about the Lord, His love and forgiveness.

Daniel and Naomi Walters looked at Callan like she was a stranger to them. Her sister was more receptive when Callan picked up Zander and Ty. She had received a phone call in advance from her parents concerned for Callan's mental stability.

Callan and the boys headed back to Michigan to join Rey. She couldn't help wondering what the Lord had in store for them.

Harold met Pastor Rey outside the prison at their usual time. Harold waited in his truck. Pastor Rey slipped into the front seat next to him. "Can we talk for a minute before we go in?" Pastor was holding three Bibles.

"Sure, Pastor."

"I have some awesome news. I was going to save it for the small group meeting tonight, but I can't. I'm bursting. At your cabin on Tuesday night or Wednesday morning the Lord baptized me in His Holy Spirit." Rey watched for a reaction from this Community Outreach board member.

Harold smiled. "I was praying you would experience the same wonderful things that Esther and I have been experiencing for years. Looks like my prayers have been answered."

Pastor Rey was half laughing and half talking when he said, "Wait a minute. You do this? You pray in an unknown language? You hear the Lord speak to you? You feel Him directing you to do things?"

"Guilty as charged. Now we better get in there. There are some prisoners who need to see the new and improved *YOU*!"

"I really don't feel any different. Can you tell I'm different?" Rey thought. Yes, I am different. I have a peace, an inner strength and boldness. This is new for me. I am perfectly fine trusting and allowing the Lord to be totally in control.

"Be prepared." Harold warned. "Things could get worse before they get better."

"Did you *know* that James has written up an agenda for the business meeting on Sunday evening? It's pretty much all about me changing my ways, or I'll be fired."

"No. Haven't heard about that, but I'm not surprised. He wouldn't want anyone who supports you on the board to be prepared to defend you. He's hoping to catch us off guard. Not to worry, Pastor, the Lord's got this one. You just wait and see."

"Harold, I'll be honest, when I found out I could feel myself getting angry. Then, I prayed. There was such a release in giving this over to the Lord. Best news of all, Callan called me at midnight last night. She was baptized in the Holy Spirit, while visiting her parents. I can't wait to hear the whole story when she gets home this afternoon."

"Praise God, my faith is soaring. Let's get in that prison and believe for a miracle."

Rey handed Harold two of the Bibles he took from the donation box at the church. "As the Lord leads you, find a prisoner to give one of these Bibles to, and I'll keep this one to give to someone. Lord, direct our paths, words and actions today."

"Amen!" Harold said. Then both men walked with confidence towards the prison.

They met with the prisoners as usual. Pastor Rey led them in a song acapella. Most of the men joined in with booming voices. Snake sat at the back with his arms crossed over his chest. He wore a scowl on his tattooed face. Pastor Rey had thought the last time they talked he had made some headway. As he watched Snake today, he wasn't sure.

A few new prisoners introduced themselves. There was a testimony from one of the regulars. Then Pastor Rey told the men about his personal struggles. The inmates listened intently.

He told part of the story of Mr. Edwards without using his name. He told of the regrets he carried from not sharing the life changing message of salvation with this man before he died.

Rey confessed to the twenty plus men in the small meeting room, "I never want to walk away from the prompting of the Holy Spirit again as long as I live. Today and always as the Lord allows me to come to this place, I will always share with you the hope of salvation through Jesus Christ. I will always give you the chance to choose. Being a Christian is not about your grandparents, parents, siblings or friends. It's about *you* choosing Christ. Only you can ask for forgiveness for the wrongs *you* have done. Accept and believe that He is the Son of God. Then you give Him lordship of your life. The Bible says that there is no way to come to the Father except through Jesus Christ, the Son.

I'm going to pray with you a prayer of salvation. If anyone wants to be saved and know forgiveness, peace and contentment, please repeat this prayer."

"Jesus, I believe that you are the Son of God.
I know that I am a sinner in need of a Savior.
Please forgive me.
I believe that you died on the cross for me.
You rose again—for me.
And you are coming again—for me.
Come in and take control of the mess that I have made.
I give you lordship of my life.
Help me to live for You from this day forward.
Thank You, Jesus.
I love You, Jesus."

The sound of the prisoners repeating the prayer sent a surge of joy through Pastor Rey. He scanned the crowd before he said, Amen. Only one inmate did not bow his head.

Snake glared at him from the back of the room. Pastor Rey kept his eyes fixed on Snake. What he saw was not the hardened criminal

Snake was trying to project. Through the eyes of the Spirit, the Lord allowed Pastor Rey to see a small boy, scared and alone. It nearly broke Rey's heart.

Pastor Rey closed the service with, "Amen." He picked up the Bible he carried in and walked to the back of the room where Snake sat alone. He took the empty folding chair next to him. "Snake, I want you to have this Bible. It was donated to our church. Read it. Watch what the Lord will do. I know you are hurting—God will heal. Give Him a chance."

The tall man stood up towering over Rey who was still seated. There was resistance in his face. Rey wasn't sure if Snake planned to punch him. He was an intimidating force with that tattooed snake slithering up the side of his face.

Snake reached out, took the Bible from Pastor Rey and turned to walk away. He stopped, looked back over his shoulder and offered this information, "I see the parole board later today. If I'm approved, I'll get out about 8 A.M. tomorrow morning."

Pastor Rey wanted to talk to Snake more, but Snake walked away before he could respond. Rey was unsure what to do with this information.

He decided to pray.

CHAPTER 21

Finally on the Same Team

"There is a time for everything, and a season for every activity under the heavens..."

Ecclesiastes 3:1 New International Version (NIV)

C allan arrived home just a few hours before the small group meeting would begin at Tom and Jean Brown's home. The small group had been meeting weekly for eight months. Callan had never attended. Not even one time, but tonight would be a different story.

Rey greeted his wife and sons like they had been gone for months instead of days. From Saturday to Thursday this couple felt the Lord had redirected, refocused and repurposed them. Zander and Ty ran into the house pushing and yelling with glee. Then it was quiet as the boys settled into playing with their toys.

Callan was ecstatic to be home. They snuggled on the couch in the family room and Callan told her husband everything. How she found the paper at the park, about the church she attended while home with her parents. She told Rey how the coldness of her parents forced her outside of her comfort zone and straight into the arms of the Lord. How the Lord spoke to her in that strange church service. Then the message in tongues and interpretation seemingly directed right at her. She told about meeting Mike and Tina Morris who knew the Browns!

She shared how she bravely stepped out of her comfort zone. She actually went to the Morris's house after church on Wednesday night.

"You know, that was all the Lord's doing? I never do things like that. Tina prayed for me, Rey. She knew things that I have never told another person...not even you." She laughed with a joy that Rey had not heard in a very long time. "The Lord never gave up on me. Never! Rey, He's held me in the palm of his hand since I was a child. He loves me."

There were far too many things that happened on her trip to call it coincidental. Callan went on to tell her husband about the beautiful evening after church on Wednesday night, when the Lord filled her to overflowing with his Spirit. She didn't want to fight it anymore. She didn't try to explain it away. She had always marked her own course from her earliest memory. Now, she had fully surrendered to the Lord. For the very first time she was in the back seat, and she loved it! She was ready for this new adventure.

There would be no formalities at the Brown's small group. Jean left her front door ajar for the members to come directly in. They had been meeting long enough that there were few secrets left among them. Except for the one Emily held. She had never asked this group to pray with her or allowed their counsel to help guide her in her relationship with Kota. Emily knew in her heart the reason. She told herself it was to respect Kota's wishes for anonymity while he sorted some things out. She knew the truth was that she couldn't bear to hear anyone in the group say out loud what she already knew in her heart. A Believer has no business dabbling in a romantic relationship with a nonbeliever. Emily used Kota's excuse to do what she knew was harmful to her as a Christian.

Everyone had arrived except Pastor Rey. Harold and Esther Smith sat in the folding chairs because the soft furniture was difficult for them to get in and out of. Emily and Marilyn were on the love seat. It was kind of funny how after so many months everyone had claimed their places. Tom and Jean always sat on the sofa. Pastor Rey sat in the recliner that faced the lake. Henry and Dorothy Samson, whenever they came, sat separate. Dorothy would sit on the sofa next to Jean, and Henry sat in the other recliner next to Pastor Rey. Things had become very comfortable for this little group.

When Pastor Rey arrived all eyes were on him. Holding his hand was Callan. Everyone in the group except Harold and Esther looked visibly surprised.

Jean hurried to the kitchen and grabbed another chair. She placed it next to the recliner where Pastor Rey always sat. Jean, always the hostess, said, "Callan, I'm pleased you could join us. This seat is for you, and the food is on the kitchen island. Please make yourself at home."

Callan smiled. Her ease set the pace for the rest of the group.

Marilyn offered her seat to Callan, but Callan said that she preferred to sit next to Rey.

After the initial eating and fellowship, Tom opened the meeting with prayer. He read a portion of scripture from Isaiah 61. "The Spirit of the Lord GOD is upon Me, Because the LORD has anointed Me to preach good tidings to the poor; He has sent Me to heal the broken-hearted, to proclaim liberty to the captives, And the opening of the prison to those who are bound; to proclaim the acceptable year of the LORD, And the day of vengeance of our God; to comfort all who mourn, to console those who mourn in Zion, to give them beauty for ashes, the oil of joy for mourning, the garment of praise for the spirit of heaviness; that they may be called trees of righteousness, the planting of the LORD, that He may be glorified. I will greatly rejoice in the LORD, my soul shall be joyful in my God; for He has clothed me with the garments of salvation, He has covered me with the robe of righteousness…"

Following the reading of the scripture, a silent reverence fell over the group. Tom waited to speak allowing the Word of God to settle on the group.

To everyone's surprise Callan spoke. "I'd like to say something. I need to ask everyone here to forgive me. My heart was not right when Rey and I arrived in Hillbrooke nine months ago. In fact, it hasn't been right for a long time. I was insecure, greedy and there was a spirit of jealousy that was rooted in me. Yesterday, God changed me."

Callan was normally controlled whenever she opened her mouth, but there was obvious emotion in her voice as she continued. "I have always loved my husband. But I loved me more. All my decisions passed through the filter of—*how will people view me*—in this situation. I wanted to be seen as accomplished and professional, rather than humble and Spirit led. Rey came to this understanding sooner than I. Now, we are both on the same path." Callan looked directly at Tom Brown, "Tom, the words you just read thrill me. They give me hope for the future. I am no longer looking for a country club church. I pray that Community Outreach will instead become a spiritual hospital—a place where hurting and damaged people will come to find wholeness." Callan held tightly to Rey's hand the whole time she shared. "I am eternally grateful to the Lord that he never gave up on me."

Then Rey shared about going to the Smith's cabin. How he met with the Lord there. He said, "I got it. The Lord baptized me in his Holy Spirit." There were no shocked expressions in this group—no further explanation was needed. If they had not received the Baptism in the Holy Spirit—it didn't matter because they were all in agreement that it was God breathed—a gift for the believer today.

Callan shared with the group her encounter with the Holy Spirit. When she mentioned her home town and the church she visited. Tom and Jean gasped. Their expressions revealed that they were hearing about this for the very first time.

Jean laughed, "We came from that church. We know people there. Callan, I can't believe that's your hometown."

Pastor Rey shared again. "Harold and I went to the prison today. I was able to share with them about my experience at the Smith's cabin. I told them how I felt the Lord's forgiveness for my failures. There was a prisoner named Snake who hasn't accepted the Lord, but I feel there is hope. He did accept the Bible I gave him this morning. I want this group to pray for him especially over the next few days. He is being paroled from prison tomorrow morning. It is my prayer that he will come to church on Sunday. Oh, and beware, if he does. He is a big guy with a snake tattooed on his face, and it's wrapped around his neck. He is a monster of a man. But, we know Jesus died for this man the same as anyone else. Will you pray for him?"

Different ones in the small group led out in prayer for Snake, and then a reverent hush fell on all present. It was Jean who spoke first.

"Callan and Emily," Jean looked back and forth at the two youngest ladies in the room. "The Lord burdened my heart for both of you this week. Here is what I saw when I prayed. Emily you were strolling along a cliff that had a steep drop off. You were walking along enjoying everything around you. You seemed unaware of the danger just inches away. You were so close to the edge at times that the ground began to give way under your feet. Then you moved just enough to stop from tumbling over the edge." Jean looked directly at Emily and continued. "Emily, God doesn't want you to see how close to the edge you can get, but how far away you can stay." Emily had tears in her eyes.

Then Jean turned to Callan. "Callan, you were running in a maze unable to find the exit or the entrance. The more you ran making aimless turns the more frustrated you became. Then you stopped. You just stopped running, sat down, pulled your knees to your chest and cried. While you were sitting there crying all the partitions collapsed to the ground and you stood up with no obstacles in your way."

Callan said, "That's exactly how I felt. When Tina Morris prayed for me all the pain and hurts I had carried for years were gone."

Jean was ecstatic. "You met Tina and Mike? This is beyond coincidental. Tom, remember the word that was given at our small group before we moved to Hillbrooke? I wrote it down in my journal. You are going to want to hear this." Jean ran to another room and returned with a floral journal that she was flipping through. "Here it is." She read.

> *"Through the years your feet have taken you many places, and your words have touched the hearts of many people. But this time your purpose will be to touch the life of one. Then the Lord will use him to touch the lives of many. The harvest will be like leaves falling from trees and waves crashing on the shore. Be watchful, be alert and seek the Lord in all you do. Pray continuously. Your prayers will be his covering; your prayers will be his rear guard. The enemy has marked him for destruction, but the Lord has marked him as a Good and Faithful Servant."*

Snake sat on the edge of his bunk. His large frame leaned forward. The small prison cell that had been his home the past four years was safe and familiar. Tomorrow morning he would be released. He had mixed emotions about life outside these walls. Where would he live? Did he have any friends left? He couldn't associate with any known criminals. That was pretty much everyone he knew. The Bible the pastor gave him sat on the small three foot by two foot metal desk that was attached to the wall. He looked at his distorted reflection along the sides of the desk. His thoughts drifted to his mother. She had always been a kind and loving person. He quickly pushed the thoughts of family away. That chapter of his life was closed, never to be revisited.

Snake leaned forward reaching for the Bible on the desk. Grabbing the book it slipped from his fingers projecting the leather-bound book to the floor. Without lifting himself from the bunk, Snake leaned down and retrieved the book. He noticed a small piece of paper sticking out from between the silver trimmed pages. Instead of pulling the note from its place, Snake held the Bible fumbling through the pages until it opened to the page holding the note. He slipped the note next to him on the bunk. His eyes were drawn to the verses on the page that had been highlighted with a yellow marker. There were handwritten notes along the side margin. The print was small and hard to read. There was something warm and comforting about the style. It was strangely familiar.

Snake's eyes were pulled to the highlighted verses. Before he could stop himself the words had jumped from the page. They invaded his thoughts: *"For God so loved the world that he gave…"*

He snapped the book closed and returned it to the cold stainless steel desk. Snake picked up the folded note. He slowly opened it unsure what he would find inside. The first two words caught him by surprise, "Dear Carl."

Snake dropped the note on the floor. He looked around to see if this was some kind of joke, but no one was interested in him or what he was reading. He could hear the usual chatter of male voices up and down the cell block.

Curiosity propelled Snake to pick the note up from the cold cement floor. He held it in his hand. The handwriting—it was hers. He was sure of it.

Dear Carl,

It has been nearly six years since you left us. I have faith-fully prayed for you—for your safety—for your salvation. I will never stop praying for you. I know my tears have not fallen to the ground unnoticed or uncounted. The Lord has heard my prayers and counted my tears. He has not forgotten me, and he has not forgotten you. He loves you. He will find a way to get through to you. You think you are forgotten, but you are loved. As much as I love you, God loves you more. He is calling out to you to come to him. Don't miss his voice. Don't allow anger and hatred to rule your life. You are at a crossroad, and you have the power to choose. Choose life not death.

Love,

Mom

Rey glanced at his watch. It was 8 A.M. on the dot Friday morning. Snake hadn't asked him to come—in so many words. Rey knew it was the right thing to do. He knew being late to the office would give more room for chatter about his fitness to pastor, but this was far more important.

The guard told him to wait by the fenced-in area behind the prison. All prisoners released would exit there. The metal door swung open. A tall tattooed man walked out. His head was held high looking directly into the sun. He breathed in the air of freedom. Pastor Rey allowed his car to idle forward towards the gate. The guard unlocked the outer gate to allow the former prisoner to exit.

In a sarcastic voice the guard said, "See you soon, Snake." Then he laughed, locked the gate behind him and strolled back towards the prison.

"Hey buddy, you want a ride?" Snake bent down to look into the window of the jeep that rolled to a stop in front of him.

"Thanks for coming, Pastor." Rey could hear the gratitude in Snake's voice. He was happy he made this a priority.

"Get in. I'll give you a ride."

Snake opened the passenger door and threw his pack in the back-seat. He slipped into the front seat filling up the space with his large frame. Pastor Rey had never been alone with a convicted felon. He felt a slight wave of fear wash over him.

"Where can I take you?"

Snake's voice was void of emotion. "You can drop me downtown."

"I hope I'm not being too presumptuous, but I know of a halfway house in downtown Hillbrooke that has an opening. I called them last night." Pastor Rey looked over at the massive man hoping he had not over-stepped his boundaries. He put the car in park to wait for further direction.

Snake gazed out the window at the local prison that had been his home for more than four years. "Sure, that's fine."

Rey put the jeep in drive. It would be a twenty-five minute drive from the prison to the halfway house.

Snake seemed deep in thought then turned towards Pastor Rey and asked, "What church did you say you come from?"

"Community Outreach Church it's out of town set back in the woods. It looks more like a hunting lodge than a church. Do you know the place?"

Each time Snake turned his head to look at Pastor Rey it looked like the snake tattoo was ready to leap from his face and strike. "Yes, I know that church. You been there long?"

"About nine long, long, long, months." He chuckled. "The Lord has been teaching me a lot as I shared yesterday morning during the group time. I wish I would have been open sooner to the leading of the

Lord. But I do know this. If my family had not come to Hillbrooke, you and I would not be sitting together in this jeep right now. Maybe the Lord brought me here because he loves you that much."

Snake jerked his head towards Pastor Rey and looked at him like he held secret knowledge that Snake wanted to keep buried—forever. Snake asked. "Whose Bible was that you gave me yesterday?"

"It was dropped off at the church in the donation box. Were you able to read it last night?" Pastor Rey took his eyes off the road and glanced in Snake's direction. He was unable to read the situation.

"I opened it. Did you know there was a personal note to somebody named Carl?"

"No. I usually fan through the Bibles to make sure there are no personal items in them or any identification. Sometimes people leave their Bibles at church, and they get put in the donation box by mistake. If the name is still in the Bible I can return it to the rightful owner. What did the note to Carl say?"

"It was a note from his mother. I was just wondering how that Bible came to me." Snake kept his eyes fixed on the road.

"That's strange. I'm not sure how that note slipped by me. Maybe, if you're name was Carl, you could say it's a God thing. Oh, by the way what is your given name? I only know you as Snake."

"It's Zac Parker for all legal purposes, but I prefer Snake as you can see." Snake gestured to the serpent slithering up his face.

"Then Snake, it is!" Pastor Rey laughed. "Would you consider coming to church this Sunday? I would love for you to meet my wife and boys. There are some wonderful people with big hearts that would like to help you get acclimated to life on the outside—if you're willing."

"Not sure if I'm ready for that." Snake replied still keeping his eyes on the pavement directly in front of the jeep.

Rey turned into the driveway of an old three story house with a wooden front porch. A bay window ran up the front of the house on all three levels. It was easy to see that a hundred years ago someone with a lot of money lovingly built this home. Now, everywhere you looked it was in need of repair.

"Snake, I know it's not much to look at, but I visited here yesterday. You'll have your own room with minimal rules. I'm going to drop you off to get settled. They know you're coming."

Snake swung the jeep door open and reached into the back seat to retrieve his meager belongings. He stuck his head back inside to say one last thing. "Look for me Sunday. I may just be there."

CHAPTER 22

Caught Fish Need To Be Cleaned

*Stalwart walks in step with GOD; his path blazed
by GOD, he's happy.
If he stumbles, he's not down for long; GOD has a grip
on his hand.*

Psalm 37:23 The Message (MSG)

*F*eeling hopeful, Pastor Rey drove away from the halfway house. The thought of Snake attending church on Sunday filled him with hope. He rolled to a stop at the 4-way, looked in all directions. A feeling of déjà vu rushed in. I've been here before. Then he knew. The house catty corner from where he stopped was the home of Bill and Mary Edwards. He had always come from the other direction, but there was no doubt about it. The porch screens still hung from their wood frames. Bill's empty chair was in the same spot on the porch. The memory of that day he parked down the street from the house crept in sending a wave of shame over him. It had been months since he thought of Bill or his family.

The pace of Rey's heart increased and beads of sweat popped out on his forehead. He brushed the droplets away easing into the intersection. With a sudden determination, he flipped his blinker on and pulled his jeep into the dirt driveway at the side of the Edwards' home.

Home visits had never been one of his strengths. He shied away from them at every opportunity, but not this time. He felt impelled by the Spirit to stop, and he obeyed.

Crazy thoughts rushed in. They're going to slam the door in my face. They hate me and my church. Don't embarrass yourself any further? This family just wants to be left alone. It's been six months since the funeral, and they haven't called or visited the church. With each step Rey took through the messy yard his thoughts continued to assault him.

Finally, he shook his head physically trying to remove the negative thoughts. Then mutely he scolded himself; YOU ARE DOING THIS—NO MATTER WHAT THE OUTCOME MAY BE!

Rey put his foot on the broken wood step. At the same time, Mary Edwards opened the front door. Her face revealed joy at the sight of Pastor Rey walking up her steps, "Pastor, you came."

Rey felt startled and a bit thrown off guard. He sheepishly asked, "Did we have an appointment?" He believed Heidi more than capable of setting an appointment, then not telling him.

Mary laughed with her crackly smoker's voice, "No. But you came to my house. That's sweet. I should have sent you a thank you note for the wonderful service. And that dinner along with the kindness of the ladies—I'll never forget it." Mary looked down for a moment then added. "I've been mean'n to come visit your church again."

"How about this Sunday?" Rey blurted it out, and even he was surprised by his boldness.

"Well, maybe. Just maybe, Reverend." Mary smiled and waved Pastor Rey into her home.

Once inside, Rey remembered visiting the home before the funeral of Bill. The home was all viewable from the doorway. The living room, dining room and kitchen combo were *lived-in* but welcoming. It reminded him of his grandma's old saying, "Our house is clean enough to be healthy and dirty enough to be happy." If that were the case, the Edward's home must be one of the happies places on earth.

Walking into the living room, Rey thought back on that first visit after Bill's death. He was ashamed, remorseful and awkwardly uncomfortable. He had not rubbed shoulders with many people like the Edwards' family. The uneasiness he felt that day reminded him of an old saying of his grandpa's.

Gramps would say this whenever he heard Christians complaining—expecting nonbelievers to act like they were already saved. He'd say, "Jesus told us to be fishers of men. Seems when Christians go fishing for men, they expect them men they're fishing for to be all cleaned before they even get'm caught. But that's not how fishing works. Fish are dirty, slippery and need to be cleaned up *after* they're caught. So don't go expecting them caught fish to come to you pan ready!"

Rey knew he had been guilty most of his adult life of this very thing.

Mary moved a load of laundry from the sofa making room for the Pastor to sit down. A group of young adults sat at the kitchen table playing cards. About six stray kids were running around in varying amounts of clothing. Mary was perfectly comfortable with her family and her home. She never suspected for a moment that Pastor Rey was being stretched outside his comfort zone.

"Reverend, would you like a cup of coffee?" Mary offered.

"No, Mary. I was just in the neighborhood, and saw your house and wanted to check in with you. I'm sorry it's taken me so long. How have things been going since the funeral?"

"This is just crazy. I mean you stop'n by today of all days. I finally got around to going through some of Bill's things. I was cleaning up on the porch. When I moved his chair to sweep this paper dropped to the floor." Mary picked up a pamphlet from the cluttered coffee table and handed it to Pastor Rey. It was titled the *ABC's of Salvation*.

Mary continued, "I read it—but don't understand it." She took the pamphlet back from Pastor Rey and pointed at the back. "Look here. See? Bill wrote his name there on that line."

Rey took the pamphlet back. His eyes drawn to the line that Mary mentioned. There it was—the name Bill Edwards obviously written with a shaky hand. Above the line where he wrote his name it said; sign on this line, if you prayed the prayer. As quickly as his eyes read those words—that random piece of paper became a cherished treasure.

Pastor Rey tried every trick he knew to fight the tears. He pinched his leg. He bit the side of his cheek. He looked up towards the ceiling—it was all futile. The tears pooled in his eyes then spilled out coursing down his cheeks.

Mary looked away—first at the floor, then the table, then towards the kid's playing cards. The Reverend was in her home, sitting on her couch—crying. She was ill prepared to bring comfort to the man of God.

Mary spoke with concern in her voice, "I didn't mean to upset you, Reverend." She paused then added. "I had questions. I thought you might have answers. Please don't be sad. I thought it might be a good thing."

Rey spotted the box of tissues nearby and grabbed a handful. He wiped his face and blew his nose. After regaining his composure, Rey responded, "Mary, it is a good thing. It's the best thing—better than I ever hoped."

Mary still looked confused.

Rey saw the little green New Testament that he read from at Bill's funeral. It was lying on the coffee table. He picked it up. "Mary, I want to talk to you and anyone else in the family that may be interested. I'll tell you all about this pamphlet, the importance of this little green book and why Bill signed his name on the back of this paper."

Mary called her family to the living room like a drill sergeant, and Pastor Rey shared the life changing story of a man named Bill Edwards.

Best Friday ever! Rey thought. In a matter of three hours he had helped a prisoner. He pushed past some of his own demons. He stopped to check on people he wasn't sure would welcome him. A huge burden of guilt he carried was gone in a moment. He was able to openly share the salvation message with a family that was legitimately interested.

He pulled into his assigned parking place at the back of the church. In a fog of excitement Rey bolted up the stairs two and three at a time. Standing outside his private entrance, he fumbled with his keys for a moment before unlocking his office door. Once inside he threw both arms in the air like he was cheering the winning point at a sporting event. Then he shouted, "Praise God! Praise God!"

To the right of him, someone moved. He jerked his head in that direction. James Fields sat in one of the wing back chairs with a sour expression of disgust. Rey did not require the prompting of the Spirit to know that this man was annoyed!

"I see you finally remembered where you work!" James voice dripped with sarcasm.

Rey didn't answer. He walked over to his massive desk and took a seat in his leather chair. He was slightly elevated above James looking down at him across the desk.

James moved uncomfortably in his lower and smaller seat. He knew what Rey was doing and it almost worked. James smirked as he lifted his 6'6 frame from the chair. "You wouldn't be trying to intimidate the father of intimidation." James had moved to the front of Rey's desk and looked down at him.

James pointed his finger at Rey twisting it to the beat of his slow, overly pronounced words. "You are messing with the wrong man. I know who you really are—Rey Douglas. Do you really think I would invite you here without checking you and that wife of yours out? You think I just heard you speak that one time at your graduation."

Rey frowned—confused by James' words.

"NO! I've followed you. I've been watching you. I visited your church in Illinois. I talked to people who knew you. People from your home church, your classmates at seminary and by the way Callan's parents are top notch in my book. You may have fooled a few people here with your religious talk."

James changed his tone to mock Pastor Rey, "God's speaking to me. God's leading me." James leaned in closer, resting his hands on the desk. Rey could feel his breath, "I know who you are. You are proud, you love money, you love power and you like to be in control. Most of all you love the praise of man more than God."

Rey was dumbfounded. James words stung.

"I picked you because you're like me. We are cut from the same cloth. And now, it's time to get back on track or get out of the way."

James' crushing words painted a picture of Rey's life that caused shame to wash over him. Rey knew there was an element of truth to every word of it.

Moments ago, he was happier than he ever imagined. Now he was cast down to the lowest place. Rey looked away from his accuser's stare focusing on the wood grain of the desk.

James turned to leave. His work was done. A satisfied smile formed on his mouth. He pulled the door shut with a good old fashion slam. His parting words hung in the air, "Still praising God now?"

Kota parked his car across the street from the Field's Insurance Office. He could feel his heart softening towards Emily. He wanted to give her everything she asked for, who wouldn't. She was sweet, kind and thoughtful. She wanted him to meet her family, go to church, read the Bible with her and pray. He needed to refresh his hatred towards her evil father to get his plan back on course.

James Fields pulled up in his sleek Lincoln. He got out of his car still wearing a triumphant smile from his verbal victory over Pastor Rey. Kota looked at his watch. He thought how nice it must be to own your own business, so you can show up to work whenever you want.

James walked with an extra bounce in his step. He was even swinging his briefcase like he was about to break into a skip. Kota was sickened by his reverie. Kota savored the cruel words James spoke about his father. His eyes narrowed as he visually followed him allowing his hatred to be rekindled. The rhythm of his heartbeat accelerated. His body grew warm, his teeth clinched. Soon Emily returned to her position as the pawn in this game, not the prize.

Jean sat at the breakfast table gazing out the window at the leafless trees. She thought, at least the snow is nearly gone. Spring is almost here. She glanced at the devotional book that was open on the table in front of her. Her brain felt like mush.

Tom had left for work hours ago. She replayed the events of the small group over in her mind. They had prayed for the service on Sunday and for the man called Snake. Emily asked for prayer, but gave no details.

Jean felt heaviness in her spirit—especially for Emily. The girl wasn't ready to talk about whatever was going on. Jean prayed for her allowing the Spirit to lead her. Then she wrote in her prayer journal.

The first time the thought came, Jean ignored it. The second time, she obeyed. Jean reached for her cell phone, dialed her old friend and prayer partner, Tina Morris. Jean believed they were on the verge of something that was going to be life changing. It was time to bring in the reinforcements.

James put his hands behind his head and reclined in his office chair. He recalled with pleasure the pain on Pastor Rey's face from the blistering words he leveled on him. He felt triumphant in a wickedly delightful way. He thought, maybe there is still hope for Rey Douglas. Maybe, I can still harness the do-gooder part of him. Maybe all he ever needed was a dose of reality. Of course, he'll need to be closely monitored for a while, but things could still turn around nicely.

James was firmly seated in the power seat. This time he would not be lax. He could feel the momentum changing. Once he made the necessary adjustments to the Statement of Faith and church outreach policies—that should get Rey Douglas focusing inward again.

James called his two cronies on the board, John Alden, his number one *yes-man*, and Peter Carver his breakfast buddy. They made plans to meet at James' house later that night. This would set things in motion for Sunday.

Following these phone calls, James felt an uneasiness invade his victory party. He tried to force the negative thoughts from his mind, but uncertainty festered. He tried the breathing and meditation exercises he learned at the corporate retreat. In the past, when he needed to refocus negative energy and cleanse his mind of impurities these techniques had helped.

James closed his eyes. He laid his open hands on the desk and relaxed his whole body by breathing in slowly through his nose. Then he exhaled quickly through his mouth. He repeated the exercise ten times. The sound of squealing tires outside his office caused him to flinch. The uneasiness was now joined by dizziness.

CHAPTER 23

It's Dangerous Living on the Edge

And remember, when someone wants to do wrong it is never
God who is tempting him,
for God never wants to do wrong and never tempts anyone
else to do it.

James 1:13Living Bible (TLB)

*I*t was Friday afternoon. Rey could hear shuffling in the hallway, people chatting and doors closing. It was the happy sounds of the end of the work week and the start of the weekend. Rey got up from his desk and walked to the picture window that looked out on the parking lot. Tiffany was walking to her car followed by a few other staff members. Rey watched then until they were out of sight.

The verbal attack leveled on him earlier in the day by James still caused an ache. He began to shake his head slowly back and forth signifying "no" to the empty office. Then out loud he yelled it, "No!"

Rey turned his head and scanned his desk. His eyes locked on his cell phone. He crossed the room in two steps, with one swipe he picked up the phone and searched for a familiar number.

"Jean, this is Pastor Rey. I need you to do something for me."

"Sure, Pastor."

"Will you contact all those in the small group, including Grace from the church office and invite them to meet me at the church tomorrow afternoon at 3 P.M.? We're going to pray for the Sunday service. It's boots on the ground time!"

"Praise God! I'm on it."

"One more thing, we're going to do something that as far as I know has never been done before at Community Outreach. I need this group to stand with me."

"You know we will, Pastor."

"Sunday we are going to end the service with an altar call. We need people ready to pray with those who come forward."

"We'll be ready!"

"I know you and Tom have done this sort of thing in churches you've attended. I could sure use you both on Saturday to help instruct the others. I want to open the altar to people seeking salvation. Also, if there are people who are struggling or want to receive the baptism in the Holy Spirit I want people ready to pray with them. I'm looking for people who are tapped into God and ready to lead others into that kind of relationship with the Lord."

"This is an answer to prayer. Consider it done."

"Kota, come in here." Kota walked into the kitchen. His mom stood next to the sink drying her hands. Just a few inches away from Mary, her cell phone lay on top of two very used oven mitts. "I thought I heard you come in. I got'a ask you something." She smiled like she knew something that was bursting to get out. "My friend, Sue, just called me. You got somethin' you wanna tell me?" There was a girlish giggle in her voice that he hadn't heard in a long time.

"No! I barely know your friend Sue. What did she say about me?" Kota hated getting involved in girlie gossip.

"She said that you were with a cute girl downtown eating at some restaurant holding hands across the table. I want'a meet her. Who is she? Sue said—she's a cutie."

Kota listened to the words with dread. The glee in his mom's voice and her playful mannerisms were in direct conflict with his plan. He wanted to hurt James Fields. He was sorry that Emily would be wounded in the crossfire, but he hadn't planned on his own mom getting caught in the battle.

He had decided not to bring Emily around his family. He knew his mother. She would love Emily's sweet personality and kind ways. Emily would have his mom purring like a kitten on her lap and lapping milk from her hand.

Kota shook his head to try to force that picture out of his mind. If his plan was going to work, he needed to stay away from her family and keep her away from his—until the deed was done. After that—he didn't care.

"Mom, don't get too excited. I go out with lots of girls and hold hands with all of them. If I ever do meet..." Kota gestured making air quotes. "...*the one*. You'll be the first to know." He paused then added, "You can even plan the blue jean, backyard BQ wedding of your dreams."

Kota checked his watch, headed for the front door and grabbed his keys. The door eased shut behind him. He needed to be ready to meet Emily when she got out of work.

Kota parked across the street from the Legal Aid office. From his car he watched Emily. She stood outside in the afternoon sun talking to a preppie young lawyer type. Kota could feel his window of opportunity closing. He needed to get things moving along.

Kota continued to watch Emily interacting with her co-worker. She had a disarming way of engaging people in conversation. Her smile was genuine—and there it was. Emily tipped her head to the side, looked down at the ground and laughed at something Preppy Lawyer said. The way the lawyer looked at Emily gave Kota reason to fear. He knew the ways of men. Preppy Lawyer liked her. Kota had to make his move now. His time was running out.

Finally, Emily disengaged. She casually strolled towards her car. Kota pulled into the parking lot from his position across the street. His window was down.

The sound of the car approaching caused Emily's head to jerk in his direction. "Em, you got plans for tonight?"

Emily's expression changed from fright to relief the moment she saw Kota. Laughing she said, "You scared me." She walked over to the car. "No plans for me. I was just heading home. You want to go do something?"

"Why…yes I do." He laughed.

Emily walked closer to his car and leaned in. Kota kissed her. It wasn't their first kiss. He reached over to hold her hand and asked. "You know how you are always asking to meet my friends and family?"

Emily nodded. Her expression was easy to read. She was pleased with the direction this conversation was going. Emily moved closer to the open window. She relaxed and rested her arms on the window frame leaning in closer to listen to Kota's plan.

Kota liked the expression he saw on her face. "Well, my friend, Mason and his girlfriend, Maya invited us over to their place for dinner and a movie tonight. Do you think we could start by meeting each other's friends? Then we can work up to family."

Kota watched Emily's face. She seemed to be struggling with something. He couldn't be sure. He reached over and stroked her arm bringing her back to the present. She leaned in and kissed him.

Kota knew whatever was holding her back was gone.

"I'll follow you." She said.

And with those words Kota felt tonight was going to be *the night*. Everything was arranged. He pulled his car into the flow of traffic with Emily following close behind him.

Marilyn read the text message from Emily. ***Be home late. Don't wait up. Going out with friends. Dinner and a movie. See you tomorrow.*** The doorbell rang. Marilyn laid her cell phone on the kitchen counter. Walking from the kitchen to the front door, she passed by James' office. She could hear him scurrying about like a busy squirrel.

Marilyn opened the front door.

John and Heidi Alden stood with big smiles. Together they said, "Surprise!" Then they both burst into silly laughter.

Heidi pushed past Marilyn walking into the Fields' home with the rights of ownership. "I can tell by your face that James didn't tell you." She paused for effect. Then she added. "He invited us and the Carvers over."

Marilyn dreaded socializing with the Aldens. Heidi rarely gave anyone a chance to say a word. The few times Heidi did want feedback following one of her many mean spirited comments, she would often say, "Am I right? You know I am." Then she was off ranting about something else before Marilyn could speak.

John Alden had a bro-crush on James. He took all his cues from him by treating Marilyn like the maid instead of the lady of the house. John laid his coat on Marilyn's shoulder when he passed by her following his wife into the ample foyer. Before Marilyn could close the door Peter and Katherine Carver pulled into the driveway. She stood with John's coat in her arm holding the door open until all the guests were inside.

James stepped out from his study. He looked at Marilyn with a smug expression. "Oops, I forgot to tell you. I invited a few people over."

Heidi laughed.

James looked at his wife. "I need to meet with Peter and John in the office. I thought you would enjoy visiting with the ladies."

Marilyn was perceptive enough to know James's plan. He wasn't fooling her. She knew it, and he knew it. The ladies were meant to keep her busy.

With a condescending tone he continued. "Marilyn, why don't you and the girls go whip up a nice dessert for us men? We'll be done talking in about an hour." With that, James directed the two men into his office and shut the door.

Marilyn looked at Heidi and Katherine. She knew who would be whipping up dessert. Fortunately, she had a frozen pie for such occasions.

What Marilyn really wanted to do was pray. Her heart was burdened. She wanted to run to Carl's room and shut the world out. She knew something bad was going down in James' office. His plan was to occupy her with these two ladies to keep her from praying or calling others to pray.

"Ladies, excuse me for a moment." Heidi watched Marilyn.

At the kitchen counter Marilyn picked up her cell phone. She opened a kitchen drawer and pulled out the phone charger. Before charging her phone, she typed in a short text messaged and hit send. She laid her phone back on the counter and immediately it started pinging like popcorn hitting a metal pan. Marilyn picked her phone back up and switched the mute button on. She looked at the messages flying in one after another. Smiling she laid the phone face down on the counter. The small group prayer chain had been activated. People were praying.

Marilyn started the coffee and took the chocolate cream pie out of the freezer to thaw. She decided to mix things up a bit. Normally, when she was forced together with these two ladies Heidi dominated the topic and controlled the conversation. Not today, Marilyn thought, not today. Her Bible was open on the kitchen table from her devotional time that morning. Heidi and Katherine had already sat down. Their heart-to-heart was about somebody's hair cut that was disastrous.

Marilyn joined them at the table. She moved her open Bible from the sideline to ground zero. "Ladies, I was reading the most fascinating scripture today. I want to share it with you."

Katherine rolled her eyes looking in Heidi's direction to get this runaway train back on course.

Heidi willingly stepped up. "Now, Marilyn we didn't come here for a Bible lecture. We came to have some fun conversation."

Marilyn didn't back down. "We can get to that later. I want to share this one verse with you first."

Surprised that Marilyn didn't give in Heidi relented. "Fine Marilyn, share your verse."

Marilyn read the scripture from her morning devotional. She referred to the thoughts she wrote down in her journal.

Heidi was not interested. She played with her spoon stirring her coffee endlessly clanging the spoon against the ceramic cup.

Marilyn could tell that Katherine was listening. She continued to share from her heart and silently prayed that the seeds of the Word would find fertile soil in Katherine.

Emily woke up Saturday morning with a throbbing headache. She rubbed her temples while walking downstairs to the kitchen. She wasn't sure if it was breakfast time or lunchtime. She did remember Kota dropped her off. It was in the early morning. Someone else drove her car home. Kota handed her the keys before kissing her good night at the door.

Emily felt dirty. The choices she made last night were her own. A sip of wine or champagne on special occasions was the extent of her drinking experience until now. She knew better. She couldn't find anyone to blame but herself. Her heart ached with remorse. She walked over to the kitchen table and sat down. Her mother's Bible still laid open from the night before. She pushed the Bible away as far as her arm could reach. She didn't want to look at it.

Emily thought about Jean's warning; it's not how close to the edge you can walk, but how far away you can stay. She thought she could handle things. Kota was a gentleman. He had never tried anything with her—before. It had always been just kissing, but they had never been truly alone. Kota's friends didn't show up until much later— when she was unable to drive.

Now after the fact, there were a dozen things she would have done differently, but she didn't. She *knew* her feelings were running deep and dangerous. She simply didn't listen—not even to herself. What was she thinking? She wasn't some rebellious teenager. She was a grown woman who loved the Lord. Why didn't she heed the warnings? She had no one to blame but herself. Emily picked up the phone and dialed Jean Brown's number. She needed to talk to someone—not her mother, not yet.

One hour later, Emily stood at the door of Jean's house. This time she didn't walk right in like she normally did on Thursdays, but rang the doorbell feeling like a stranger more than a friend. Jean opened the door. Emily barely made it across the threshold before Jean wrapped her arms around her. Emily cried out her regrets mingled with grief. What she gave away last night she could never get back. Jean held her until Emily was ready to let go.

Snake was assigned his room at the halfway house. The director reviewed the rules with Snake, then handed him a paper with all the rules written out. He gave Snake a key and motioned in the direction of the stairs. The key had the number 302 crudely etched in the top.

The director said, "Third floor, first room on the left." Then he returned to typing on his laptop computer.

Snake climbed the stairs, found his room and unlocked the door. This room wasn't much bigger than a prison cell, but he was the one who locked the door at night—no one else. He walked over to the window. Looking out at his view of the ally he saw rows of garbage cans. The backyard was nearly nonexistent. Snake thought—no matter. I won't be playing catch with anyone. A smile formed on his lips at the very thought of throwing a ball with another person. He unpacked the few items he owned and settled into his new room.

He put the Bible Pastor Rey gave him on the bed stand between his chair and the bed. He had not read a single verse since that first day when the note fell out. The note to Carl was tucked inside the Bible for safe keeping. He had pulled that note out many times in the past 24-hours to read it.

Just to the right of the door, there was a framed cork board full of tacks. Snake took a pin from the cork board and posted the rules where he could see them. Pastor Rey had told him to expect some rules. These rules were a breeze compared to the last four years.

The doors were locked each night at 11 P.M. Each resident had to be inside the house by that time. If you missed one night, you weren't welcome back. Meals were served at 8 A.M., noon and 6 P.M. You miss a meal you don't eat. Snake would have to have some type of income within two weeks or he was out on the street. The director of the house would help him find a job, if he could. He would have to take whatever he could get.

Snake woke up a free man for the first time in many years. He showered, got dressed and sat down to put his shoes on. There was a knock at the door.

"Come in. It's open." Snake slipped his big foot in his size 15 shoe. He looked up to see the director of the halfway house peeking into his room. The man opened the door wide enough to fit his head through the opening. He kept his feet firmly planted in the hallway. The guy was kinda nerdy, but he was respectful to all the guys in the home.

"It must be your lucky day," the director said. "It's Saturday, and a job opportunity just came in. They're looking for someone with computer skills. I saw from your paperwork that you earned a degree in Computer Science while you were in prison." He paused.

Snake didn't answer. He didn't hear a question.

The director continued, "Well, if you want to interview for the job, they said you could stop by about 1 P.M. today. Ask for Mr. Amos. They know you were in prison, so no worries. I'm sure when they see your little friend there," the director pointed at the tattoo on Snake's face. "They would probably guess you had some sorta past. I'll need to know if you get the job. Here's the information." He laid the papers on a small table just inside the door.

Snake wondered why he didn't step inside the room. No matter. He was perfectly happy the director wasn't trying to be his BFF.

Kota spent the night at his friend's house. They had been very accommodating when he told them he needed some alone time with his girl. He thought he would feel better about his plan coming to fruition. He didn't. His mom was in the kitchen making lunch when he walked in sleepy and unshowered.

"Kota, where did you sleep last night, in the ditch? You're a mess. Go get cleaned up. I have something I want to ask you."

Mary looked up from the table when Kota returned. He had showered, shaved and was a handsome young man. "Sit here with me." She pointed at the place directly across the table from her. "I want to tell you what happened yesterday."

Kota sat down, and his mom told him about Pastor Rey's visit, the pamphlet with his father's name written on it and the invitation to come to church on Sunday. She wanted the whole family there. Kota never wanted to step foot in that church again, but he couldn't resist his mother's plea.

He finally agreed knowing how awkward it was going to be when he saw Emily. She had tried to call him twice, but he let it go to voicemail. On second thought, maybe the church would be the best place to let James Fields know about the fun he'd had with his precious daughter. Even if there wasn't a baby in the making, the deed was done and that would be a blow to Mr. High and Mighty. Time would decide the rest.

Harold and Esther Smith were the first to arrive at the church on Saturday afternoon. They unlocked the office door and made their way to the conference room. They wanted to be sure everything was ready. Harold noticed a folder on the table. He opened the folder and read the heading: Business Meeting Agenda. He stopped reading, picked up the file and stuck it in a drawer out of sight. Nothing was going to interfere with what the Lord had planned for them today.

Pastor Rey and Callan arrived next. Then one by one the others came in and found seats around the conference table. Those in attendance were Pastor and Callan, Harold and Esther Smith, Tom and Jean Brown, Henry and Dorothy Samson, Grace from the church office and Marilyn. Emily wasn't able to make it. Everyone in attendance agreed to the role they would play.

Pastor Rey explained the recommended steps for leading someone to the Lord. Then he had the Browns explain the steps for praying with people who were going through personal struggles. Everyone received anointing oil and were organized into teams of two for Sunday. Grace and Marilyn became a team since Emily wasn't available for the training. Following the instruction time, the teams of two each prayed together for the service on Sunday.

Heidi pulled into the church parking. She hated doing church work on the weekend, but this was important. Driving to the back of the church she wondered why there were so many cars in the parking lot. Had she missed a meeting? She couldn't remember anything planned for Saturday at 3:30 P.M. The church doors were unlocked. She entered. Her eyes darting to the right and left feeling like she was walking into an ambush. She hurried to her desk to find the papers she needed.

The sound of people talking drifted into the church office. Heidi followed the muffled voices down the hallway to the closed door of the conference room. She stood to the side of the door, leaned against the wall and listened. Within seconds she realized—people were praying in there. These prayers were not the *thanks for the food* kind of prayers. These people were weeping, moaning and crying out to God. She felt a rush of anxiety. She wanted to throw open the door and expose their hypocrisy, but opted instead to report her findings to James Fields. He'd know what to do.

Heidi hurried out of the building, got in her car and fumbled through her purse searching for her cell phone. When she couldn't locate it, she moved her jacket from the passenger seat. It was on the seat hidden under her coat. She snatched it up and dialed James' cell phone.

There was no answer. The voice mail picked up. Heidi waited for the beep and left a message.

"This is Heidi. I just stopped by the church to pick up something I needed, and Pastor Rey is having a prayer meeting in the conference room. I can only guess from the cars who's in there. It looks like the Smiths, Samsons, Grace, and Marilyn. Probably the Browns too, just thought you'd want to know. Oh, and it's 3:30—Saturday afternoon. Call me, if you want me to do anything more."

CHAPTER 24

It's Sunday!

I was happy when the people said, "Let us go to the
LORD's Temple."

Psalm 122:1 Easy-To-Read Version (ERV)

*S*unday morning Pastor Rey watched the sun rise. It had been
a restless night. He finally surrendered to the Lord and got
up to pray. He prayed for the congregation to be receptive to his message and for the altar time. He prayed that the Lord would draw people
in from the north, south, east and west.

This Sunday was Callan and Rey's first Sunday together as a real
ministry team. They had been married over six years, but this week
they finally were ONE—unified and in-sync. Rey heard Callan stirring in the bedroom. Soon the boys would be waking. His solitude
was about to be broken with the hurried sounds of a typical Sunday
morning.

"Rey?" Callan called from the bedroom. Rey hurried in not sure
if someone was sick. They had a joke between them about their own
version of Murphy's Law. It went like this—if something disastrous
was going to happen it usually happened on a Sunday morning. They
had experienced high fevers, vomiting, sore tummies, sore throats,

seal-like barking coughs and once a trip to the ER for stitches when Zander pushed Ty off the top bunk—always on Sunday mornings.

Rey answered, "Coming."

Callan was moving the hangers in her closet back and forth looking for that perfect outfit. She stopped, turned and looked directly at her husband. "I think you should drive separate to church this morning. The boys and I will come later. I don't want you to have any distractions that could hinder what God wants to do in the service this morning."

Her sensitivity and concern left Rey flabbergasted. These attributes had never been a part of Callan's DNA prior to her experience at the home of Mike and Tina Morris.

"I'm going to let the boys sleep as long as possible. They will need to be rested in the event the service runs longer than usual. You go ahead. Don't worry about us. I'll handle things on this end."

Rey looked at his wife with gratitude. He drew her into his arms and held her.

Callan slipped her arms around her husband and returned his affection. Then she pushed away and waved her hand in the air and said, "Now get going."

Rey was the first to arrive at Community Outreach Church on Sunday morning. He unlocked the outside doors, turned on the necessary lights and walked into the sanctuary. He knew he was not alone.

Prayers began to pour from his lips as he walked up and down the rows. Whenever he felt prompted by the Spirit—he stopped. Touching a seat, he would pray as the Spirit led. Then move on to another. When he reached the front, he knelt at the altar and laid his face on the carpeted-step. Rey stayed there a long time praying for those who would find freedom at the altar.

Walking up the steps to the platform, he went to the keyboard and placed his hands on the keys. He cried out to the Lord inviting His to be a part of every aspect of the day. He asked the Lord to draw people into worship preparing them to hear the Word.

Finally, he stood behind the podium with his eyes closed and his face lifted. He petitioned heaven, "Lord, allow Your anointing to fall on me. I can't do this in my own strength. I am totally reliant on You. I surrender. I plead for Your Holy anointing." He began to groan and weep as the power of a Holy God settled on him. When he opened his eyes he looked across the sanctuary. Eldon Chambers, the Music and Fine Arts Director, stood with his head bowed, wiping tears.

"Eldon, will you pray with me?"

Eldon joined Pastor Rey at the altar. One by one, as the worship team arrived, they joined the prayer time.

Pastor thanked the members of the worship team. Then gave instructions about how the service would close. There was no resistance.

Rey could sense the excitement. Expectancy was in the air like birth was emanated, but first travail.

Pastor Rey went to his office, a sense of acceptance swept over him. He was ready for whatever the Lord had in mind for this church and its pastor.

The morning sun cast a waterfall of light on the calm waters of Deer Lake. But no one in the Brown's house was looking. Tom and Jean sat at the breakfast table facing each other. Jean rested her hand on top of Tom's.

Their eyes were closed and heads bowed. Taking turns they prayed for a supernatural outpouring of the Holy Spirit. They prayed for lives to be forever changed, for hearts to be mended, for people to know the forgiveness of the Lord, for physical healings, for unity, for peace and for the love of God to be poured out on all the people who came to Community Outreach in Hillbrooke, Michigan this particular Sunday morning.

The Browns held in their hearts, the assurance that Pastor Rey truly was the pastor they had prayed for nine months ago. They trusted the Lord and knew His callings and plans were coming to completion. The air was bursting with possibility.

"God is victorious!" The shout came from a place deep within Jean bursting forth like pent-up water. She repeated it two more times as she danced around the kitchen.

Harold and Esther Smith sipped coffee around their kitchen nook. They took turns reading parts of Isaiah 41. When Harold's turn came back around he began at verse eleven. With each word his volume increased until he ceased reading the Word and began proclaiming, *"Be sure that all who are enraged against you will be ashamed and disgraced; those who contend with you will become as nothing and will perish. You will look for those who contend with you but you will not find them. Those who war against you will become absolutely nothing."*

And Esther said, "Lord, let it be so."

Grace woke up refreshed. The Saturday training and prayer time awakened a hope within her that had been looking for a way out. She felt empowered by the Lord. She finished her breakfast and plugged in her curling iron waiting for it to heat up.

The phone rang in her bedroom. She checked the caller ID. It was Heidi Alden. She wondered what Heidi would want with her on a Sunday morning.

"Hello Heidi. Is everything okay?"

"Hey Grace. I wanted to warn you that Pastor Rey's days are numbered at the church, and if I were you, I wouldn't go hitching my wagon to his falling star. I saw your car at the church yesterday, and I know what you were doing there."

"It wasn't a secret meeting." She told Heidi. "We were praying for the service today. What could possibly be wrong with that? And I haven't hitched my wagon to Pastor Rey, but I have hitched it to the Lord. And it will be *His* voice that will guide me from now on. Hope to see you at church this morning. I'm expecting great things. But right now, I have to get ready for the service. I believe wonderful things are going to happen this morning. Bye-now." And with that Grace hung up and finished getting ready for church.

James was in a rare mood. He had already tried to engage Marilyn a few times, but she refused to bite.

Now he turned his attention to his daughter. "Emily, you look mopey today. You should stay home no one would blame you, if you're not feeling well." He stood at the kitchen island and poured a cup of coffee then added, "Don't be like your mom. She thinks she's the United States Postal Service, come wind, rain, sleet or snow nothing keeps Marilyn Fields from church." Then he laughed at his own comparison.

Emily never lifted her eyes from the countertop, but spoke in a tone that revealed desperation. "Dad, if there ever was a Sunday that I needed to be in church—it's this Sunday."

James let out a discussed huff. He walked to his office slamming the door behind him hard enough to rattle the kitchen windows. He yelled from behind the closed door, "I'll drive myself to church."

Marilyn watched her daughter leave the kitchen with slumped shoulders. She watched her for a moment then followed her up the stairs.

Emily went into her bedroom and Marilyn walked in behind her. Emily turned and faced her mom. Without saying a word Marilyn wrapped her daughter up in her arms and held her longer and tighter than normal.

Emily couldn't remember needing her mother more than she did at that moment. She told her mom everything.

"Let's sit on the bed and talk." Marilyn sat first and patted the place on the bed next to her.

Emily's emotions were raw with pain. Marilyn took her daughter's hand and held it while she talked.

"Honey, the Lord specializes in cleaning up messes. He doesn't just cover them up to be discovered later. His word says that *He* remembers them *no more*. It's like it never happened. I understand your pain. If only we could forgive ourselves as quickly as God forgives us." Marilyn squeezed Emily's hand tighter and asked, "Do you love Kota?"

"Yes—I think I do." Emily stopped fighting her emotions. Through tears she confided, "He hasn't returned my calls since that night."

"Em, when you were a little girl you had a toy that was magnetic. You could draw on the screen with a pen. When you were done drawing there was a knob at the bottom that you could slide from side to side. Just like that the screen was wiped clean. Every doodle, stick people, practice letters and shapes were gone—erased. Even if you wanted to bring those images back—you couldn't. The only way to get them back was to draw them again." Marilyn waited a moment to see if Emily was able to hear what she was saying. Maybe her pain was too much at this moment to hear advice.

Emily looked at her mom to continue.

"I know you get what I'm saying, Em. Sins and personal failures we want to erase quickly. In theory it is easy to slide a knob and have a clean slate. Jesus made that available to us. Unfortunately, I also know the residual pain from choices. This can take a long time. Jesus has cast our sins into a sea of forgetfulness—but we are not that merciful to ourselves. I'm here for you Em. Whatever you need—I'm here." Emily hugged her mom. They prayed together.

It was the second time in two days that Emily was bathed in God's merciful grace, his unmerited favor. She did nothing to deserve it, but He gave it to her anyway—full and free.

Mary Edwards selected her best pair of black stretch pants. She completed her church outfit with the floral print top that had a giant bow at the hip. The freshly permed and colored hair looked perfect. She looked herself over in the mirror. A satisfied smile formed on her lips. She was ready.

Mary called out a warning. "Come on everyone. We are leaving this house in ten minutes."

Every seat at the table was filled by cereal-eating kids. The adults filtered out from various bedrooms and bathrooms. They formed a line in the kitchen for a quick sip of coffee and a cigarette.

Mary mentally took attendance and saw one of her litter was missing. She bellowed. "Kota, get out here. NOW!"

He came dragging out of the bedroom with uncombed hair, a wrinkled shirt and a five o'clock shadow.

Mary reached up and grabbed her son's chin. A smile formed on her lips as she gave his face a loving shake. She released Kota and at the same time yelled, "WE ARE LEAVING HERE IN FIVE MINUTES— SO GET YOUR BUTTS IN THE CAR."

The church parking lot was filling up quickly. It looked like everyone who ever called Community Outreach their home church decided this was the Sunday to be in church. The dial-a-ride van pulled up to the front doors of the church. The back door of the van opened automatically. A very large man stepped out. He was like nobody this church had ever seen.

The woman greeter opened the glass door with a welcoming smile, but when she fully examined the tattooed man, the color drained from her face and her smile faded.

The tattooed man breezed past her without stopping for a handshake, a bulletin or a word of welcome. Walking with purpose, Snake entered the sanctuary and found a seat near the back on the far right side near the wall. Snake positioned himself here to keep his tattoo in full view of anyone who tried to get close to him. He came out of respect for the Pastor. He wasn't interested in making nice with anyone here. The slightest turn of his head gave him a panoramic view of most the room from the back to the front.

The pre-service music was playing softly. People were mulling about talking and laughing. Snake was feeling vulnerable, trapped and unsure if he made the right decision in coming. He tried to keep his eyes fixed directly in front of him. Hoping he wouldn't have any confrontations to deal with in this service.

Occasionally, he glanced around looking for a familiar face. Then he saw her—it had to be her. She wasn't a kid anymore. She was prettier than he remembered and all grown up.

Emily, it's you, sweet Emily. Then his mom came in and sat next to her. Snake knew that she had never given up on him. God made sure he knew it. How that letter actually got to him was still a mystery. His mom looked great, actually the same as the day he left six years ago.

Marilyn put her arm around Emily drawing her close. Emily laid her head on her mom's shoulder. Snake fought back the emotions that tried to overtake him.

The music started. The congregation stood to sing. Snake remained seated. He thought that his height might draw even more attention to him. He heard the back doors to the sanctuary open, turning; he saw a large group come in. In the mist of the group he saw his old friend, Kota Edwards.

What was that guy doing at this church? Maybe things really had changed. Looking past the Edwards family he saw his father. James Fields was standing in the back of the church talking to an usher in a secretive manner. Then his father pointed at the Edwards' family. Snake didn't need to be a skilled lip reader to see the words forming on his lips. His father still had the same judgmental expression Snake remembered from his youth. A slap of emotion stung his face, as he remembered that familiar feeling of being a bad kid about to feel the wrath of his father. He wanted to bolt out of this place and never return. Pushing his hand into his pocket he felt the note. He pulled it out and read the words again. *Dear Carl*—the words washed over him.

A hand touched Snake on the shoulder.

"Snake—you just made my day." Pastor Rey stood in the aisle. He gave Snake's shoulder a tight squeeze. "Thank you for coming. Let me take you out to lunch. Then I can drive you home after church. I know you don't have a car."

Snake nodded his head.

Pastor Rey walked to the front of the church. Snake could see Emily and Marilyn both looking in his direction. They couldn't possibly know it was him. He had grown seven inches, and gained fifty pounds over the past six years. He took a deep breath and kept his eyes fixed on the back of the man standing in front of him.

The singing was nice, but Snake didn't know any of the new style songs. When he attended here as a child, they only sang hymns and usually only two or three per service. Snake glanced over his shoulder at the clock on the back wall of the sanctuary. They had been singing for twenty minutes.

Many people had closed their eyes, some even slightly lifted one hand. He wanted to close his eyes too. The words of the songs were meaningful. He kept his eyes open not wanting to be unaware of his surroundings should someone get too close. The tempo of the music changed.

Finally, a song he knew, Amazing Grace. Snake sang a few lines. Then the words and music changed again. The people started singing with a passion. The words were very appropriate for Snake's situation. It was something about chains being gone and being set free. That God had ransomed people and loved them. Snake could not remember feeling this way when he was young in church—not once!

There were a few more songs. Then the man leading the music said some stuff and prayed. The people were encouraged to greet each other right in the middle of the service.

Snake thought this was the strangest thing yet. The people were moving all over. Talking to each other in the middle of the service—he saw someone moving toward him. God help me, he thought.

"You have got to be kidding me. You're out. Why didn't ya call? You need a place to stay? It's great to see you." Kota lowered his voice, "What the hell are you doing at this church?"

Snake didn't stand up to talk to his old friend, "The pastor came and visited me while I was in prison. He invited me."

Kota leaned in close to his old friend. He spit the words out between clinched teeth. "You don't owe the man nothing."

Snake was shocked. This was not the same Kota he remembered—gentle and kind just like his father. What happened to him? Even prison didn't turn him mean, but something about this church did.

"Let's hook up later. Don't run off. I'll see you after the show is over." Kota turned to go back to his seat. Standing directly at the end of the pew was Emily. Kota had nowhere to go.

Emily smiled waiting for him in the center aisle and her father stood at the back of the church watching the whole scene play out.

Kota felt the eyes of James Fields on him. He thought, well, this is as good a time as any. Kota moved towards Emily who looked unsure. He reached out and embraced her in a way that was obvious to everyone watching this couple was not meeting for the first time.

A warm smile brightened Emily's face. "Would you like to meet my mother? You met her once before at the funeral dinner, but I'd like you to meet her again—officially."

Kota was infected by her smile. "Sure!" Emily took Kota's hand. Kota followed. Emily introduced him to her mother.

The big screen in the front of the church displayed the numbers 0:15 letting people know that the greeting time was ticking down.

"Kota, I'd like to meet your mom too. And my dad is in the back. I can introduce you to him."

Emily started walking towards Mary Edwards who was smiling like a kid in a toy store. Kota stopped her. "Maybe it would be better for introductions after the service when we have more time."

"Ok, sure. Come sit with me." She held tight to his hand. He followed her like a child.

Kota glanced back at his mom who was giving him the thumbs-up sign while nodding. Kota shook his head and rolled his eyes.

However, James was not giving him an encouraging thumbs-up but rather a death glare which Kota found quite satisfying. Kota gave James a nod and a wink, putting to rest any questions about their relationship.

Mary interpreted Kota's nodding and winking as a confirmation to her. Mary's thumbs-up changed to silent air clapping. Kota's momentary feelings of *triumphant revenge* changed when he looked at his mom. Things were getting complicated.

Snake watched this all play out with great interest. There was no way Kota knew that Emily was his sister. He never told the Edwards family his real name. He liked Kota as a friend—but not for Emily.

Snake looked back at his father whose face was reaching stroke-level red. As much as he loved seeing his father suffer, he wanted no harm to come to his sister.

CHAPTER 25

The Altar

...Only a few would welcome and receive him.
But to all who received him,
He gave the right to become children of God.
All they needed to do was to trust him to save them.

John 1:11-12 (TLB)

*P*astor Rey walked the short distance from his seat in the front row to the platform at Community Outreach Church. The sanctuary was reverently quiet except for a few random coughs. He stepped up to the podium and rested his hands, one on each side of the rustic wood. He had stood in this place every Sunday for the past nine months. It was a privilege he did not take lightly to stand here and expound the Word of God. His Bible and sermon notes lay open on the sacred desk. He glanced down at his opening line. This was the day he had waited for, prayed about and now it was here.

Rey lifted his head and looked out at his church family. His eyes were drawn to the back of the sanctuary where James Fields leaned against the wall.

James met the Pastor's eyes appearing ready for a fight. Rey had a mental picture of James disrupting the service. Then he thought,

234

James would never call attention to himself, but he may get others to do his bidding.

Holding tight to the podium, Pastor Rey scanned the faces of his flock. He saw the Browns and the Smiths. Both couples appeared to be praying. He could see their eyes were closed, head slightly tilted forward. He could feel their prayers strengthening him.

Rey glanced down at his notes again, cleared his throat and this time focused on the Edwards family and Snake. These faces were not angry. He did not fear these people were plotting against him. They were simply hungry—hungry and ready to receive the Word. The table was set, the seats were filled and all eyes were on him. Rey whispered a silent prayer then opened his mouth to speak. He trusted the Lord to do the rest.

"This week the Lord has done amazing things in my life and in Callan's. I'm going to share it all with you, but first I have a confession to make. When this church invited me to be your pastor nine months ago, I was ill prepared to lead. In Psalm 78:72 the Lord describes his servant David like this…*he shepherded them according to the integrity of his heart, and guided them by the skillfulness of his hands.* It was always my goal to be this kind of pastor, but when I came—I had very little integrity and even less skill."

Rey saw that people were shifting about in the pews, looking uncomfortable with his words. Many looked down not wanting to make eye contact. Their eyes darted around looking for a safe place to land. Rey felt the discomfort of the people. He pressed on.

"My heart was polluted with greed and full of pride. During the past few months God placed me on the Potter's wheel, and with the skill of His hands He began to apply needed pressure to my life. Being on the Potter's wheel is *not* fun. In fact, I would go as far as to say *it is painful*." Rey used his hands to illustrate the work of a Potter applying pressures on imaginary clay while he spoke.

"It's there that the Potter takes the lump of clay and with the skill of his hands molds the shapeless form into a useful vessel—one that will bring honor." Rey looked out at the congregation. They were back with him—for the most part.

"My first Sunday at Community Outreach was also the first for another family. They had recently received news that their beloved husband and father had only months to live. I never dreamed that Sunday following the service as I greeted folks, Bill Edwards and I, would meet and say goodbye at the same time."

Pastor Rey saw Kota sitting with Emily. He cringed at the mention of his father's name. Rey had seen hatred like this before. Kota's face was red. A snarl formed on his lip like a twitch.

Pastor continued. "I could have stopped to visit Bill. I could have prayed with him. He wanted me to. He had questions, and I had the answers." With brokenness evident in Pastor's voice he paused—then resumed his confession.

"Bill didn't fit my demographics for Community Outreach. I chose not to go to him in his time of need. Bill died without the benefit of pastoral comfort."

Rey looked to the back of the church. The Edwards' family was crying. He directed his words to them. "Mary, Kota and girls forgive me. I failed your family when you needed me most."

There were few dry eyes at this point. Sniffles were heard front to back and side to side throughout the sanctuary. It was hard for Pastor Rey to admit his failure, but necessary for his healing and hopefully the church family's as well.

In the back, James smirked when he realized Rey had not pointed a finger at him for his role in this fiasco. He chuckled to himself at this man's stupidity. Pastor Rey was falling on his own sword. James occasionally looked in the direction of his daughter sitting shoulder to shoulder with Kota Edwards. This was another mess he would have to clean up later.

Pastor Rey pressed on, "In the days following Bill's death my guilt was overwhelming. My personal failure to Bill and his family was epic. And my remorse was consuming. I cried out to the Lord in my time of need. I asked the Lord to forgive me—and He did. I promised Him that I would never allow a travesty like this to happen again. Even though I vowed to change, I still carried the pain of not knowing Bill's eternal destination—until this week."

Kota was so tense hearing the pastor confess that his shoulders were arched upward. He dropped Emily's hand and squeezed his own hands together in his lap. He wanted to jump up and shout—hypocrite! He told himself; just sit here, do it for your mom. He fostered his plan for revenge. When this service was over he would confront James, embarrass him and his family in front of these people they held so dear. Then he would leave and never come back. He calmed himself by rehearsing his plan for revenge over in his head.

Snake listened intently trying to reconcile the two images of Pastor Rey. There was the stranger that Pastor Rey described in his message and the kind man who visited him in prison. These were two different men. The Pastor that Snake knew was caring, humble and would go the extra mile. The picture Pastor Rey's words painted were of a self-centered, self-absorbed and heartless man. These two men could not be the same person. Snake angled his head slightly to see the face of his friend. He knew Kota loved his father. These words must be agonizingly painful for him to hear.

Pastor continued, "After the funeral, I cried out to the Lord and asked him to forgive me for what I had done. I purposed in my heart from that moment, I would reach out to help whoever, whenever, wherever, the Lord directed me. That's when I began to visit the prison.

Harold Smith and I visited every Thursday morning. The Lord blessed this ministry. About the same time the Browns opened their home for a small group Bible study, prayer and fellowship. These two men, Harold and Tom, have been like Aaron and Hur to me. When I was tired and weak they held up my arms through prayer and words of encouragement." Pastor paused. He looked back and forth at these men. "Thank you—you are mighty men of valor to me."

Standing in the back, James thought, this couldn't be going better for me. This foolish man is all but hanging himself. It's madness. This Pastor is rash and naive to admit to these dumb sheep his faults. A shepherd needs to be a fearless leader, a warrior and brave. This man is a blathering crybaby telling all his weaknesses to the grunts, the peons. He is playing right into my hand and for a moment James Fields forgot that the son of Bill Edwards had embraced his daughter four rows in front of where he stood.

Following a slight pause, Pastor resumed. "The next thing the Lord needed to do was bring Callan and me into agreement. That could only happen through supernatural intervention. The way the Lord worked on both of us separately—while we were away from each other, this is nothing less than a miracle. I went up north to the Smith's cabin to pray, and Callan went to her parents. We were unaware that God had a divine appointment for each of us. In the course of 24-hours we both experienced what is described in the book of Acts as the Baptism in the Holy Spirit."

Rey looked out at the congregation. Most of the people listened intently. He prayed for a divine revelation of truth to be imparted to them.

"Some very sincere souls have rejected this Pentecostal experience. In fact, I must confess a few months ago, I would have been one of them. The Baptism of the Holy Spirit with the initial evidence of speaking in tongues has been debated since the turn of the 20th century.

The question is always the same. Is it for today, or did it end at the completion of the New Testament?"

Pastor Rey could tell by the facial expressions of the church folk that they had *never* debated the topic of the baptism of the Holy Spirit. He couldn't remember in the past nine months having anyone come to him with so much as a question about this experience.

He pressed on. "Pentecost was a Jewish Feast that happened on the 50th day following the Passover. It marked the beginning of the season of harvest. It is not coincidental that the outpouring of the Holy Spirit came on the day of Pentecost and was followed by a great spiritual harvest of souls. The outpouring of the Holy Spirit was not for the thrill of the experience, but rather it was preparation for a great harvest."

Pastor Rey paused to scope his audience. They sat in anticipation ready for what would come next. He continued to preach the message he'd prepared from the book of Acts. He shared his personal experience along with sermon points and scripture references to enforce the validity of the message. A crinkling sound was heard throughout the sanctuary as the parishioners searched the pages of their Bibles for the truth. It sounded like a gentle rain. It was sweet music to his ears.

Pastor Rey forced himself to stay on task, "Why did God use this sign of other tongues?" Pastor gave a moment for the people to ponder the rhetorical question. "There was a partnership that God wanted to make with the believers, and it was miraculous in its' very nature. This miracle grants the worshiper the opportunities to pray beyond their individual capacity. Think of how limited we are in our known language. Our praise may consist of—you're great—you're awesome—you're wonderful—you're mighty. The Holy Spirit under the direction of God the Father is limitless. He can take the intercessor or worshipper beyond their own limitations. The Holy Spirit expands the believer's prayer life to praying the actual heart and mind of the Father."

James stood fidgeting like a child at the back of the church. He shifted from one foot to the other hoping an end to this service was near. Why is Pastor Rey babbling on about this stuff? James wished he would just close the service with the usual doxology and get this thing over. He had more than enough ammunition in this one service to put an end to this pastor and his crazy teachings.

Pastor Rey began to close. "At the beginning of this service I shared a personal failure with you. I said that I did not have the courage to do the right thing under pressure. I am changing that behavior right now. I understand what it is to be forgiven. Jesus has done this for me. And He didn't just forgive me; He's given me the precious gift of His Holy Spirit. Now, I am on a personal mission to reach my community with the message of forgiveness through Jesus Christ. Through God's grace he invites each of us into a divine partnership with the Holy Spirit. Then, through this partnership He fills and enables the believer. I wish someone would have taken the time to explain this to me when I was first saved."

Jean Brown smiled, nodding her head in agreement.

Tom said, "Amen!"

"Each person's experience will be different when they receive the Baptism in the Holy Spirit. For me it happened at night in a cabin up north. For Callan it happened in the living room of Christian Believers. This past week I have shared with others my experience. It was thrilling to find out that Callan and I are not the only people in this church who have accepted this gift by partnering with the Holy Spirit. Their personal stories of baptism range from alone in a bedroom to walking in the woods. That is the God we serve. He will meet you where you are. In Luke 11 verses 11-13 Jesus said this, 'Which of you fathers, if your son asks for a fish, will give him a snake instead? Or if he asks for an egg, will give him a scorpion? If you then, though you are evil, know how to give good gifts to your children, how much more will your Father in heaven give the Holy Spirit to those who ask him?'"

The room was quiet.

"God is challenging us to get close to him. We are not alone in our struggles. He is with us. He will never leave us. It's time to come down from the bleachers and take your place on the field of service."

Rey picked up a small toy he brought with him from home. It had been lying on the pulpit the whole time he spoke. He held it in his hand while he shared his last story.

"A few nights ago, I went in to pray with the boys at bedtime. When I walked into their bedroom, I stepped on this little action figure that belongs to Ty." Pastor Rey moved the toy around in his hands while he spoke.

"I reached down and picked it up. I held it while I finished hurrying the boys into bed. Ty was distracted by the toy. He interrupted me to say—Dad, when you turn off the light that man will glow in the dark. I said—oh, really? He said—do you want'a see? I thought he was just stalling to stay up a little longer, but I played along and said sure. He scurried over to turn off the light. And just as he predicted—the little man glowed. It *was* pretty cool. Then in the dark I heard Ty say—See Dad, the darker it gets the brighter he glows. Then he added—Dad, you know why he can glow in the dark? I did know why, but I asked him to tell me anyway. He said—because you have to put him by the light. That's how he gets his power. Then when it's dark he glows." Pastor Rey paused.

"If we want our lights to shine in the darkness then we need to spend time in close proximity to the Son who declares He is the Light of the world. The Lord tells us in His word—that if we seek Him, we will find Him—if we draw near to Him, He will draw near to us. When we accept Christ into our lives, the darker it gets the brighter HE glows in us and through us."

"Instead of closing with the doxology we are going to do something different this morning. It's been that kind of service don't you think?

I would like to give each one here an opportunity to meet with the Lord in a personal way. You may be here today and have never been challenged to ask Jesus to be Lord of your life. I want to give you an opportunity this morning to do that very thing. Also, if you are struggling with sin issues, things that are pulling you down like an anchor, there is hope for you today. If you would like to receive this gift of the Holy Spirit like Callan and I did we will pray with you for that as well."

Pastor Rey called for the altar workers to come forward. They responded without hesitation. Harold and Esther walked to the far right side of the platform. The rest of the prayer team fanned out across the front facing the congregation. Eldon came to the keyboard and began to play the song; *My chains are gone. I've been set free.*

James nearly choked when he heard this. He had no idea what an *altar worker* was—were they like janitors, repair people, another fine example of this pastor's apparent lack of decorum.

Pastor Rey asked the people to stand. "We are here to pray with you. You are not alone in your struggle." He encouraged the people to come.

Callan stayed in the center aisle to direct people as they came forward.

Emily reached over and took Kota's hand. "Will you come with me?"

Kota shook her hand loose. Then without saying a word, he walked to the back of the church. He stood against the wall opposite from James, watching from a safe distance and near the exit.

Alone, Emily walked to the front of the church. Callan directed her to pray with Jean and Tom Brown.

People began to move from their seats. They formed a line for prayer. Mary Edwards flanked by two of her daughters and four of her grandchildren, stepped out in one big group and walked to the front.

Callan directed them towards Harold and Esther Smith. Esther opened her arms and Mary accepted her embrace. Her daughters joined the hug. The grandkids watched unsure what to do. Grace stepped over and gathered the children around her to talk to them at their own level. This left Marilyn standing alone.

Then it happened. A man in the back stood. His head rose above the crowd. Only one other man in the church was close to his equal. He walked towards the front with a slow thoughtful pace. It was Snake. Callan directed him to pray with Henry and Dorothy Samson, but he went to Marilyn instead.

Marilyn was not afraid of this fierce looking man. She could see his life had not been an easy one. She touched his arm to make a connection with him, trying not to look him in the face. She fought the urge to gawk at the snake tattooed. Looking down she asked, "How can I pray with you today?"

Snake didn't close his eyes, but looked directly at Marilyn and said, "Mom—it's me—Carl." He pulled a piece of folded paper from his pocket and opened it.

Marilyn recognized the paper from her journal and her own handwriting. It was the note she wrote less than a week ago. A gasp escaped Marilyn's lips. Now, she looked directly into the face of the tall man who stood in front of her. She knew it was her son.

The sound of Marilyn's gasp drew Emily's attention away from the prayer of Dorothy Samson. She looked in her mother's direction with concern. Marilyn tenderly touched the face of the tattooed man and gazed at him.

The expression on her mother's face told Emily all she needed to know. This was Carl. Emily took a few steps towards the tall man. She wrapped her arms around his waist burying her face into his side. Mother, son and daughter wept together.

From the back wall of the church James' large frame moved towards the altar area. Pastor Rey was unaware what was happening, but he was reasonably sure they were seconds away from a brawl—at the altar. James moved with determination and with each step his indignation grew—this has gone far enough. This sloppy, emotional religion has crossed the lines of propriety. My wife and daughter are making spectacles of themselves, and the whole church is looking on—it ends today—it ends now.

James reached the altar, placed his hand on Snake's shoulder and forcefully swung him around. All eyes in the church were on these two men. James and the tattooed man stood face to face. James tightened up his fists ready for a fight. Then he froze. There was something familiar about the eyes looking back at him. There was no mistake that this man was—his son. James stumbled backwards falling into the front pew. His face displayed shock. His eyes sorrow.

Snake's face was wet from tears. The man with the tattoo of a snake slithering up his face was Carl, his son. James could scarcely look at the man. It was his child, his boy. The one he believed was dead. He had resigned all hope years ago. He coldly shut the door. James never allowed himself to imagine there might be a day of reconciliation.

Snake stepped towards his father, knelt down on his knees and reached out his hand.

James knew the choice was his.

CHAPTER 26

Restored

I know what I'm doing.
I have it all planned out—plans to take care of you,
not abandon you, plans to give you the future you hope for.

Jeremiah 29:11 The Message Bible

Five years later, Snake stood at the grill in the backyard of his humble home. The coals were white hot. He arranged the hamburgers on the rack over the fire and drenched them with salt. He looked up from his work and yelled across the yard. "Em, when is that creep you married gonna be here?"

She quickly replied with sisterly love, "It takes one to know one."

Emily was wrangling a little girl who was about three months past her fourth birthday. Emily's daughter was beautiful just like her mommy. She had a head of black curls and big brown-eyes. Under Emily's other arm, she held a roly-poly baby boy.

Snake smiled as he watched his little sister mothering her children. There was a grace and beauty about her just like their mother. Snake felt an awe and respect for her. She had made mistakes, but what the enemy thought would destroy her—God redeemed from the ashes.

The Fields family was reunited following that momentous Sunday at Community Outreach in Hillbrooke. A few months later God brought Kota back into Emily's life. It took a while for wrongs to be made right, but patience and forgiveness won out over hatred and revenge.

Snake heard a car pulling up to the front of his house, followed by car doors opening and closing.

Swinging her granddaughter in the air Marilyn said, "Grandpa and Daddy are here. Now we can eat."

Rounding the side of Snake's house, walking side by side was James Fields and Kota Edwards. Kota had been working with James for three years and had shown everyone that he was an amazing salesman.

Snake accepted the job he was offered five years ago as an IT and web designer for the Superior Solar Energy Plant. He advanced in his job to the position of supervisor. He was giving back to the community by teaching advance computer skills to teen boys at the Hillbrooke juvenile delinquents' home.

Pastor Rey and Callan along with their boys arrived at the picnic. The church had become one of the largest in the city. Now, it truly lived up to its name, Community Outreach.

Callan was all smiles carrying a bowl of macaroni salad. Pastor Rey balanced a crock of baked beans with one hand behind her. Zander and Ty were now ten and eight. They were still rambunctious boys, but they both had tender hearts for the things of the Lord.

Snake shook his head in mock disgust. "I told you not to bring anything. I have it all covered."

Rey chuckled. Then pointed at Callan, shrugged his shoulders and made a wimpy face attempting to show he was helpless in the situation.

Snake sighed. "Just put them over there on the table with the food my mom and sister weren't supposed to bring."

Callan walked confidently to the picnic table. "We women have no faith that a man can prepare a meal without our help."

James Fields found a comfortable seat at the picnic table. Snake glanced in his father's direction. It was a picture he could never have imagined five years ago. James looked happy and content pinching samples from the array of dishes on display.

Snake's father was still a work in progress. The day they were reunited—life really began for the Field's family. The words *Born Again* took on a whole new meaning to Snake that day at the altar. Both father and son were profoundly changed for the good.

James gradually learned to accept the wrongs he had done, and like Zacchaeus in the Bible he spent years attempting to right those wrongs. James resigned his position as head of the Community Outreach board. It proved harder for him to let go of this power position than anyone could have imagined. Everyone, including James, knew it was the right first step.

The second step for James was to focus on his relationship with the Lord. By putting the Lord first in his life it resulted in the healing of this fractured family. It also gave him the ability to move on to step three. He went to the home of Mary Edwards and apologized to the whole family for the things he did behind the scenes while they were grieving. This step softened Kota and moved him to action.

Kota contacted Emily shortly after he found out she was expecting a baby. The next months moved slowly as betrayed trust and broken love was mended. When Kota and Emily's daughter was born, he was at her side. They were newly married, passionately in love with each other and the Lord.

Marilyn opened the screen door with her foot while balancing a tray of condiments. She let go of the door, and it slammed behind her. She crossed the yard and placed the tray on the picnic table just out of her husband's reach. James and Marilyn's home was bigger and grander than their son's, but this was Zac's special day. For some reason, he wanted the BBQ at his house. She had pictured a day like this only in her most private dreams. She was overjoyed to be sitting at her son's home, eating a meal cooked by him—mostly cooked by him. Her family was reunited and better than before.

Marilyn refused to call her son Snake—opting instead for Zac, the name Carl had chosen for himself. Only Snake's immediate family called him Zac. Everyone else liked the name Snake and thought it suited him quite well.

Marilyn sat close to her husband at the picnic table. She had the perfect seat to look out across the small backyard. Memories were being made. Emily and Kota were on a blanket under a shade tree with their two children. Kota was lying on his stomach and his little girl was flopped over his back. Her chubby fingers running through her father's hair. Emily held her son up in the air at arm's length speaking sweet words to him. The baby cooed back. It warmed Marilyn's heart to see her daughter happily married to this kind and gentle man. These were the moments that filled a mother's heart.

Marilyn's happy thoughts were interrupted by her son Zac banging a metal spoon on the side of the grill.

"Family, I called you all here not just for this amazing meal, but to tell you some good news."

Anticipation was visible on each face. He had everyone's attention. Zac took a breath and then blurted out, "I met a girl and we have been dating for a few months."

Marilyn jumped up, nearly throwing James backwards onto the ground. She screamed with glee. Then she covered her mouth to muffle the excitement.

Speaking through her hands she said. "When can we meet her? What does she look like? How did you meet?"

Snake smiled. Playfully he warned his family, "She'll be here in a few minutes, and I *don't* want you going crazy. You might scare her off."

Emily laughed. "Really—us scare her off. If she's stuck around you for a few months—then she's fearless."

Moments later the back door opened. All eyes were drawn to a girl in her twenties. Her hair was long and black. She had it pulled back in a ponytail. A butterfly tattoo graced the left side of her face. Her sleeveless shirt revealed both arms adorned with a collection of colorful tattoos ending just above the wrist.

"Everyone this is Fauna Reynolds. We met on a Christian dating website. Fauna—this is my family."

Coming in 2017
Hillbrooke The Healer

Group Discussion Questions:

Pastor Rey had a spiritual experience as a teenage that impacted his career choice. Can you identify an experience with God that impacted your life? If so, when and how?

In the book of Romans it says, "…by the obedience of one many are made righteous and by the disobedience of one many are made sinners." Although this has reference to the first Adam and the second Adam (Christ), the principle is true for all believers. How did Jean and Tom Brown's obedience impact others?

Marilyn Fields heard the good news of salvation and immediately embraced the Lords forgiveness compared to her husband who was a work in progress. When you accepted the Lord was it more like Marilyn or James?

Callan did not initially embrace all the new things that were happening in her world. Why do you think she pull away? Have you ever been in a place like Callan where you resisted before accepting what God had for you?

Kota Edwards allowed anger and revenge to overtake him when he heard James Fields speak heartlessly about his father. Do we have the right to lash out when others have 100% done wrong? Does revenge ever really make a person feel better or make the wrong—right?

James Fields seemed like a hopeless cause. Have you ever met a person whose actions seemed beyond redemption? How did you handle interacting with this type of person?

Snake chooses a path of crime blaming his poor choices on a controlling father while Marilyn lived in an abusive home with an alcoholic father. Snake and Marilyn each chose a different path. What made these two characters respond differently?

Emily ignored the warning of the Holy Spirit and made a decision that would affect the rest of her life. Have you experienced a situation when you heard or felt the Lord warning you to stop? Did you obey or chose your own way? What was the outcome?

Heidi seemed to be playing church and using it for her benefit. What are the dangers that await a person who plays with the things of God? Can you think of an illustration from a story in the Bible of a person who played with the things of God? What happened to them?

Marilyn's Bible is taken from her prayer room by her husband out of spit, but God has a plan for good. Do you recall any time in your life when someone wanted to do you harm, but God turned it around for good?

The Holy Spirit plays an important role in this book. What are some of the things in this story that you can attribute to the working of the Spirit?

Pastor Rey experiences fasting for the first time. Have you ever fasted? Could you identify with Pastor Rey's frustration? Did anything good come from your fasting experience? Can you identify individuals in the Bible who fasted?

The Edwards family and later Snake were not welcomed at Community Outreach Church. What can **_you do_** to make sure your church is a welcoming place?

Which character in the book did you identify most with and why?

The Altar plays an important part at the close of this book. Is the Altar a necessary part of the Christian experience? What happened at the Altar in the Old Testament? What happens to the believer when they come to an altar today? Can you think of a New Testament scripture that deals with the believer and the altar?

Pastor Rey and Callan were both brought up in the church and desired to use their lives for the Lord, yet they both struggled to follow the leading of the Lord. Do you elevate your pastoral staff thinking they are above the daily trails of the average believer? Do you pray for your church leadership on a regular basis? They need your covering. Take a moment and **Pray Now**!

Scriptures:

Chapter 1:   Jeremiah 29:11-14 The Message (MSG)
Chapter 2:   Psalm 37:23 New English Translation (NET)
Chapter 3:   Joshua 3:7 The Message (MSG)
Chapter 4:   Jeremiah 8:18-19 The Message Bible (MSG)
Chapter 5:   Ecclesiastes 4:13 Contemporary English Version (CEV)
Chapter 6:   Psalm 142:1-2 The Message (MSG)
Chapter 7:   Isaiah 30:18 The Message (MSG)
Chapter 8:   Isaiah 55:9 The Message (MSG)
Chapter 9:   Psalm 78:70-72 The Message (MSG);
             Isaiah 42:1-4 The Message (MSG)
Chapter 10: Psalm 122:1 The Message (MSG)
Chapter 11: Matthew 5:16Living Bible (TLB)
Chapter 12: Jeremiah 31:19The Message (MSG)
Chapter 13: Psalm 103:8-12 The Message (MSG)
Chapter 14: Matthew 12:20 Living Bible (TLB)
Chapter 15: Matthew 25:35-36 The Message (MSG)
Chapter 16: Amos 3:3 New King James Version (NKJV)
Chapter 17: Job 36:16 The Message (MSG)
Chapter 18: John 7:37-38 English Standard Version (ESV); Isaiah 58:6
Chapter 19: Jeremiah 29:12-13 The Message (MSG)
Chapter 20: Psalm 100:4 & 5 New King James Version (NKJV)
Chapter 21: Ecclesiastes 3:1 New International Version
             Isaiah 61 New International Version (NIV)
Chapter 22: Psalm 37:23The Message (MSG)
Chapter 23: James 1:13 The Living Bible (TLB)
Chapter 24: Psalm 122:1 Easy-To-Read Version (ERV)
             Isaiah 41 New King James Version (NKJV).
Chapter 25: John 1:11-12 The Living Bible (TLB)
Chapter 26: Jeremiah 29:11 The Message (MSG)

Made in the USA
Middletown, DE
08 May 2016